ISBN: 9798518413764

To my beautiful wife Jo and our wonderful children...
I dedicate everything.

'The fact is, I don't know where my ideas come from. Nor does any writer. The only real answer is to drink way too much coffee and buy yourself a desk that doesn't collapse when you beat your head against it.'

DOUGLAS ADAMS

Prologue

It would be easy to say the ocean was unsettled on this particular night. But, a better way to summarise the roaring plumes of white froth attacking the black rock would be to say the ocean was *royally* pissed off.

The sky echoed the ocean's temper; huge clouds of dark grey and green swirled by the biting wind, snuffing out the moonlight, as though it was thinking *Me too*. This ranting from the elements was nature's way of keeping itself busy while an ancient magic awaited its curtain call.

A sorcerer wrapped his dark green cloak tight as he stepped across the damp wooden footbridge that crossed the raging water beneath. He looked up at the solitary, monolithic stone tower that served as his quarters. The building sat upon a single rock surrounded by ocean, the footbridge being its only access. Turning around, the sorcerer peered back up the stone steps that ascended a steep rocky hillside and to a high-walled castle at the peak. 'He asks too much,' cursed the cowed man, under his trembling breath. 'It must end.'

Pausing before a large oak gate, he rummaged around inside a deep pocket within his cloak. Producing an iron key, one of many on a knotted loop of twine, he rattled it into the lock. Glancing back towards the castle, once more, his heart sank.

The gate opened with a low groaning creak, as if somehow it also knew what was about to take place inside. Crossing a small, darkened courtyard, the sorcerer hurried up the stone steps, leading to an archway and then into the cold, lonely tower.

A single bolt of lightning cut into the night, the final curse word of the furious sky.

Chapter 1
Welcome Back, Tom

For most of us, waking up consists of an alarm clock going off, followed by a reluctant arm reaching over to the intruding device, hitting the snooze button then giving it ten minutes before forcing ourselves away from our bed. A bed that, after a good many hours of being slept on, becomes its most warm and snug. Hence, the regret of having to part company with it until we return, at the end of another long day, to begin the process all over again.

This isn't a luxury the entire population of our world shares; for some, a place to curl up under a thick duvet and dream the night away is, in itself, a dream.

On a bright, crisp Friday morning in April, a slim young man lay battered and bruised like a discarded toy. The loud cawing of birds took the roll of an alarm clock, which meant there was no way of hitting a snooze button.

Opening his eyelids, the pupils puncturing his brown eyes shrank to dots as the sunlight stung his retinas. As his senses reactivated, he soon realised that as far as a good night's sleep goes, broken slate and damp heather were no substitute for a bed. Topping things off, the mother of all headaches was doing a sterling job at replicating the beat of twenty drummers.

He groaned. His vocal cords allowed a single word to slowly escape. 'Shiiit.' His internal monologue filled in the rest. *Think I'll just do nothing for a while.*

It was at this point that something white and furry leapt onto his chest, startling him up onto his feet. 'What the..?' he blurted out, stumbled, then fell back down. Looking to the ground in front of him, he saw it was just a rabbit.

The rabbit backed off and tilted its head to one side, as though assessing the human sat before it. It looked up to the sky through its pink eyes, then sat down.

Pins and needles filled the young man's legs, but the burning pain in his spine, as he sat there, forced him back up onto his feet. Placing both hands on his lower back, he corrected his posture with a crack. Confused, battered and alone, he stared down at the rabbit. 'You okay, little fella? Enjoying the show?' Being something of a unique creature, the rabbit nodded.

Not aware of the rabbit's unusual behaviour, the young man brushed the dirt from his grey jeans and the elbows of his brown peacock jacket. Something niggled his brain. He held his hands out in front and studied the unfamiliar digits. 'Oh, shit.' His heartbeat rocketed. 'Who *am* I?' He took a deep breath and gulped, trying to stem the onslaught of panic. 'Keep calm. Just keep calm. Think.'

Patting the pockets of his clothes, he found a slim, black leather wallet from his jeans. The young man opened it and searched through the contents. Producing a credit card, his hands trembled as he examined it.

'Mister T. Last?' The memory of his name jumped centre stage into his mind. *Thomas*, he thought, *Tom*.

Searching unsuccessfully in the wallet for an address, Tom returned the otherwise empty wallet to his pocket. 'Phone. My phone.' He rummaged around his clothes, the ground immediately around him, then in a wider radius. No luck.

The rabbit, still intrigued by the young man's behaviour, looked on as Tom felt something jangle in his jacket. Reaching into an inner pocket, he pulled out what appeared to be car keys.

He sat down on a large piece of slate, and the rabbit seemed curious enough to come and sit beside him. Exhaling, Tom tried to compose his racing mind. *Okay, what do I remember?* He decided to do a mental checklist. *I woke up, here... wherever 'here' is? And, before that? Er... Before... That?* But, try as he might, his memory drew blanks.

'What about you?' he asked, giving the rabbit a little neck scratch. 'You got any family? Friends?' The rabbit looked up at Tom then down to the ground.

A minute of silence passed as Tom tried to compartmentalise his thoughts. He broke it with a set of vocal interjections. 'Eee... Ooo... Aaa... Huh? What accent is this?' asking his furry new friend. 'Southern? Posh?'

The rabbit, deciding it had more pressing matters to attend to, wiggled its nose then ran off towards a cliff behind him.

'Hey!' Watching as the creature scrambled up a steep narrow path, Tom yelled out, 'Fine. Don't help out then.' He picked up a small stone and tossed it to the dirt in front of him.

As he sat alone, feeling confused and vulnerable, Tom tried to make sense of his surroundings. Behind him, the tall cliff had a narrow footpath snaking to the top; in front, slate and heather thinned into mossy patches of grass with the odd bush here and there, ending next to a stream. Beyond that, a woodland ascended the slope away up the other side of the valley. In other circumstances, this would be an idyllic location, but for Tom it was deeply troubling. He took a moment and listened. Birds chirped, the stream babbled, wind gently swayed the leaves of the trees. Tom tried to focus for any sound of civilisation, cars, people, but to no such luck.

He stood and wandered down to the stream. Kneeling down, Tom looked at the clear water as it flowed across a shallow bed of slate. He cupped his hands, lowered them into the stream and splashed the cold water onto his face, helping awaken his senses. Filling his hands once more, he gulped it down.

'So, you're Thomas Last, hey?' he said to the rippling reflection of the grubby face, wincing back from the water. 'You look like crap, mate.' He tried flattening his tussled dark brown hair into some level of neatness, then studied his features. *Narrow face, not too ugly, I guess*, he thought to himself. *What am I, twenty? Twenty-two?* He assessed the scuffs and grazes to the shaved skin of his jawline. Rubbing his fingers across his hairline, he felt a tender bruised lump. 'What happened to you?' he whispered, staring at his unfamiliar reflection again. The image rippled once more, as tears hit the surface. Tom dried his face with the bottom of his black T-shirt, then stood up. 'Come on,' he said, willing himself, 'get it together.' Turning around, he looked back to where he'd woken up, his eyes drawn to the pathway up the cliff. *Follow the white rabbit, I suppose?*

Soon, he was navigating his way up the narrow path of the cliff, every steep footstep reminding him of the condition his body was in. The ascent was slow, but it wasn't as though Tom was in any kind of rush, and the task helped as a distraction from his confused mind.

After only a couple of misplaced slips and stumbles, he stood at the top. Only then, could he take in the broader view. In the distance, a patchwork quilt of grass, heather and gorse covered hills that shrank to the horizon. But no sign of buildings.

He looked back down the cliff, drawn to the trail of loose slate that led to the spot where he'd woken. Beginning not far from where he was stood, the flat grey stones had been dispersed in an almost straight line all the way down. *I must've fallen?* he thought, as the faintest of memory – a match-light in a cavern – struggled to be noticed. He bellowed out into the peaceful valley, 'What the hell has happened to me?' Turning around, he faced the nearby wood. 'Bollocks to this.' With a big sigh, he peered through the gaps amongst the evergreens. Spotting a viable route across the needle-carpeted earth, he began to walk.

As Tom now meandered his way through the trees, the smell of pine and chirping of birds acted as a natural cure for his headache – now only ten drummers. He found what appeared to be a track, with the soil looking more compacted, the pine needles fewer. Up ahead, Tom could see the woodland opened out into a clearing. A number of trees had been sawn down, leaving ten or so as just mere stumps. This allowed Tom a better view beyond.

After passing this clearing, Tom saw the area in front of him had been levelled to just dirt and grass now. Tucked away over at the far left of the open space, by a thick hedgerow of hawthorns and bindweed, sat an old, dilapidated shed. The rusty corrugated metal gave it an abandoned appearance. Being the first man-made structure he'd seen, it was enough for Tom to go investigate.

When he reached the shed, he studied its weather-beaten slatted doors; a metal slide bolt holding them shut. Studying this more closely, Tom noticed the grease smeared over the old bolt. 'Not that abandoned then,' he muttered to himself, as he slid the latch open with a clunk. As he pulled open the double doors, his eyes widened at what was inside.

'Cool,' he gasped, stepping into the shed. Tom ran his hand along the wing of a green classic sports car, wiping a thin layer of dust from the paintwork as he did so. The vehicle's chrome wing mirrors had all but completely rusted. The steel-wire wheels, as Tom bent down to look at them, had also succumbed to age. Standing up, Tom gave the dust on the windscreen a wipe over with the sleeve of his jacket. The interior seems decent enough, he thought as he peered inside.

Walking around the shed, Tom couldn't see anything else in there. He flicked a switch on the wall but noticing the light-bulb suspended from a metal rod across the corrugated ceiling was smashed, he looked back towards the car. 'Wonder who owns you?' Then a thought crossed his mind, *The car keys*. He removed them and studied the emblem on the keyring. 'Triumph.' He smiled. 'Surely you can't belong to me?' The key slid into the driver's door and, with a little persuading, it unlocked.

For the first time that morning Tom had comfort as he sank into the driver's leather seat. He slid his fingers around the polished wood steering wheel. 'What *is* going on?' Holding his own gaze in the rear-view mirror, the bloodshot eyes peered back. 'One thing at a time,' he muttered.

Spotting an aged paper booklet in the footwell of the passenger seat, he read the title: *Triumph GT6. Owner's manual.* Next, wondering what else was inside the vehicle, he rooted around for a couple of minutes, but with no success. *Maybe there's something in the boot?*

A loosely rolled-up blanket covered the boot compartment. He moved it aside to reveal a green satchel. Unbuckling it, Tom lifted open the flap, then immediately dropped it. 'Oh...

kay?' He ran back round to the entrance of the shed and, peering out, froze there for a moment, making sure no one else was around.

He took a deep breath and went round to the back of the shed, to the boot of the car and opened the satchel again. 'Now that… is a shitload of money,' he whispered to himself, before giving a low whistle at the contents. Placing a hand on one of the many bundles of cash that filled the canvas bag, Tom removed it and flicked his thumb along a wad of crisp fifty-pound notes. 'Twenty notes per bundle…' he counted, massaging his temple with his other hand, 'er… and eleven bundles. So, that makes… over ten grand.' Realising he'd said this last part aloud, he hastily stuffed the wad into his pocket, closed up the satchel and finally the boot of the car. *I should probably get out of here.*

Sitting back in the driver's seat, Tom's fingers trembled as he slid the key into the ignition and turned it on. He figured out how to squirt the windscreen washers and activate the wipers. Once the dust had cleared enough from the windscreen, Tom gripped his left hand onto the gearstick. *Right, think I still know how to drive.*

The engine moaned and clattered as Tom twisted the key further round. 'Come on,' he prayed, 'start.' He pumped the accelerator and tried again. On the third attempt, he slammed his foot down hard, yelling out, 'Just start, already.' The car suddenly revved into life, spluttering like an old smoker's cough as soot plumed from the exhaust pipe.

Tom crunched the gearstick into first. Trying not to stall the car, his brain notified his foot to use the clutch pedal. The car juddered out of the shed, like a grumpy bear awoken too early from hibernation. Assuming the overgrown track he'd spotted was the way out, he steered the GT6 towards it.

After a couple of minutes, Tom got to grips with the car just as the bumpy track levelled out into a country lane. At the end of this, he reached a junction to a main road, framed by a tall hedgerow.

On the opposite side of the junction, Tom spotted an old,

white, wooden road sign. Turning right would take him to a motorway, to his left the nearest village. Hearing his belly groan, he answered back, 'Good plan.'

Pressing his foot down on the GT6's pedal, Tom turned the steering wheel counterclockwise, and headed towards the village of Penworthy.

At the side of the junction, the white rabbit appeared from behind a small bush. It stared down the road, watching as the GT6 vanished from view. It shook its head, looked up to the sky, then scurried off as fast as it could towards the village.

Chapter 2
The Copper Kettle

A stern-looking crow flapped its way down from the morning sky and perched on a vacant tree branch. Twitching its head round, unsatisfied, it hopped off and settled on top of an old mossy cornerstone beside a road.

Engine roaring, Tom's car raced around the corner, startling the crow back up into the air. It looked down at the green vehicle with disapproval and let out a caw.

Questions queued up inside Tom's mind demanding an answer, the most pressing one, of course, *What the hell is going on?* He mulled this over as he drove along the country road. *Did I really take a header down that cliff? Would explain why I woke up there. The missing bits of memory... doesn't feel right though.*

Changing gear, Tom next considered the car. *Why is it so dusty? How long had it been there? What if I've just stolen it?*

His next thought: the money. *What if I've just stolen a car AND that cash?* He shook the thought from his mind.

Ahead, a road sign read, 'Welcome to Penworthy Village. Please drive slowly', to which someone had graffitied below, 'Or you'll miss it!'

Tom pulled up at a mini-roundabout and waited a few seconds. In the centre of the roundabout, a stone pillar stood with a large metal clock face mounted on top which read ten o'clock.

Right, think. I don't know for certain what's happened, or how long I could've been lying at the bottom of that cliff for. Park the bloody car somewhere quiet, concentrate on food, then I'll figure out what to do next.

The loud beep of a horn brought him out of his thoughts. Looking in his rear-view mirror, the impatient van driver behind him gestured for Tom to drive. Waving a sign of apology, Tom pressed on.

Driving through a quaint high street, he passed rows of shops. By the look of the buildings, the village must be centuries old. He spotted some locals entering a post office, others chatting outside a hairdressers and a greengrocer loading stock onto a display cart. Tom felt a pang of jealously as he observed people having a normal day.

Spotting a sign hanging above a bay-windowed, single-storey shop, Tom found what he was looking for. Slowing the car as he drove past, he peered inside the café. Continuing along the street, Tom turned the car onto a narrow side street and found a quiet car park.

After locking the GT6, he walked back down towards the high street. The closer he got, the more his heart filled with hope. Thoughts of eating, and interacting with anyone, gave him some comfort.

'Morning,' said Tom, after rounding a corner and approaching a couple of old gentlemen stood outside a newsagents. The two fellows regarded Tom's grubby clothes with disdain then, ignoring him, they continued with their own conversation. He sighed, crossed the street and headed towards the café.

The interior of the *Copper Kettle Café* looked like a chintz-bomb had exploded, covering everything in gingham: tables, chairs, curtains, even the lightshades on the ceiling and wall lights, all adorned with the same white and salmon pink pattern.

Tom studied the handful of customers scattered around who eyed him back with varying degrees of disapproval. A few whispers and tuts did the rounds, before they continued with their breakfasts, morning papers, or both. Walking towards the counter, Tom was welcomed over by a warm rosy smile from a sturdy old lady stood behind it.

'Well, I would say good morning but from the looks of it, you've not had the best of starts,' said the lady, in a thick West Country tone. 'Tell you what, you sit yourself down over there, my love.' She flipped to a fresh page on her jot pad and, with her tiny pencil, pointed to a free table beside the window. 'Let old

Beryl here get you a nice hot cuppa and a menu, eh?'

'Thanks, er... Beryl. Tea, please.' Tom helped himself to a small sugar bowl from the counter, then made his way to the table. Beryl hummed tunefully as she placed a teapot under the tap on a large chrome urn.

Seated at the table, Tom tried to compose himself. He needed a shower and a comfy bed. There was enough money in his pocket to mooch around the village for a few hours, get his bearings and, hopefully, find somewhere to lie low for a few nights. But for now, all that could wait until after breakfast.

Beryl came over. 'There you go,' she said. 'One pot of tea.' She placed a tray on the table, consisting of a mug, steel pot, jug of milk, and extra hot water.

Handing him a menu, she said, 'I'd recommend "The Big Mutha".' She tittered at her poor attempt at an American accent. Resorting back to her Cornish accent, 'It's got four fried tomatoes, three slices of bacon, two bangers and one extra-large fried egg. That comes with toast, fried bread or just plain old buttered bread.' She licked the tip of the pencil, then hovered it over a pad, awaiting his response.

'That all sounds amazing.' Tom smiled. 'Thank you.'

'My pleasure.' Beryl beamed. 'Just visiting Penworthy, are you?'

Tom averted eye contact by pretending to pick something off his hand. 'Yeah, sure.'

'Thought so,' said Beryl. 'I always enjoy seeing new faces.'

Me Too, thought Tom, *just not when it's my own.*

'Just a tip though, m'dear,' Beryl whispered, drawing close. 'Maybe get kitted out properly from the hiking shop down the street, before going for a trek over the moors.'

'How do you know I was there?' answered Tom.

'The dirt on your jacket, looks like you've been rolling around up there. You'd be surprised the amount of people go wandering around up there in their Sunday best. It's amazing no one gets seriously hurt.' She chuckled to herself as Tom sat stone-faced, then returning to her waitress role, concluded,

'Anyway, how do you want your bread?'

'Just regular toast with butter, thank you,' replied Tom.

***

'Mrs. Malory, my dearest Beryl,' boomed a voice by the entrance, as the door to the café shut to. 'How are you this most glorious of mornings?' The man gave a regal wave at everyone sat around, who in turn mumbled a greeting back. Removing a long slim brown overcoat, he placed it on a hook on the wall.

'Hello there, Leonard, fine spirits as usual?' said Beryl, leaning against the counter.

'How is Charles doing?' asked Leonard, combing his fingers through his long white hair, attempting to neaten it. He gave Beryl a wink. 'Still away with the old boys golfing, is he?'

'Yes, back next weekend.' Beryl pretended to busy herself by wiping the counter. 'Says the weather over there is awful. Rain, rain, bloomin' rain. I told him he might as well just stick to golfing in this country.'

'Well, come on now, Beryl.' The wrinkles on Leonard's forehead shifted to one side, as he raised a bushy eyebrow. 'We both know he hardly plays when he's away with the lads. His idea of going for a round is stepping into the nearest bar.' His laugh cut the chatter in the café.

Beryl blushed and smiled, as she glanced around the room at her customers. 'The usual then, Leonard?'

He acknowledged her, then turned away from the counter. Tugging the white cuffs of his shirt from out of the sleeves of his immaculate green Harris tweed jacket, he gave the room a quick smile. Glancing over to the young man sat wolfing down his breakfast near the window, Leonard spotted a vacant table beside him. He made his way over and sat himself down.

'You reading that, my young fellow?' he asked, leaning to his right and pointing to the newspaper on the table.

'Help yourself, mate,' said Tom, passing it over.

Leonard ironed the paper out flat on his own table. 'You

12

all right there, my lad?' he said, without taking his eyes off the headlines.

Tom swallowed the last bit of toast from his plate. 'Me? Yeah, just a difficult morning, is all.'

Leonard turned the page over. 'If you say so.'

Tom glared at the resplendent man – all decked out in his immaculate green suit ensemble – sat there thumbing through the newspaper. 'I'd rather not talk about it,' he said.

Leonard lifted his head from the paper. Looking at Tom, he gave his chin a contemplative scratch. 'I do apologise, dear lad, didn't mean to pry.' He flourished his fingers at Tom. 'Continue with your tea, undisturbed.'

'Sorry,' replied Tom. 'I didn't mean to sound so blunt.'

Beryl brought Leonard's morning latte over. Thanking her, he turned back to Tom. 'Let's start over, shall we?' He offered a handshake. 'Professor Leonard Goodwin.'

Tom, remembering how he'd wished for someone to talk to, reciprocated. 'I'm Thomas Last,' the name, still feeling uncomfortable in his mouth, 'Tom.'

'Pleasure to make your acquaintance, Tom.' Leonard sipped his drink, then gave Tom a warm smile. 'May I offer you a fresh pot?'

Feeling somewhat at ease talking to the old gent, Tom decided to take Leonard up on his offer.

***

After a third round of drinks, Leonard – now relocated at Tom's table – considered what had just been confided.

'Well, I suppose it's not uncommon, Tom.' He wrapped his fingertips around the tea tray. 'As you say, falling from that height, it's highly likely a blow to the head may trigger a trauma of some sort. So, what're you going to do? Shouldn't you seek medical attention, just in case?'

'Dunno,' replied Tom. 'I just want things to be back to normal.'

'Well, maybe you could check the registration on your car. That would at least give you a home address maybe?'

'Yeah, I guess I could do that.'

'You must, Tom, if you're to piece things back together. I believe,' Leonard waggled his fingers like he was typing something, 'one can do that all on a computer, these days.'

Tom scrunched his face. 'Um...'

'Hmm? Ahh, one thing at a time, eh?' Leonard studied Tom's forehead. 'I have to say, Tom, if you did suffer a blow to the head, it's healed up nicely.'

'To be honest, Leonard, I feel okay.' He rolled his shoulders. 'Even the pain in my spine's gone. As for my memory, hopefully it'll come back soon. If not, I guess I should go see a doctor.'

'Well, there's one thing for certain,' Leonard nodded towards the café counter, 'Beryl's cooking works wonders, eh?' He swilled down the last of his coffee. 'Tell me, you mentioned you might stick around for a few days. It's entirely up to you, but I have a room vacant at the lodgings behind my house. There's a young man what stays there, must be close to your age. I'm sure he'd appreciate having someone, how shall I say, *cooler*, hanging around for a while. He helps out about the place, does a few odd jobs for me, doesn't go out much though. We could keep an eye on you, should you need anything. What say you?'

Tom deliberated this Good Samaritan's offer. Leonard seemed honest enough, and it would save him having to search elsewhere for accommodation. 'Sure, why not.' He thanked him, then insisted on paying for their drinks.

***

'It's very kind of you to offer me a lift, Tom,' said Leonard, as they crossed the street. 'I usually enjoy taking in the fresh air on the way here and back. But, I do admit, the chance to ride in a classic car is, well, it's rather exciting.'

'Please,' replied Tom, appreciating the turn of luck, 'it's the least I can do. You're the one who's being kind.'

They arrived at the GT6. Taking the keys from his pocket, Tom looked at the old professor, who was stood admiring a Harley-Davidson motorbike parked nearby.

'Would you look at that,' exclaimed Leonard, shaking his head.

'Not really into bikes, Leonard,' replied Tom, glancing at the air-brushed star-spangled banner on the vehicle's metallic blue petrol tank.

'No, no, me neither, Tom. I'm referring to what's strapped to the back of it.' He knocked on the lid of a cylindrical box. 'This is a real antique. And, someone's just tethered it to the back of this monstrosity of a motorbike and left it here.'

Tom gave the wooden box a look. 'Worth something, is it?'

Leonard tutted. 'It's a genuine Victorian burr-walnut hat box, Tom. Yes, it's worth something,' he snorted. 'About a thousand pounds.'

Tom paid the box closer attention. 'I hope you're not thinking about nicking it, Leonard?'

Leonard's back straightened. 'Har-har. Oh, God, no. I used to teach history. I have something of a penchant for objects like this. I've collected a few in my time.' He folded his arms, stepping away from the bike. 'It just bothers me when people don't treat old things with respect.'

Tom couldn't help but wonder if Leonard was including himself.

'So, here's your mystery vehicle.' Leonard ran a finger along the dust on Tom's car. He showed the dust on his fingertip to Tom, while raising an eyebrow.

'Hey, I'm sure if I could remember,' Tom said, frowning, 'I'd be more apologetic for not respecting it.' He opened the passenger door for Leonard, then walked round to the other side and got in.

'Indeed,' said Leonard, wincing at the rusted wing mirror as he got inside.

Chapter 3
The Whirlpool

The tyres crunched across the gravelled driveway.

'Here we *are* then,' said Leonard. 'My humble abode.'

Tom parked the car close to the front door of the cottage. Looking up at the grey thatched roof, it made the old building look as though it had a mop-top haircut. He pointed to the ivy snaking up from the side of the porch and around the window above. 'Could do with a clean, Leonard.'

Ignoring the remark, Leonard enthused, 'It's actually the oldest house in the whole village. Built a little over six hundred years ago. Just the window frames alone are well over a hundred years old, well, most of them anyway.' Unclipping his seat belt, he added, 'Come on, I'll show you to where you'll be staying.'

Tom got out of the car and looked around at the rustic setting. The trees surrounding the un-mowed lawns that lay either side of the drive made a gentle rustling sound. His thoughts recalled the woods from earlier which had led him to discover the car he was now standing near. He snapped back out of his thoughts and opened the boot of the GT6.

After retrieving his satchel, Tom followed the professor along a slabbed pathway that skirted the left side of the house. The wildflowers that grew beside the garden path, a combination of purples, oranges and white, looked like a close-up of a George Seurat painting.

Reaching the rear of the cottage, Tom's attention was drawn to the large, black, wooden-clad shed, butted into the wall of the house at a right angle.

'My workshop, Tom,' commented Leonard. 'Looking a little run-down these days, isn't it? Don't fret, that's not where you'll be staying.'

Holding up a hand to direct Tom across a brick-paved

courtyard, Leonard guided him towards a separate building. Once an old barn, it had now been converted into a sizeable dwelling. 'Here's your lodgings,' announced Leonard, 'and there is the young chap I was telling you about.'

On the doorstep of the cedar and red-brick structure, a paunchy, apprehensive young man sat rolling a cigarette. He pulled out a lighter from his black hooded top, was about to light the rollie, when he clocked the two heading over.

'Ah, Ed,' boomed Leonard, 'perfect timing.'

Ed placed the cigarette behind an ear, giving his limp sandy hair a flick back from his eyes, then eased himself off the step.

'Allow me to introduce you,' continued Leonard, 'to your new temporary housemate, Thomas Last.'

Tom held out his hand. 'Hi, Ed, just call me Tom.'

'Hey, mate. Ed White.' Shaking his hand, Ed saw the state of Tom's clothes. 'You just got back from Pit Fest, or something?'

Tom returned a vague look. 'Huh?'

'The rock festival?' said Ed. 'Total mud-out this year. I was stuck here, though, helping the prof—'

'That's enough prattling now,' interjected Leonard. 'Would you believe, Thomas here is suffering from a touch of the old amnesia. Therefore, has absolutely no idea what you're going on about, no doubt.' He shot Ed a silencing glare, before signalling for him to step aside. 'Now kindly let us in, thank you.'

Ed obliged.

'Sorry about that,' Leonard said, ushering Tom inside. 'You'll get used to him wittering on.'

'I *am* stood right here, Prof,' said Ed.

'More's the pity,' grumbled Leonard. 'At least make yourself useful and go pop the kettle on.'

Ed walked over to the left of the large open-plan room where the kitchen area was situated. He opened one of the cream cupboard doors near his head and selected some mugs. Next, he grabbed a kettle. Cursing as he spilt some water onto the granite worktop, Ed grabbed a tea towel and immediately wiped it. As he stood filling the kettle with water at the sink, he stared out of the window in front of him, whistling a tune as he did so.

'You can leave your satchel by the door for now, Thomas,' instructed Leonard. 'Pop your jacket on the hook there too. Let's go sit down, shall we?'

Tom did so, then looked over to the right of the room where two green leather sofas surrounded a dark-oak coffee table. Leonard led the way, giving the varnished exposed beams a knock. 'All original, these,' he commented.

Tom nodded, studying the bric-a-brac displayed on an antique-looking shelving unit. 'Some of your collection, Leonard?' asked Tom, lifting up a brass gimbal.

'Oh,' exclaimed Leonard, 'careful with that, it's—'

The loosely attached sections of the mechanism separated and clattered on the shelf.

'Balls,' mumbled Tom, faffing around trying to piece the thing back together.

'Just leave it,' Leonard said, with a wave.

Picking up a bolt that had dropped on the slate floor, Tom placed it beside the rest of the unassembled parts, then hurried over to the sofas.

Leonard settled back into a creaky rocking chair next to a stone fireplace, waiting for Tom to sit down.

'Do you collect art too, Leonard?' said Tom, studying the oil paintings that, as he sat looking around, hung on every one of the magnolia walls. 'Not sure about the fox-hunting one, though.' He pointed to the largest one, above the mantlepiece, which depicted a group of gammon-faced men on white horses, cheering at a pack of dogs ripping a fox apart.

'To be honest with you, lad, I think it's a cowardly way to hunt,' replied Leonard, rummaging around inside his jacket. 'Outnumbering the poor defenceless quarry hardly gives the damned thing much of a sporting chance, if you ask me.'

'Oh, right,' said Tom, rapping his fingers on his knees as his supply of small talk depleted.

Leonard produced a pipe from his jacket and placed it on a

small table beside him. 'You want to know why I own it?'

'Well, I suppose so. I mean, if you don't like the sport…?'

Opening a small tobacco tin, Leonard began packing the bowl of the wooden pipe. Once full, he struck a match and brought the flame down on to the contents, the orange flicker reflecting in his eyes. 'It was gifted to me by an old friend.' Leonard drew on the tip of the pipe. 'Sadly, he's no longer alive.' His sigh sent smoke drifting across the room.

Tom turned to the muted television in the opposite corner of the sitting area. The image on the screen captured his attention. A short, cheerful-looking man was talking into the camera, while behind him a group of people were sifting away in a muddy trench. 'Hang on,' exclaimed Tom. 'I recognise that place.'

'Sorry, lad?' muttered Leonard, puffing out smoke.

'On the telly. At least, I think I do?' Tom's eyes widened as he stared intently at the screen. 'There's something familiar about it.'

'What? *Dig This*?' Leonard quizzed, taking another puff on his pipe. He studied the look of concentration Tom was giving the television screen, then said, 'It's an archaeological show.'

'Maybe I used to watch it? My memory seems to think so.' Tom rubbed his forehead.

'The advert says it's on this evening.' Leonard tapped the contents from his pipe into a glass ashtray on the table. 'Maybe you should watch it, could help trigger your memory. Can you recall anything else about it?'

Tom tried focusing on the image in his head. 'Not much. It was when they were digging in that field, something about it just clicked.' He felt the initial hope fade. 'I don't know, could've been nothing.'

'I beg to differ. Something twigged there, just for a moment. I saw it in your eyes.' Leonard leant forward on the rocking chair. 'Look, don't get disheartened. You're welcome to stay here for as long as needed.'

'Thanks. I can pay you for letting me stay.'

'Oh, good Lord, there's no need to talk about that right

now.' Leonard wafted some smoke from in front of his face. 'What kind of person would I be, taking money from someone in need of assistance, hmm?' He looked over to the kitchen at the opposite of the room. 'How long does it take to make a cup of tea?'

Ed was busy humming away to himself as he stood idly letting the teabags brew. 'What's that?' came his reply, suddenly realising he was being watched.

'The tea, lad,' huffed Leonard. 'How long?'

'Coming right up.' Ed removed the bags from the mugs.

Leonard looked at Tom, whose face had grown pale. 'You all right there?' He clicked his fingers, bringing Tom back out of his thoughts.

'Sorry.' The reality of Tom's predicament swirled within his mind. He let out a long breath, hoping to expel the anxiousness plucking at the minor chord inside his head.

'Maybe you should just skip the tea and go lie down, Tom,' suggested Leonard. 'Give your brain a chance to catch up, yes?'

'It's just,' Tom gulped, pushing back the panic in his voice, 'with everything that's happened, I haven't really given much thought to family. How bad is that?' He looked towards Leonard, but avoided eye contact. 'Are they worried? Do I even have parents? Friends?'

'Tom, Tom, Tom,' repeated Leonard, holding a flat palm upright. 'Stop right there. You're going to burn yourself out. Clear your thoughts, one thing at a time, yes?'

Resting his head against the back of the sofa, Tom tried as best he could to compose himself. 'Look, I'm glad I met you, Leonard. You've been so kind, I'm sorry to dump all this on you.'

'Say no more about it, Tom.' The old man's warm smile helped reassure Tom's galloping mind. 'Glad to be of service. Might I suggest though, at least take it easy this evening. Stay right here, make sure you get an early night. In my opinion, the events of this morning have affected you more than you realise. Tomorrow, I could get a doctor to come check you out, if you're up to it?'

Ed came over and placed a tray of tea and some slices of carrot cake, on the coffee table. 'Sorry it took so long.' He gave the professor the first mug, then sat down.

Tom took a sip of tea, then helped himself to some of the cake. Both had a holistic effect on him, the panic dropping down a gear, for now.

***

After they'd finished off the tea and cake and updated Ed on Tom's situation, Leonard excused himself to get on with what he had planned that afternoon.

'Mate, that's one crazy story,' said Ed. 'If you want, tomorrow I could show you around the village, get your bearings and that. Or… we could just go to the pub, get ratted and let me kick your arse at pool. Either is good.'

Feeling exhausted, Tom just nodded at Ed's offer. If anything, he just wanted to be left alone. He faked a yawn. 'Do you mind if I crash out for a few hours?'

'Oh, of course,' said Ed. 'We can chat about that later. C'mon, I'll show you to your room.'

Tom grabbed his satchel and jacket, then glanced at his grubby jeans. 'Don't suppose you have some clothes I could borrow?'

'Sorry, mate.' Ed pulled on his own T-shirt. 'I think mine will be far too big for you. What's in your bag?'

Tom held his satchel tight to his chest. 'Just a few belongings in here, no clothes though. Would it be cool to use your washing machine then?'

'Yeah, no probs, mate,' replied Ed, pointing towards the kitchen. 'Leave your jeans on the landing, I'll stick 'em in with mine in a bit. If I put the dryer on too, they'll be done in no time. There's a brush for your jacket somewhere upstairs, if you're that picky. If you want to take a shower, I could stretch to lending you a dressing gown tonight?'

'Thanks, that's kind.'

21

'Yeah,' said Ed, cringing. 'To be honest, I just don't want to see you parading about the place in the buff.'

'Oh, I see.'

Ed walked over to the iron spiral staircase in the centre of the room, near the wall opposite the entrance. 'Come on then.'

They headed up the stairs and stood on the claustrophobic landing. Ed pointed to a wooden door. 'There you go, Tom. No one ever uses that room, but there'll be clean sheets and stuff in the wardrobe. I'll just grab that gown from my room. Back in a mo.'

Opening the door, Tom stepped through and dumped his stuff down on the grey carpeted floor. He studied the cream-coloured bedroom, lit with natural light from the small, curtained window. A pine wardrobe, stood pushed up against the side of a small vanity unit in the corner of the room, provided the only break in the otherwise blandness of the bare walls.

When Ed returned, Tom asked, 'Don't s'pose you know what the time is?'

Ed dumped the dressing gown on the floor and checked on his phone. 'Twenty to one, mate.'

Rubbing an eye with his palm, Tom said, 'I don't know how long I'll be out for, but just in case I oversleep, could you come wake me up around five?'

'I'm not room service, mate.' Ed sighed as he pocketed his phone.

'Sorry,' said Tom, realising how much of a burden he must be. 'I didn't mean to—'

'Mate, it's cool, seriously.' Ed smiled. 'I'll be hanging out all afternoon. But if you'd like, as a welcome gift, how about I pop out and grab us takeout for dinner. Chinese cool?'

'Umm… yep, sure.' Tom thanked Ed once again, then retired for some much-needed rest.

***

In his dreams, everything span. His body was falling faster and faster, through a strange spinning tunnel that whipped him around. In the centre, he could just make out what appeared to be a large hole. The wall of the tunnel melted into liquid, as though now a whirlpool. Cyan sparks rippled across the mirror-like surface. Tom sank into it as he spun. All he could do was try to keep himself afloat.

The liquid, thicker than water, as reflective as mercury, gave off an incandescent light which seemed to crackle whenever he moved his limbs. All around him, he heard a pulsating noise.

At the centre of the whirlpool, the hole suddenly ejected a flash of light that shone past him. Becoming more anxious now, Tom was closer to falling through it. He struggled to fight against the current. *Shit, shit, sh…*

Another flash.

As Tom approached the centre, he could now see through it. He saw what appeared to be fields and woodland, hundreds of feet below. His breathing became rapid, his heart beating faster.

He tried kicking his legs out, thrusting his arms against the liquid. It felt thicker at the centre, although that could've been fatigue. He heard a voice. Muffled, but definitely a voice. *It's calling for me*, he thought.

There it was again, off in the distance, beyond the outer edges of the whirlpool.

'It's dragging me down,' he cried out. 'Please, help.'

Too late, he'd reached the hole. The pulsating sound was at its loudest. He could feel it coursing throughout his whole body as he slid inside. His arms reached out in desperation, trying hopelessly to grab anything that might stop him. At last, he grabbed hold of what felt like a person's forearm.

'It's okay, man, wake up,' the voice yelled. 'Wake up, mate.'

***

'Wuh?' Tom sat upright in his bed with a jolt. 'What's happening?' Panting, he opened his eyes.

'From the sounds of it, you're having one bitch of a nightmare, that's what. I could hear you from downstairs, mate.' Ed tugged his arm back from Tom's clammy grip. 'You okay?'

'Sorry.' His heart racing, Tom looked around and let out a relieved sigh.

'Hey, look, no need to apologise,' said Ed, perching on the end of the bed. 'You're safe, awake, and most importantly, I got us takeaway and it's getting cold.' He stood up and headed over to the door. 'I've put your clean jeans over here. Get changed and get yourself downstairs, yeah?' With that, Ed left the room.

Tom stood up off the bed, his legs shaky. He paused a moment to compose himself. Splashing some water onto his face from the vanity unit's small sink, he looked at himself in a mirror on the side of the wardrobe. *It was just a dream*, he told himself, *nothing to panic over*. He got dressed, then made his way downstairs to where Ed had laid out the food on the coffee table.

***

As they both sat tucking into their takeaway, the channel announcer on the TV said, 'Coming up now, Toby Johnson and his team are back to show us what they've discovered in the first of a three-day live special. It's *Dig This*.'

Tom, his mouth half-full of food, waggled a fork at the TV then gulped. 'Hey, that's the show that was advertised earlier, when I was chatting to Leonard.'

Ed wasn't really paying attention, a battered pork ball in sweet and sour sauce was far more important. 'Yup, that's great, man.'

The opening titles had an aerial shot panning up over the British countryside, set to a Celtic beat. Giant shovels fell from the sky, landing at various historical sites. The camera zoomed out to reveal the shovels had spelt out: 'Dig This!'.

'Hello, I'm Toby Johnson,' declared the presenter, all professional grin and winks. He swung out his arms. 'Welcome to *Dig This* live. We've had an exciting day today, here in Cornwall.'

'Bloody 'ell,' sniggered Ed, commenting on the middle-aged presenter. 'Look at his clothes. That yellow Kagoul. At least the orange wellies match the colour of his make-up. He looks like a rubber duck.'

Tom ignored Ed and pressed the volume button on the remote.

'We're at a site five miles outside the village of Penworthy,' said Toby, making his way across a field. 'From our research, we believe there may have once been an Iron-age settlement on this very spot.'

Ed pointed a salty chip at the television. 'Hey, that's the Penmoor hills. It's not far from here.'

This comment warranted Tom's attention. 'The place out of the village, past that mini-roundabout with the clock on?'

'Yeah, man.' Ed paused to eat the chip. 'Go on for a few miles along the road through some woodland, eventually you come to a load of hills. It's definitely Penmoor. I'd recognise it anytime. I used to go camping up there when I was a kid.'

Tom knew something was familiar about the advert earlier. And now, it turned out they were filming at the area close to where he'd woken up that very morning.

'Do you want this last bit of duck?' Ed tapped the blackened meat on his plate. 'There's crispy, then there's cremated.'

Tom politely hushed him.

On the TV screen, Toby was stood next to a couple of fold-out tables placed under a temporary gazebo. Various objects dug up by the team earlier that day were spread out as a makeshift display; pieces of broken pottery, a couple of rusty bits of metal that were caked in mud. There were larger items too. Old crumbly pieces of wood soaked black with age, and what appeared to be wooden bowls.

'As you can see,' said Toby, pointing towards the artefacts, 'the team have made a great start already. All of this here is just from trench one. Let's bring in Jeremy Huxley, our resident historian, to run through what we've found.'

A man with cloud white hair circling his bald-topped

head, and dressed in a brown threadbare suit, appeared on the screen. His hand vanished into the bushy white hairs of his beard as he scratched his chin. Shuffling over to the tables, he gave an uncomfortable gaze at the camera. He placed a pair of half-rimmed glasses on, before picking up a piece of clay pot. In his broad West Country accent, he started to inform Toby what he knew about its history.

After a couple of minutes, Ed had seen enough. He began clearing up the left-over takeaway off the table.

'Mate, I'm gonna chuck all this away, wash up, then go take a shower.' Carrying the pile over to the kitchen, he added, 'You enjoy them two hipsters get all excited about their junk.'

'Thanks again for the food,' said Tom, distracted by the programme. 'I'll see you in a bit then, yeah?'

'No worries.' Ed dumped the plates and cutlery into the empty porcelain sink, ran a hot tap over them, then turned back to Tom. Seeing his new housemate was engrossed in the show, Ed tutted and went upstairs.

On *Dig This* Jeremy had finished assessing all the various items found in the archaeological trench from that day. 'A wonderful start. Wouldn't you say, Toby?'

'Indeed. Thank you, Jeremy. Here's a fascinating find,' said Toby Johnson. The camera cut to a rusted metal box on the table. 'While one of the girls was excavating, she unearthed this old purple biscuit tin. Nothing too unusual about that, you might think?'

'I doubt Iron-age man had much care for custard creams, eh, Toby?' Jeremy said, chuckling.

'Well, you may be surprised. It's not so much the tin but what we found inside that's got the team here baffled.' Toby removed the lid from the rectangular tin and lifted out something swaddled in a piece of grey cloth. Gently unwrapping it, he revealed an old dark brown book. 'Take a look at this.'

Jeremy's eyebrows leapt high above his half-rimmed glasses as he took the object from Toby. 'Good gracious.'

'We don't know how it came to be here,' said Toby, turning

to face the camera, 'or why someone would want to bury it. Some of our crew estimate it to be eleventh century.'

The same size and weight of a paperback novel, Jeremy cradled the old artefact in his hands, as if holding a newborn. 'The craftsmanship of the leather, Toby,' he stammered, 'and... and the condition of this binding, it's remarkable.' With a quivering finger and thumb, he gently opened the book. 'The vellum pages are practically unspoilt, for its age, I mean. I'm inclined to agree with the team, it looks eleventh century.' He composed himself as he tried to control his excitement. 'Look here at this inscription on the inside cover, it's written in Old English.' Silently, he mouthed the words to himself.

Toby flapped a hand at the cameraman to zoom in on the text, which read: 'boc of æfre'.

'What does it *mean*, Jeremy?' Toby enquired.

'I'm not entirely sure? The literal translation is *Book of Always* or *Book of Forever*, maybe. But, I've never encountered anything quite like it before.' He turned over the pages. 'There doesn't seem to be anything else written in it. See for yourself.'

'It's blank?' said Toby, craning in to study the pages.

'As am I,' chortled Jeremy. 'Wonder why anyone would discard such a historic item, in a biscuit tin of all things?'

'Our first thought upon discovering it,' said Toby, 'was that it may have been stolen, then hidden here perhaps?'

A blur of memory shot through Tom's mind. *Stolen. Hidden.* He sat bolt upright on the sofa, his eyes transfixed at the television screen.

'Well, there you have it,' said Toby, to the camera. 'Our first day here has certainly proved to be an intriguing one.' He turned back to the historian. 'I have to say, Jeremy, for a book so old, the condition it's in has got everyone here baffled. Can't say the same for the biscuit tin it was found in.'

'Ha, very true.' Jeremy laughed. 'Judging by the rust, I would take an educated guess that tin's been underground for a good few years, but nowhere near the age of its contents.'

Toby shook his head. 'It certainly is a mystery as to why

someone would bury such an interesting object, and here of all places?'

'It beggars belief.' Jeremy caressed the pages with his fingertips. He held the book so the cameraman could get a better close-up. 'Just look at the sheer quality, Toby, it's such a shame there's nothing written on the pages. Anything that could give us a better understanding to its origin.'

'Huh?' Tom's eyebrows drew a deep wrinkle of a frown. 'What the hell's happening to those pages?'

Chapter 4
Ink

Tom must have been hallucinating. *Yes, that was it*, he reasoned, *a hallucination.* It couldn't have been his name, surely not? *A coincidence then? It must be another Thomas Last, not the most original of names. Thomas is popular, and Last probably is too.*

As Toby and Jeremy chatted, the camera had been fixed on the book. The open page had briefly shimmered with golden light, just long enough for Tom to notice. Then maroon words had begun seeping from the pages. When fully visible, these words formed a list of names – each one a different signature in various types of handwriting – all written in the same blood-coloured ink. At the bottom of the page, clearly visible on the television screen, was Tom's name. Recognising the familiar signature immediately, from the credit card he'd retrieved from his wallet earlier that day, he sat and rubbed his eyes.

The two presenters had said, just moments before, how there was nothing written in the book apart from the inscription on the inside cover. Yet, right in front of them the pages had come alive with writing. Toby and Jeremy continued to talk, seemingly oblivious to the bizarre occurrence.

'Well, there we have it,' said Toby, now winding up. 'A good selection of Iron-age artefacts to sift through and an old blank book from the eleventh century. Not bad for our first day. Join us after the break, when we'll be chatting to geographical historian Jane Jenkins, who'll elaborate as to what the Iron-age settlement, here on the Penmoor, would've been like.'

Flapping his arms at the television, Tom shouted, 'What the hell is wrong with you all?'

Ed came back downstairs. 'They need to get a better hobby, that's what's wrong with them, mate.' He looked over at Tom, who was now sat with his hands cupping his mouth. 'I've never seen anyone get worked up over a history show before. If it was football, I'd understand.'

'Just shut up a minute,' snapped Tom, then immediately back-pedalled. 'Sorry. I'm sorry.'

'Whoa, okay there, buddy?' asked Ed. 'You've got a weird look on your face.'

'Weird?' Tom snorted. 'What I've just seen on that show is bloody weird, Ed. You won't believe it.'

Ed walked over to the TV. 'Oh I'm not so sure, mate. I've seen plenty of crazy shit in my life. Doubt a couple of boring old farts on the telly could top that.'

With the television muted, Tom began to recount what he'd seen. 'They just unearthed some old book from the ground.'

'Right,' replied Ed. 'And?'

'They all said the pages were blank. Like, none of the people on the show could see anything written inside the book.' Ignoring Ed's raised eyebrow, Tom continued, 'Here's the thing, though, I saw a whole bunch of names suddenly appear on the pages. See what I mean by it being weird?'

'Erm, oh... kay,' said Ed, unsure what to say.

'Look, I know how it must sound,' Tom aimed a hand towards the television, 'but, it was right there on the screen. A list of names and...' He paused a brief moment, preparing for Ed's response. 'The last one was mine.'

'Sure it was, if you say so.' Ed winced then rubbed his temple. 'Look, let's think rationally for a second. You're suffering from amnesia, right? Maybe some sort of psychotic episode too?' He saw Tom's eyes glare at him. 'Hey, it's all right, no need to—' He ducked as a cushion flew over his head.

'If you don't believe me, watch for yourself.' Tom swiped the TV remote off the sofa and thumped the button to unmute. 'Then you'll see.'

Ed stood, arms folded, staring at the screen. He remained silent for fear of another angry cushion from his new housemate. Together, they waited for the ad break to finish.

An immaculately dressed entrepreneur, overly accessorised with gold jewellery, was showing off a wall full of sports shoes. It cut to him driving away in a gold Rolls-Royce with a registration plate that read: SHO3 80SS. 'That's, the man with the million-dollar shoe,' a voiceover announced, 'tomorrow night at nine o'clock.'

Ed shook his head. 'What a load of sh—'

'Shhh,' interrupted Tom. 'It's back on.'

On the screen, Toby and Jeremy had been joined under the gazebo by a woman who resembled a Girl Scout leader. 'Jane,' welcomed Toby, maintaining a well-rehearsed smile, 'glad you could come along.'

'A pleasure to be with you,' she replied, beaming at him. 'What a glorious array of treasures you have for me.'

'Bloody hell, it gets worse,' mumbled Ed. 'Look at that haircut. One plait on someone her age is bad enough, but two? What style would you even call that, Austrian milk-farmer?'

'Shut up and watch,' huffed Tom.

Jane stepped over to Jeremy, who placed his hand on her back, directing her to a table. 'Dude, check it out. That guy totally wants to explore her trench,' joked Ed.

Tom frowned at Ed's crude hand gesture.

'Oh, Jane,' Ed impersonated, in a seductive tone, 'how I want to sift through your debris.'

Tom shook his head and turned back to the show.

The camera panned across the table of Iron-age finds. Next to them sat the book, still open on the same page as before.

'Is that it?' asked Ed, nodding at the television. 'Looks pretty blank to me, mate.'

'What?' Tom shot over to the screen and pressed his finger repeatedly against it. 'Are you taking the piss? Look at it.'

Ed signalled for him to calm down. 'Tom, really, you're freaking me out now. There's nothing written on those pages. They're just plain pieces of paper inside some old book.'

The camera still had the strange artefact in shot as the team discussed a rusty brooch sat beside it. Tom was not going to give up so easily. 'My name is right there.' Again, he poked at the screen with his finger. 'Below someone called...' he squinted at the signature above his own, 'Lance... Goldstorm?'

'This is a joke, right?' scoffed Ed, who wandered off to the kitchen. 'The famous magician? Pull the other one, mate.'

'Wait,' called Tom, following him across the room. 'You've heard of that guy?'

'Well, duh. Didn't you hear me? I said *famous* magician.' Ed opened the fridge and took out a beer bottle. He flipped off the cap with a metal opener attached to one of the cupboards. 'Goldstorm was a huge star when I was a kid. His tricks were gruesome but that was the appeal.' Ed thrust the bottle into Tom's hand, then went back to the fridge to grab another. 'He once jumped off the Eiffel Tower *without* a parachute. There was a curtain set up at the bottom,' Ed removed the cap from his own bottle and took a swig before continuing, 'but the curtains failed to close. Everyone witnessed him impact into the ground. Blood. Splat. Everywhere. Only then, after a brief pause, did the curtains finally close. Onlookers were losing their shit, man. Women were screaming, men crying, just going crazy. And then, suddenly the curtains were thrown back and there was Goldstorm, looking like a right smug arsehole, dressed in a fresh tuxedo and casually sipping champagne. I swear, it was coolest thing I'd ever seen. The guy was invincible.'

Tom, now glad of the beer, took a long gulp. 'So why would both our names be written in some random book unearthed on *Dig This*?'

Ed leaned back against the kitchen work surface. 'I think the real question here, mate, is why did you imagine seeing both your names in that book?'

'I know what I saw, Ed. I'm not going crazy, if that's what you're implying.'

'But you have to see it from my perspective, Tom,' said Ed. 'If neither me or anyone on that show noticed anything strange on those pages then surely that leaves only one answer. I dunno, maybe what happened to you this morning scrambled your brain.'

Tom had heard enough. 'Thanks for the beer.' he said, scowling as he plonked down the bottle. 'I need to be alone.'

'But it's not even seven o'clock?' shouted Ed, watching Tom stomp off up the stairs. 'Tom, come on, man,' he called after him. 'Don't be like that, mate. At least finish your beer first?'

Tom slammed the bedroom door shut. He sat on the bed, head in his hands. *I'm not going mad.* After some time had passed, he knew what needed to be done. Tomorrow, he would need to wake up early.

Journal of a Sorcerer
I

'The crystal dagger grew blood-red as I thrust it into her young heart. While the acrid stench of death will haunt my nostrils for many days to come, it is the young girl's dying screams, I fear, which will haunt me forever.

'As though I had captured the very light of the moon, the crystal transformed into a bright white light, consuming her spirit. Following the instructions on the ancient scroll, I captured more of the girl's blood inside an inkhorn before mixing it with a common tannic base...'

*

'I have retired to my chamber. I shall use the arcane ink to inscribe the king's register. This should bind the Eternus spell within the pages.'

*

'The servants have brought me food and provided me with a rare, sweetened wine, a gesture from the king, they said, to show his appreciation.

'I plan to drink the entire jug this evening, not in celebration, but to numb my thoughts for what is to follow. May the Lord show mercy for the part I have played in this.'

Chapter 5
Going Undercover

A golden beam shone onto Tom's face through the narrow gap between the thick material of the bedroom curtains. Slowly opening his eyes, he rolled onto his back, stretched out his legs, feeling safe under the thin cotton sheet – a complete contrast to how he'd awoken the day before. But within minutes of lying there, it didn't take long for the memories of yesterday to drip-feed their way back into his head. Thoughts about the missing parts of his memory, the mysterious list of names in that book on *Dig This* and what he was intending to do next. Tom got dressed, gave his jacket a quick dust-off with his hand and, checking the coast was clear, crept downstairs.

In the kitchen, the two empty beer bottles from last night were now accompanied by a dozen more on the breakfast bar. *Bloody hell*, he thought, *Ed had a good night*. He stood there for a minute and ate a banana from a nearby fruit bowl.

Noticing the digital clock on the oven, he whispered to himself, 'Have I really been asleep for nearly fifteen hours?' Finishing off the banana, he poured himself a large glass of water, downed it, then quietly slipped out the front door.

Stepping out into the bright light of the morning, Tom hurried across the courtyard. He was about to round the corner of the cottage when Leonard called to him, from the rear door of the house.

'Ah, good morning, Thomas,' the old professor greeted him, beaming like the clear morning sun. 'Up early, aren't we?'

Tom smiled, acknowledging him. 'Yeah, thought I'd go for a drive, try to retrace my steps.'

'I see.' Placing his hands on his hips, Leonard drew a big lungful of the fresh morning air. 'Good plan,' he boomed. 'No joy refilling that grey matter of yours after a night's rest then, I take it?'

Fidgeting on the spot, Tom had the image of the book in his head. 'No, just a couple of little flashes, but nothing important.'

'Oh, I shouldn't worry too much, I'm sure it'll all come back eventually,' said Leonard, noting Tom's uneasy stance. 'I'll leave you to your investigation then. But, the offer's still there if you want me to contact my doctor for you?'

'Thanks, but I'll be okay for now.'

The professor turned to head into the wooden-clad workshop, when Tom stopped him.

'Actually, Leonard, you didn't happen to catch that show, *Dig This*, last night, did you?'

'It was on, yes,' said Leonard. 'Can't say I was paying much attention though. Why do you ask?'

'Don't suppose you saw the bit where they found an old book wrapped up inside a biscuit tin, did you?'

Leonard nodded. 'Yes, I did see that part.' He let out a slight chuckle as he recalled it. 'Most unusual indeed.'

'I thought I saw something odd on the pages.' Tom noticed the professor's expression. 'It doesn't matter. Probably nothing.'

'Can't say I spotted anything unusual about it, other than why some idiot had buried it, of course. What was it you thought you saw?'

Tom paused. Given Ed's reaction, he wondered how to word it. 'I thought I could see writing on the pages, but it must've been a mistake. Ed thought I'd gone bonkers. Maybe he's right?'

'Well, sorry to disappoint you, but they seemed perfectly blank to me.' Leonard shrugged. 'Apart from the Old English inscription. I'm fluent in that language, by the way.' He appeared to be quite proud of that last part. 'Maybe whatever caused your memory loss is messing around with your brain a little, hmm? See how you get on retracing your steps today. If you're still having problems, I'm always here to help.

'If you'll excuse me now, Tom,' urged Leonard, turning to

leave. 'I really should get started. I have a little project to shout and grumble at.' He pointed towards the workshop door. 'Something I've been working on for well over ten years now.' His voice trailed off, as he sauntered away.

Tom shook his head as the door to the wooden shed shut to. He headed off around the cottage to the driveway, and to his GT6.

**

Snaking its way through the woodland, the road eventually opened up to reveal the scenic Penmoor hills up ahead; varying sized domes of green, punctuated here and there by the white cloud-like dots of grazing sheep. As Tom drew closer, he slowed down behind a white van, indicator flashing, in front. As it turned right, into a narrow road, Tom noticed a large red vinyl sticker on the side of it. 'Channel Seven,' he read out loud. *That's the Dig This channel.* Allowing an oncoming car to pass by, Tom turned into the narrow road, following the van.

The road ended onto a small quiet car park. Tom crept the GT6 across the bumpy ground and parked the opposite side to the van – not to appear obvious he'd followed it. Peering into his rear-view mirror, he saw a gruff-looking man open the back doors of the *Channel Seven* van and slide out a long metal stand. The man paused and, removing his black baseball cap, wiped his sweaty forehead with the sleeve of his red fleece jacket. Placing his cap back on, he reached into the van once more.

Struggling to carry the metal stand, a spotlight and a flight case the man now lugged his way over to a wooden gate, adjacent to the entrance. He rested the equipment down against a drystone wall, then proceeded to swear loudly at the chain that held the gate locked.

'You all right there, mate?' Tom asked, as he walked over.

'Bloody morons,' cussed the crewman, his thick Glaswegian accent embellishing his frustration. 'I wish they'd stop locking this sodding gate. Three times now I've told them to leave the damned thing open. Three times. I mean, come on, it's not a difficult thing to remember, is it, sonny?'

'Totally agree.' Tom nodded. 'They're always doing stuff like this, though, aren't they?'

'You part of the team then?' said the crewman, giving Tom a brief couldn't-care-less examination. 'Can't say I've seen you before.'

'Er… Yes, archaeology student, just helping out here for today.' He pointed to the equipment. 'I'll give you a hand, if you want?'

'Aye.' The crewman sighed, sizing up Tom's thin frame. He pointed to the metal stand. 'Grab that, if you can.'

After they'd lifted the equipment over the gate, Tom and the crewman walked up a grassy track, leading into an open field. *It's exactly like I saw on the telly*, thought Tom, taking in all that was going on ahead. The field rose steadily, and at the far corner Tom could see the turf had been stripped back in a couple of places. Surrounding these shallow trenches, people were trowelling away.

From up ahead, the crewman was stood. In one hand he gripped the heavy flight case, using the other to steady the awkwardly shaped spotlight that he'd balanced on his shoulder. He shook his head at Tom, who was stood staring at the filming location. 'Try to keep up, son,' shouted the man. 'Don't get me wrong, I do appreciate the help, but I haven't got all day.'

Tom quickened his pace, switching his grip on the stand every few steps. 'Did you see that book they discovered in that biscuit tin?' he said, puffing. 'We get some weird finds on these digs, eh?'

'Yeah, sure, that book thing,' the crewman replied, his frustration subsiding the closer he got to the gazebos in the far end of the field. 'To be honest though, sonny, as long as I get paid, I really couldn't give a rat's arse about what you lot pull out the ground.'

'Well, I thought it was interesting,' said Tom, 'especially since the pages were blank. Who knows what it might've originally been made for, right?' The crewman, however, was no longer paying any attention.

They reached the gazebos. About twenty feet to their right a caravan was parked; the black and green grime on its faded cream paintwork made it look as though it had itself recently been unearthed. A few feet beyond the caravan was a silver catering van with its side panel hoisted up. Inside this, a man was busy hovering over a grill, frying bacon and, from the smell of it, burning onions.

Looking around, Tom could see a herd of archaeologists at the furthest trench chatting to Toby Johnson. Placing the metal stand down, next to the other equipment, Tom turned back to the crewman. 'Don't suppose you know where it is, do you? The book, I mean. Wouldn't mind having a quick peek before I start for the day. Would help me with my, um… assignment.'

The crewman chuckled to himself. 'They'd have packed it away by now.' He left Tom standing there and walked off in the direction of the catering van. 'But, you could have a nosey in there, sonny,' he said, stopping to point to the grubby caravan. 'That's usually where stuff ends up. Just don't let security catch you rummaging through things, they get a bit arsey, y'know.'

'Thanks.' Tom headed to the caravan door, waited until he was sure no one was watching, then let himself in.

The musty smell of outdated fabric upholstery filled Tom's nostrils as he scanned the drab interior. Several pairs of wellington boots were slung on the grey carpeted floor, a pile of waterproof clothes dumped on seats. Sat on a small, central dining table was a large blue plastic container. *That has to be it*. Tom went over and began to remove the scrunched-up packing paper from inside. He peered in. 'Where are you,' he whispered, removing a few historical items. He moved some bubble wrap from the bottom, hoping the book would be there. 'Damn it,' he hissed, looking instead at a broken wooden plate.

Outside the caravan, someone could be heard talking. Tom hurried over to peer through the net curtain-covered window. Not noticing a low shelf above, he banged his forehead against it. 'Gah, stupid bloody thing.' He winced, thumping the underside of the veneered shelf with his fist. A metal box, that was balanced on top, clattered apart onto the floor. 'Shit.' He panicked, hoping the loud noise hadn't been heard outside.

Looking to the floor, Tom felt adrenaline coursing. It was the biscuit tin, and still wrapped up inside, the book. He lifted it out from its swaddled cloth, feeling a shiver as he ran his fingers across the cover. He drew in a long, steady breath, sliding a thumb slowly along the edge. 'Please,' he whispered, 'don't be blank.'

His attention swung from the book to the voice outside the door of the caravan. In a hurry, Tom grabbed the lid to the biscuit tin, replaced it, then shoved it back on top of the shelf. 'Bollocks,' he cursed, spotting the cloth that had been left on the floor. Picking it up, he stowed it in his jacket pocket and sprinted over to a wardrobe door at the far end of the caravan. Entering, he shut it just as the door to the caravan opened.

Don't find me, don't find me, he repeated, his thoughts paused only to allow his ears to fully operate.

The floor creaked as someone mooched about. Tom, realising he wasn't actually hiding in a wardrobe, sat down on a chemical toilet. In his head, he imagined the toilet door swinging open and him cracking a joke, to whoever was there, about wanting privacy.

'Hello, Nigel?' came the voice from the other side of the door. It was Toby Johnson. 'Listen to me,' he continued, 'I want someone removed from the show. Can you arrange that?'

Tom listened as Toby paced the caravan talking into his phone.

'That sodding Jane Jenkins. Yes, the local historian.' He went silent for a couple of seconds, then in a raised voice, spat, 'Because, she keeps trying to grope me, Nigel. It's becoming a nuisance. I can hear the crew tittering behind my back. I shouldn't have to put up with this, Nigel. I used to be on the UK's number one, highest-rated comedy show, remember?'

The sound of his pacing stopped. 'She's basically a sex-pest, Nigel,' yelled Toby. 'She squeezed my arse-cheeks three times during yesterday's filming. Take this morning, for example. I peered out of my hotel window, and there she was across the street, bold as brass, doing things… awful, degrading things, I might add, to a poster of me at the bus stop.'

Tom pinched his lips together, restraining a snigger.

'Never mind "what things?", Nigel,' scorned Toby. 'You're the producer, now take care of it, man.'

Hearing the caravan door slam shut, Tom released a childish burst of laughter. Composing himself, he turned his attention back to the book clutched in his hands.

Letting the cover fall open on his lap, he stared at the blank pages and waited.

It took only seconds before the familiar maroon ink seeped out of the pages, forming writing, just as it had done the night before. Tom's brain struggled to compute what he was witnessing first-hand. Right in front of his eyes, a list of signatures in clear view. He flicked the pages over until he reached the final name, his own signature. Everything he'd seen on the television screen, all of it, had been true. He wasn't traumatised, deluded, or whatever Ed thought he was.

***

The GT6 raced back along the country road. Tom's foot was pressed firmly down on the accelerator pedal, his eyes checking the rear-view mirror, worried someone had seen him hurriedly leaving the site. Every few seconds he glanced at the passenger seat, *What are you?* he thought, bewildered by the mysterious artefact sat there. *How did my signature get in there?* He rounded a tight bend; not paying full attention, the car veered into the centre of the road. 'Whoa, easy, Tom,' he told himself, as he brought the GT6 back over.

He wished he could remember signing the book, but whatever had caused his amnesia had done a thorough job of removing that memory too. There was also the way the ink appeared in the pages. *Must be some kind of trick ink*, he rationalised. *But why hasn't anyone else seen it?*

Tom emerged from his thoughts just in time to see a huge bird fly straight at the car's windscreen. He wrenched the steering wheel to avoid hitting it. The tyres of the GT6 screeched as his hands fought to regain control. Within seconds, the car zigzagged off the road and onto a grass verge. Turf pelted up against the windows, blocking Tom's view of the oncoming sheer drop.

There was a sudden bang as the wheel rims impacted, side on, into a metal barrier. The speed the car was going caused the whole vehicle to flip over it, like a gymnast over a vaulting horse. Glass exploded around Tom, his arms flailed about trying to protect himself. The roof collapsed in, forcing his head to crack into the dashboard.

Spinning, rolling, bouncing, the car now descended. Tom's limbs cracked and twisted as they were thrown around. The GT6 came to a stop, its final resting place upside down at the bottom of a gorge.

The brief silence was pierced by Tom's screams echoing through the valley. Blood filled his eyes, as he hung upside down pinned by his seatbelt. The weight of his body was pushing his head against the ceiling. It took all his strength to lift up the least-mangled arm and unclip himself.

His knees fell against the steering wheel as he slumped. Spluttering, he spat a broken tooth from his mouth then took an excruciatingly rasped breath.

Unable to see or hear, his sense of smell went into overdrive. The potent, stinging fumes of petrol filling Tom's nostrils mainlined the danger straight to his brain, *Get the hell out, now.*

With the driver's door crumpled shut, the only means of escape was via the passenger side door. Luckily, this had been flung open during the cascade. Tom threw his arm across, grappling hold of the door frame with his fingertips. He pulled with all his remaining energy, crying out in pure anguish as his muscles protested. Clambering free from the wreckage, but able to go no further, he rolled onto his back. As he lay on the petrol-soaked earth, his lungs wheezed out a final breath.

Chapter 6
Healed & Sealed

Her voice sounded soft, soothing even, like…

'Honey?'

That's exactly how it sounds, thought Tom as he rolled his head.

'Hello, can you hear me, honey?'

Whoever she was, the voice was definitely speaking to him.

'There's no phone signal here, but don't worry I'll get help to you, somehow.'

'I can hear you, but everything's black,' said Tom. 'Keep talking so I can locate you.'

'Try opening your eyelids,' she answered. 'That'll make it easier.'

Tom blinked a couple of times, then shut them tightly. The golden light burnt an after-image, a silhouette of a young woman, into his retinas. 'Are you real?' he asked, easing his eyelids open again.

'Given your situation, it would really suck for you if I wasn't,' she replied. 'Just don't move, okay?'

His pupils managed to focus on a smile. 'You're… an angel?'

'Aw, thanks. Most people don't recognise us straight away, not in our plain clothes,' she said, referring to her yellow summer dress. 'We ditched the white robes and sandals centuries ago, budget cuts from head office. I keep the wings back in my car. My name's Zoe.'

His sight becoming clearer, Tom studied the young woman – maybe a year or so younger than himself – knelt over him. 'Am I alive?' he said, still somewhat disorientated.

'Very much so,' said Zoe, scanning his body. 'You don't

seem to have any visible injuries. Judging by the mess your car's in, you should lie there until I can get an ambulance. And, sorry to disappoint you, but I'm not an angel.'

Zoe's frizzy brown hair was bathed in a golden halo, from the sunlight behind her. 'You could've fooled me,' muttered Tom, under his breath.

'I'm Tom, by the way.' He backtracked to something she'd just said. 'Hold on, no visible injuries?'

'I know,' Zoe pointed to the battered GT6. 'Your car's completely totalled. There's glass and metal all around here, but you don't have a scratch on you. Well, from what I can see anyway.'

'But, but, there was blood?' stammered Tom, tripping over the words. 'It was everywhere. And my bones, I felt them break.' He clutched his forearm. 'I don't understand?'

Zoe rested her hands on his chest. 'I think you're in shock. Listen to me carefully, there's no blood on you,' she reassured, 'but you need to lie still.'

'Lie still?' Tom grew agitated. 'Wait, I can't feel anything.'

Zoe tensed. 'Okay. I think the crash might've damaged your spine. Just stay calm, please.'

'No,' snapped Tom. 'That's not what I mean. I don't feel... hurt.' He chanced moving a leg.

'Don't do that, Tom, you could make things a whole lot worse.'

Ignoring her, Tom raised his leg. 'It's not broken. See?'

Her arms reached out, trying to restrain his kicking foot. 'What're you doing? C'mon, don't lift the other one.' But, protest as she did, she couldn't stop Tom from forcing himself onto his feet.

'There,' he said, standing up. 'This is so weird.' He felt inside his mouth. 'My teeth are all here, what the hell?'

'Um... okay?' Zoe stood up, wincing at Tom's behaviour.

'Don't you see?' he blurted. 'I'm not injured any more.'

Zoe watched as he ran over to the wreckage and looked inside. 'What are you doing?'

'In here,' he rambled. 'I remember smacking my head on

the roof, then hearing my skull crack on the dashboard.' He moved his hair out of the way for Zoe to see. 'Well, any signs of injury?'

'No?'

'Exactly. I felt bones in my arms and legs snap as they were flung about.' He wiggled them, one by one. 'Do you see any evidence of that?'

Zoe gave him a quick glance, then a brief head shake.

'Don't you find that weird?'

Zoe had heard enough. 'No,' she said. 'I find how you're acting *now* weird though. I'm going back up to the road to try to flag someone down. Please, Tom, just stay here.' She stomped away back up the steep slope towards the road; her Doc Marten boots emphasising every quickening step.

Tom scrambled into the GT6 and retrieved the book. Hurrying after her, he shouted, 'Wait, you don't get it.'

'No, Tom, I don't.' Zoe said, clambering up over an outcrop of rock.

'Zoe,' Tom called out. 'Let me explain. There's some sort of magical thing going on with me.'

Zoe stopped.

Finally, thought Tom, as he lifted himself over the outcrop. Catching up with her, he waved the book in her face. 'This was on the show *Dig This*, last night,' he said, speaking nineteen to the dozen. 'I stole it this morning. There's this crazy ink inside it that only I can see.'

Zoe turned towards him and grabbed the book. 'Listen, mate,' she said, giving him an authoritative glare. 'I don't know what the hell you're going on about. One thing's clear though, you've obviously sustained some kind of head injury. Clearly, it's making you delusional. Now, for the last time, sit down and wait until I can get help. Jesus.'

'But, I'm not imagining it,' he protested. 'I just need you to hear me out. Please, there's been some really crazy shit happen to me lately, I admit, but I'm not bonkers. I just need a lift back to Penworthy, then I'll be out of your way. I promise.'

Zoe took a deep breath, a micro-reset. 'Fine. I still think you shouldn't be walking after what's just happened, but I guess I could give you a lift. You must let me call an ambulance the moment we get back though; it'll take them a while to get to you from the nearest town.' She slapped the book back into his hands. 'Deal?'

'Deal.'

Even though Tom didn't need it, Zoe insisted on helping him up the final steep grassy embankment. However, just before they reached the road, Tom stumbled and lost his footing. Placing a hand out to stop his fall, his palm landed flat on a piece of glass. Cursing, he quickly pulled the shard out.

'Whoa.' Zoe helped him up. 'You all right?'

'Cut my hand open.' He held up his palm to show her the blood. 'Glass from the wing mirror over there.' Tom wiped his hand on his jeans, then checked the wound. 'It's deep, but nothing too serious.'

'My car's just up here,' said Zoe, hurrying him along. 'As soon as we get in, I'll sort it out. Come on.'

They reached a yellow Mini, parked up on the grass verge. Clicking a button on her car key, Zoe unlocked it. 'Hop in.'

Once inside, Zoe leaned over to the glove box, opened it and removed a packet of wet wipes. 'Here, clean the cut with these,' she said, handing them to him.

Tom removed a wipe and began rubbing the blood away, feeling a sharp sting as he did so. 'What's on these things,' he asked, wincing at the growing pain in his hand. 'It really burns.'

'Stop being a wuss.' Zoe rummaged around some more, then handed Tom a paper tissue from a pack. 'Use this, should help slow the blood. Tom?' Looking at him, she noticed how pale his face had grown. 'You okay? You're not gonna puke in my car, are you?'

The pain in his hand had escalated to searing agony. 'It's getting worse,' he said, grimacing. Pulling a tissue from the pack, he dabbed at the cut. As he stared at his palm, it looked as though the blood was changing colour. 'Erm, Zoe?'

They both focused on the wound, an orange glow rippled across the congealed blood. 'I'm no doctor,' said Zoe, her brown eyes widening as she gawped at what was happening, 'but that ain't normal.'

'Gahh.' Clutching tightly at his wrist, Tom's arm muscles tensed. He spat the words, 'Holy shit,' before clamping his teeth together.

'How are you doing that?' Zoe watched, in awe, as a small white spark flickered into life on Tom's hand. Crackling, it moved along the open wound, as though being welded.

Pulling a bunch of wet wipes from the pack, Zoe pressed them down hard onto Tom's palm, seemingly extinguishing it.

Tom's muscles relaxed as he held the wipes. Dropping his hand onto his lap, he heaved a sigh and opened up his palm. 'Thanks.'

'Never mind *Thanks*, look at your hand,' spluttered Zoe, in amazement.

He stared at the now flawless smooth skin. Flipping his hand over and back, Tom squeezed his fingers. 'Healed,' he whispered in surprise.

'What the hell just happened?' Jerking back, Zoe scrambled for the door handle. She kicked the door open and retreated.

Tom swung open the passenger door. Jumping out, he tried to calm her. 'Wait, it's okay, Zoe, just don't freak out.'

'Don't, sodding, freak out? Are you kidding me?' She glanced up the quiet road, then paced back and forth along it. 'Your hand… literally just healed itself. In case you weren't aware, that kind of shit isn't natural, Tom.'

Staying on his side of the car, Tom placed his outstretched arms on the roof. 'I know, but that's what I was trying to tell you before. Something really weird, or magical, er… probably both, is happening to me. I remember seeing blood and feeling my bones break during the crash, before I passed out. Next thing I remember is you being there and somehow I'm fine.'

'So what are you saying?' Zoe walked up to the driver's door. 'You have some sort of superpower?'

'No,' said Tom, trying to remain calm. 'That's what *you're* saying.'

Zoe was shaking, what she'd just witnessed seemed real enough. But, it must be some kind of trick – and she happened to be an expert on magic tricks. 'Let me tell you something, Tom. Below my family's flat is our shop. A magic shop. We sell stuff for both professional and wannabe magicians alike. Most of the things we sell are utter crap. But, some of the professional stuff can actually pull off a fairly convincing trick, y'know? What you just did though beats all that, hands down. Sorry, no pun intended.' She aimed an index finger at him. 'Now, be honest with me, what is *really* going on here? Did my dad put you up to this?'

Zoe's father 'did' magic. As a child, the first trick she saw him do was make a bunch of flowers appear in his hands, seemingly from nowhere. Her four-year-old self beamed at the spectacle. Then, three years later, she recalled her disappointment as he emptied a large cardboard box onto the shop floor. The exact same flowers slid out, all packaged in cellophane. He wasn't the great magician she thought he was; he'd pretended. After that, she saw trick after trick unpacked and dispelled as her belief in real magic dwindled to nothing. She shook the memory from her mind.

Tom scratched his head. He tried to come up with an answer, flicking his eyes at his hand and then Zoe, um-ing and ah-ing.

'This is the part where you explain, Tom. Start talking.' She thrust her arms into a folded position and, with one eyebrow raised, glared at him.

'Okay.' Tom drew a deep breath. 'Yesterday morning, I woke up in the Penmoor with no idea who I was or how I got there. I have amnesia, apparently.'

'Right,' said Zoe. 'So you must've sustained some kind of brain injury?'

'I guess so.' Tom shrugged. 'I mean, it looked like I'd fallen pretty hard down a cliff.'

'But you don't have any injuries?'

'Exactly. After what just happened to me in the car crash, it seems I genuinely have some kind of ability to heal, like, really fast.'

'No shit.' Zoe walked over to him.

Tom held up the tissue she'd given him. 'You saw the blood on my hand vanish, and see,' unravelling the crumpled paper, 'the blood's gone from this too.'

Zoe raised a hand to stop Tom for a moment, while she processed this. 'Okay, so let's just say, for a minute, that what you're saying is true. What's the deal with the book?'

Tom grabbed the book and passed it to her. 'When I arrived in the village, I was offered a place to stay by an old professor. You might know him, Leonard Goodwin?'

'Sure, I know of him. Well, actually I know the guy who lodges at his place, Ed White.'

Tom smiled. 'Yep, he seems cool. They both do.'

'I beat Ed at poker down the local pub.' Zoe shook her head. 'He still owes me. But, he's okay. The old prof's a bit of an eccentric country type, friendly enough, though.' She opened up the book and looked at the inscription. 'And, this thing was on some TV show, was it?'

'Yeah.' Tom winced and scratched the back of his head. 'So, last night I was watching the show *Dig This*, when that thing was found. The presenters said how unusual it was that the pages were all blank.' Tom saw Zoe looking at the Old English words. 'Apart from the inscription.'

'Did they translate it?' asked Zoe, studying it more closely.

'Something like, book of forever.' Tom pointed for Zoe to turn the pages over. 'If you look at the rest of the book, you'll probably see nothing written, though, right?'

'Um, yeah?'

'That's the thing, Zoe, I can see something. There's loads of names. People's signatures.'

Zoe frowned at him, then at the book. She held it up flat, in front of her face. 'There's definitely nothing written in there, Tom.'

'But, you're wrong.' He quickly back-pedalled, 'I mean, everyone is. When the book is opened, the words appear for me, in blood-red ink. The last person to sign it was me.' Tom placed his finger on his signature. But, all Zoe could see was an empty page.

'So you just decided to wake up this morning,' said Zoe, in a sarcastic tone, 'and say to yourself, "You know, why don't I go and steal that book? Prove what I'm seeing is true. Forget logic and common sense, or that I could just be imagining things, let's go break the law".'

'Well, I wouldn't say I was imagining it,' said Tom, feeling a little hurt by this, 'but, yeah.'

'And I suppose after nicking the book, you sped away and that's how you ended up down there?' Zoe pointed back down to the wreck of the GT6.

'No, actually I ended up down there because a bird flew at my windscreen, so I swerved to miss it.' Tom grabbed the book from her, then turned to walk off.

'And, where do you think you're going?' called Zoe.

'I don't have to explain myself, Zoe,' shouted Tom, as he headed away down the road. 'I know I'm not mad, or imagining things.'

Zoe leant her elbow on the roof of the Mini, watching Tom shove the book in his jacket pocket as he stomped off. 'Gah,' she grunted. 'I know I'm going to regret this.' She walked round to the driver's side of the car, reached in and pipped the horn.

Tom stopped and turned round.

'Well, don't just stand there looking like a lost puppy.' Zoe waved him back. 'Get in.'

**

Ten minutes after Zoe and Tom had left, a motorcyclist arrived at the scene of the crash. A person, masked by a helmet and clad in blue biker leathers, dismounted the growling Harley-Davidson. Removing the ignition key, the stranger then gave the cylindrical hat box, strapped to the back of the bike, a light tap. Clambering over the buckled metal barrier, the biker began to descend the steep slope towards the wreckage at the bottom.

Chapter 7
Cheap Tricks

'Bloody Saturday shoppers,' tutted Zoe, at a car parked across the entrance to a narrow side street. 'Can't they see the large words saying "No Parking" written on the road? We'll just have to park further down and walk up.'

The Mini shot down the high street and swung into the last space between two cars.

'Listen, Tom, before we get out I should give you a heads-up about my dad,' said Zoe, switching off the engine of the car.

'Sure,' he answered, taking his eyes away from the succession of window shoppers on the busy pavement.

'My parents were once a professional magic act, but they just run their shop now. Dad can't help slipping back into his theatrical side, which can be a little overbearing at times.' She unclipped her seatbelt and opened her car door.

'Hey, you know I mentioned the other signatures in the book?'

Zoe, humouring him, gave a dragged out, 'Yeees?'

'When I told Ed the name of the signature above mine, he said it belonged to a famous magician. Maybe your dad might know him?'

'Oh, right,' replied Zoe. 'Who was it?'

'Lance Goldstorm?'

Zoe pulled the car door shut with a slam.

'I take it you've definitely heard of him then?' said Tom, as he leaned away from her.

'Do *not* mention that name to my dad,' she answered, her expression emphasising the warning. 'Understand?'

'Um…' Tom felt as though he'd just trodden on a landmine; the slightest wrong word would trigger it. 'Okay?'

Zoe closed her eyes briefly. Taking a sharp breath, she explained, 'Lance ended my parents' career, or so Dad says. Mum and him argue about it still to this day. Dad hasn't accepted the fact that his shot at fame's gone, whereas Mum has.'

'Sorry.' Tom lowered his head. 'Didn't mean to upset you.'

Zoe's expression eased. 'Sorry for snapping, it's just they had another bust-up about it this morning. Dad unpacked a product, some sort of hovering skull trick, he said how it reminded him of the good times. Mum told him how these *are* the good times, which of course she said while shouting.' Turning her head away, she muttered, 'Good times.'

'Look, I promise I won't say a word,' said Tom, clutching the book.

'Let's just go,' said Zoe. 'Maybe you can convince me you're not mental, over a cuppa.'

Heading off back up the street, overtaking the steady current of pedestrians, Zoe and Tom took a right down a cobbled side street. The oak-framed fronts of the Tudor shops were all beautifully restored, even down to the leading of the diamond lattice windowpanes. As Tom followed Zoe, he studied the mostly black-and-white buildings and felt as though he'd somehow travelled through time. The further they walked along, the quieter it got.

Zoe halted in front of her shop. If the other shops were pedigree dogs, this would be the mongrel. The scruffy, faded black paint on the exterior beams had flaked and peeled patches. The rusting metal sign hanging above the shop window no longer swung. Tom looked at the weathered image on it, a reimagining of a skull and crossbones with an ace of spades for the skull and two magician's wands for the bones. Looking at the hand-painted lettering above, Tom read out, 'Cassam's Magic Emporium.' He peered through the large grimy window at the contents on display; the items for sale looked as though they should belong in a curiosities shop, or maybe exhibits in a museum.

As a centrepiece, Tom saw a larger-than-life black top hat, placed upside down. As he stared at the bizarre prop, a mechanical white rabbit slowly rose up from inside of it; a freaky looking robotic thing, it turned its head to seemingly look at Tom before lowering back down into the over-sized hat once more.

A tinkle of a shop bell brought Tom's attention back to Zoe, who had opened the door and was stood waiting for him in the doorway. 'I see you've just met Roger,' she said with a nod.

Tom shuddered. 'Get many window shoppers here, do you?'

'Not really,' replied Zoe.

'That doesn't surprise me.'

'Come on.' Zoe tilted her head towards the door. 'Let's go in.'

***

A mixture of old polish, mustiness and cheap aftershave lingered in the air of the shop; a smell which leaves one in no doubt the premises had traded in better times.

Tom surveyed the layout. He walked over to a revolving display cabinet in the middle of the shop floor. The six hexagonal glass shelves contained – amongst other items – ten packs of cards, each pack designed for performing different tricks; a flat plastic sliding box labelled 'The Incredible Disappearing Coin Trick' sat on the same shelf as 'The Amazing Finger Guillotine Illusion' and 'The Famous Vanishing Ball In Cup.' All the items on the expensive-looking display unit were anything but that.

Stacked upon bowing shelves on the left-hand wall of the shop were piles of boxed magic sets. Tom read the names of some of these: 'Merlin's Box Of Illusions' written on one, while another claimed 'Twenty Fantasmagorical Illusions To Astound Your Friends'. Tom's favourite of these: 'Ultimate Street Illusionz', the description claimed it contained 'Ten Trickz For Da Gangsta Street Magician'.

In the corner, Tom saw what appeared to be the torture section. A large red cabinet, taller than he was, had what looked like an Egyptian Queen depicted on the front of it. Tom stared at the strange old thing. 'What's that for?'

'It's called a Zig-Zag cabinet,' explained Zoe. 'Someone steps inside, then after the doors are shut, the illusionist slides two large blades into it, making it look as though they've just sliced the person into three.' Zoe removed a square steel blade from the side of the cabinet, level to where a person's shoulders would be. Tom refrained from mentioning how bendy the blade was, as she placed it back inside the cabinet.

'The illusionist can then slide out the middle section to the side, like so...'

Tom watched as Zoe heaved the box-like section across. His attention turned to the device to the right of it.

'I'm sure I don't have to tell you what that is?' said Zoe, pointing to the tall wooden frame housing a deadly-looking blade suspended at the top.

'A guillotine. It's fake, right?' Tom tapped his finger on the razor-sharp blade that hung from the top of the wooden frame. This caused the steel to ring like a tuning fork.

Zoe, stood next to him, whispered, 'Give it a try, if you're not sure.'

Rolling his shoulders back, Tom stiffened his stance. 'Erm... no,' he replied, clearing his throat. 'I'll pass, thanks.'

'Come look at this stuff,' she said, grabbing his arm and pulling him to the opposite side of the shop. 'These are my favourite ones.'

Displayed along this wall, the items included rope tricks, various sleight-of-hand illusions and props. Also, there were rows of books and DVD's on performing detailed magic, filling a tall bookshelf.

Tom picked up a set of three steel rings that were linked together. 'Oh, I've seen these before.' He turned them over in his hands. 'The trick is figuring out how a magician unlinks them, yeah?' He tugged at the rings, trying to part them. 'They must have hidden sections that open,' he said, feeling around each ring for a hairline crack or a join.

'Come on, genius.' Zoe amused herself for a minute,

watching the expression on Tom's face change from smugness to frustration. 'They're just three simple rings of metal,' she said with a smirk. 'Can't be that difficult.'

Nowhere around any of the rings could Tom find a way to slip each one away from the other. He gave in. 'Okay, okay, I get it. The trick is, they can't be unlinked. You just pretend they've been separated by holding them at an angle, or something. Go on, show me how it's done then?'

Zoe smiled and took the rings from Tom. She gave him a wink. 'You forgot to say the magic word.'

Tom shrugged his shoulders. 'Please?'

'Not that word, you numpty.' Holding up the joined rings, Zoe feigned a look of concentration, then took a deep breath.

'ALI CASSAM,' a voice boomed, in a thick Jamaican accent, silencing Zoe. The sudden interruption caused her to drop the rings onto the floor. Now separated, they rolled along the wooden floorboards and came to a stop next to an outlandish pair of alligator skin, Cuban-heeled shoes. 'But, just call me Ali,' the voice continued. 'I'm the proprietor of this fine establishment.'

The shoes weren't the only elaborate item of clothing worn by the tall gent stood by the shop counter. Tom lifted his eyes from the garish footwear, followed the black pinstriped suit past the blood-red tie and stopped at a silver tooth, which glinted inside the widest grin he could ever remember seeing.

'You're tall... sir,' Tom muttered, before his mouth thought better and shut itself up to avoid further embarrassment.

'Who is this, Zoe?' growled Ali, his accent easing back a little.

Zoe shifted her weight to one leg, crossing the other. 'Dad, this is Tom.' She held her hands on her hips. 'Be nice.'

Ali leant against the counter. He gripped the rim of his red trilby hat with his thumb and forefinger, tipped it back from his eyes and assessed the nervous-looking young man who'd befriended his daughter.

Tom gulped, feeling like he was in a scene from a western; the part where two gunslingers were about to kick off in the saloon. 'Nice to meet you,' said Tom, breaking the tension and offering a handshake.

Ali left Tom hanging. Instead, he removed his hat and placed it on the counter. Giving his bald head a brief scratch, the assertive shopkeeper cracked his knuckles. 'And what is your intention with my precious angel today? Well?' he said. 'Answer me, son.'

Zoe shook her head. 'I'm so sorry about this, Tom. He's just messing with you, ignore him.'

Tom was more inclined to *not* ignore the great bear of a man.

Letting out a belly roar, Ali's broad shoulders bounced like a skyscraper in an earthquake. Striding over, he swung a huge hand into Tom's. 'Your face,' he guffawed. 'I really had you worried there.' His expression softened as he welcomed Tom. 'So, how can I be of service, my friend?'

'So... Anyway,' said Zoe, rolling her eyes, 'this was fun. Tom, let's go through to the back. I'll get the kettle on.'

'Um... Thanks again, sir.' Tom unclenched his gluteus muscles, then followed Zoe through a door behind the counter, avoiding eye contact with her father.

***

Clicking the button down on the kettle, Zoe gestured at a small, pine dining table and chairs.

Pulling out a chair, Tom sat down and removed the book from his jacket pocket. 'Thanks for trusting me, Zoe,' he said, placing the old artefact on the table. 'I know how crazy this all sounds.' He studied the kitchen, which, comprising of paintbrushed yellow cabinets, a worn black-and-white tiled floor, all lit by a yellowing fluorescent strip light, looked even more outdated than the shop front.

Zoe moved some unwashed dishes out of the way from

beside the sink, then grabbed a couple of clean mugs from off a draining rack and popped a teabag in each. After pouring the boiled water, she sat down at the table. 'Let me take a look at that book,' she said, sliding it round.

'You won't see anything other than the inscription at the start.' Tom slumped back in his chair as Zoe scanned the pages.

'What did the guys on the show say the inscription said again?'

'Book of forever, or something,' said Tom, leaning forward again and placing his arms on the table. 'I just wish I could remember signing it. And what it's for.'

'You're sure it's just a list of names, nothing else?' Zoe held the book up to her eye level, tilting it to the light. She tried to see if the pages had indents that a pen may have left.

'Yes, just names. Some signatures, others written out.'

'But it's blank, Tom,' she exclaimed, letting the book fall flat on the table. Pinching the bridge of her nose, she composed her thoughts for a moment. 'Okay. You have to see things from my point of view. You're the only person who sees anything other than empty pages.'

Tom knew the routine by now, having to defend his sanity once more. 'I'm not mad, I can see the ink on there right now.' He pointed to a name on the open page. 'Here, someone called William Craddock, and here Zander Du… um, *pricks*?'

Zoe tutted, 'You're just making these up, aren't you?'

Tom thumped the book with his fist. 'No,' he shouted, then whispered an apology. 'It's a real person, it's right there. D-U-P-R-I-X.'

'It's pronounced Du-*pri*, moron,' snorted Zoe.

'Oh, well, sorry for not remembering French lessons either,' muttered Tom. 'Or anything else, it seems.'

Zoe could see this was getting them nowhere. 'Okay, time out,' she said, sliding her chair back and standing. 'I'll get the tea.'

Tom sat, head sunk in his hands for a minute. Suddenly, bolt upright, he turned to Zoe and blurted, 'Goldstorm, of course.'

Zoe rushed over, shushing him. 'What did I say before?' she hissed. 'Do *not* mention his name in here.'

'Hold on,' said Tom, 'hear me out.' He checked towards the door to the shop. 'Don't you see? He's the key.'

'What?'

Pointing at the book, Tom continued. 'His name in here confirms what I thought about the book and the healing ability. They're all linked.'

Zoe frowned, then shook her head.

'Think about it. My name's in this book, whether you believe me or not. So is Lan...' Tom stopped himself from saying it, 'so is *his*. Last night, Ed told me about the Eiffel Tower stunt Lan... *he* did. At the time, Ed thought the man was invincible. That must be what this book is, a secret list of people with special powers. Hence the inscription, right?'

Zoe mulled this over. 'So,' she said after an awkward pause, 'what you're now telling me is you, and *him*, are part of a group of super humans?'

Tom sighed. Saying it like that did make it sound ridiculous. But, at the back of his mind, bells were ringing. 'What if the reason everyone else can't see what's inside this book is because they don't have the power to?'

The theory hung there. Tom watched Zoe tapping her thumb and forefingers together, as she considered this.

Zoe looked deep into his eyes. One of the qualities Zoe was proud of was how she could read what people were feeling. And right now, Tom was giving off a mix of fear and confusion. But as she looked more closely, there was something else tucked away in those tired brown eyes. Honesty.

'You know,' said Zoe, looking at the book, 'it's funny, really.' She turned her attention back to Tom. 'I can't tell you how many times, over the years, my parents hated how Goldstorm's illusions were referred to as death-defying or beyond belief.'

Tom gave her a slight smile. 'Well?'

'Well,' Zoe returned the smile, 'after what I saw happen to

your hand today, maybe you're right. *Maybe.*'

'A great illusionist...' boomed Ali, as he stepped into the kitchen. Tom shunted the book off the table and onto his lap. Zoe spun round to greet her father. 'Oh, what now?'

'Once showed me,' continued Ali, 'how to make an inanimate object come to life.' His eyes opened wide, like roller blinds recoiling, as he strutted his way over to them. Holding his hands out, he wiggled his fingers at Tom, pretending to summon up some kind of mystical power.

Zoe's face blushed. 'Don't panic, Tom, he does this. Sorry.'

'It's fine,' said Tom, humouring the big guy.

'Every time I invite someone new round,' whispered Zoe, 'Dad thinks he has a new audience member.'

Completely blanking his daughter, Ali towered over Tom. His accent returned to its heritage. 'Tell me, young Tom, have you ever witnessed the power of voodoo?'

'Err? No.' Tom discreetly lowered the book down onto the floor under the table.

With a quick flourish, Ali produced a magician's wand from thin air. 'You see in my hand an ordinary black-and-white wand.'

Tom nodded in agreement.

'But no,' bellowed Ali, thrusting the wand right in front of Tom's face. 'This, my friend, is no *ordinary* wand.'

Tipping his head back, Ali began chanting, 'Serpen-tah, serpen-tah, serpen-tah, serpen-tah.'

Tom leant in towards Zoe. 'He's very convincing.'

Ali, still chanting, thrust his head forwards, his eyes now pure white.

'In case you were wondering,' said Zoe, unimpressed by her dad's ritual, 'we sell those contact lenses out front.'

Tom ignored her and held his breath.

Gripping the wand horizontally in his right hand, his left hovering over it, Ali started wiggling his fingers above the black-and-white prop; the skull charms on his bracelet jangled as he did so.

'Now,' hailed Ali. 'On the count o' three.'

Tom's eyes narrowed, engrossed by the motionless wand. 'One.'

Zoe placed her elbow on the table, resting her head on her hand.

'Two.'

Ali paused. The huge grin on his face unsettled Tom, just for a second.

'Three.' Ali threw the wand at Tom's chest.

'King snake,' blurted Tom. At least, that's what Zoe thought he'd shouted, as he leapt up off the chair, knocking a black-and-white cobra from his lap.

Ali erupted into laughter. 'Relax, man, it's fake.' He bent down and picked up the stripy rubber thing. 'Pretty good trick though, eh?'

Zoe slowly clapped her hands. 'Fan-tas-tic,' she groaned. 'After the however-many-eth time, it still makes people jump.'

'Oh, come on, Zoe,' said Tom, catching his breath and sitting back down. 'It was just meant to surprise me. I enjoyed it.'

'Thank you.' Ali smiled, bowing. 'I've been Ali Cassam, I'm available for birthdays, weddings, et cetera.' He held out a flat palm, then with a flourish, produced a business card. 'Should you wish to book me, Mister, er... sorry, I didn't catch your surname?'

'It's Last. Thomas Last,' replied Tom.

Ali gave his neck a rub, his eyes narrowed on Tom's face.

'You finished then, Dad?' said Zoe. 'Because, you're being weird and we were both busy discuss—'

Ali held up a finger, cutting her off. 'Thomas Last.' He mulled the name over a couple of seconds or so. 'Thomas... Last?'

Tom slid his chair back a little – tucking the book behind his foot as he did so – this wasn't going to end well, he felt.

'Dad?' Zoe's eyes darted between him and their nervous-looking guest.

'It is you,' gasped Ali, 'isn't it?' His mouth dropped faster than the proverbial penny. 'Don't think about leaving. I'll be right back.'

Chapter 8
Read All About It

'I should go.' Tom bent down under the table to reach for the book.

Zoe, trying to figure out what her dad was up to, urged him to stay. 'He can't possibly know you, Tom. He'll come back downstairs saying how it was actually someone called Thomas Lent, or Toby Last, you'll see.'

'Coo-ee.' The abrupt chirpy sound of a woman's voice caused Tom to bang his head on the table.

Zoe walked over to the door. 'Great,' she mumbled. 'That's all we need.'

Eyeing Tom's bottom sticking up from under the table, the woman dropped her shopping bags down onto the tiled floor. Selecting a strand of bleached blonde hair, she twiddled it and purred, 'Hell-oo.'

'Mum.' Zoe threw her a cut-throat glare.

Tom got up, giving his knees a quick dust-off. 'Um… hello,' he said, smiling awkwardly. He averted his eyes from the overly tight white dress the woman was wearing. 'I'm Tom.'

'Gail,' Zoe's mum replied. 'Find what you're looking for?'

'Sorry,' gulped Tom, looking at Zoe to step in.

Gail pointed a manicured finger at the table, 'Under there, my love.'

Retrieving the book, Tom gave it a quick wave about. 'Oh, yes,' he said, and stowed it back inside his jacket pocket. 'Thanks.'

'And that's three for three, for uncomfortable introductions,' Zoe said with a sigh. 'Sit down, Tom, please. Feel free to close your mouth anytime.'

Gail turned to Zoe. Her thinly plucked eyebrows gestured the universal code of a prying mother: *Who is this?* 'So, Thomas,' she said, still glaring at Zoe. 'How do you know my daughter?'

'We've only just met,' interjected Zoe. 'Tom had some trouble with his car today. I'm helping him out.'

'Decided to take it for a spin in the countryside,' Tom added. 'Ended up spinning it right into a gorge. It's a complete wreck.'

'I see,' said Gail, slipping off her pink lace shrug and draping it over the back of a chair. 'Well, you should consider yourself very lucky to be alive, young man. Would you like me to stitch up that tear to your jacket?'

Tom hadn't even noticed the rip in the elbow of the fabric. 'Oh, no, that's okay.' He added, 'I've been meaning to get a new one. It's fine.'

'Anyway, I assume you're not badly hurt. Can't be doing with having to call an ambulance; I have better things to do today.' Gail beckoned Zoe. 'A word in private, my love.'

'Mum,' said Zoe, scowling. 'I'm twenty. Not your little kid any more.'

'I'm perfectly aware of how old you are. But, while you're still living here, you stick to the rules. The shop... Now.' Gail turned her head back to Tom. She swished her hair off her shoulder as though in a beauty product commercial. Giving a fake smile, she excused herself.

Zoe shook her head, then looked towards Tom. 'Be right back.'

Tom sat nervously drumming his fingers on the table. In the next room he could hear the sporadic loud hissing of Zoe and Gail's argument. Above him, he could hear the plodding of Ali thumping about searching for something. *Wait until Zoe comes back in*, he thought, *then just make your excuses and get the hell out.*

The argument escalated, then abruptly ceased.

Zoe entered the kitchen. 'Finished with your tea?' she huffed.

'Well, actually, I've barely touch—'

Zoe took their mugs to the sink and rinsed them under

the tap. She paused to stare out the window. 'Sorry, my parents are super protective of me when it comes to friends with different genitalia to mine. Dad scares them away, whereas Mum just outright embarrasses me.' Zoe stepped back over to him. 'If they had it their way, I'd be single until I died. Not that us two have anything...'

'It's okay,' said Tom. 'I get it.'

Sitting down opposite him, Zoe continued, 'Thing is, they're constantly arguing with each other. Not exactly the perfect couple.'

'Sounds like they're projecting their own faults onto you.' Tom went to hold her hand, but Zoe whipped it out of the way.

'So what are we going to do about your predicament then?'

Ali thundered down the stairs, calling out, 'I found it.'

'What are you doing with my tablet, Dad?'

'Hush, girl,' said Ali, placing the device on the table. 'Could hardly carry the office computer down here, could I?'

Tom looked at the lit-up screen. 'A newspaper article?'

'Correct.' Ali slid his finger along the screen, scrolling down the page. 'One of the plus sides to being an illusionist is we got good memories. See, what did I tell you?'

Tom looked at the article on the small screen.

'There was a plane crash,' explained Ali. 'Must've been about ten years ago now. I have a fascination with phenomena and the unexplained. But, I'll never forget this one.'

Zoe rolled her eyes as if she was thinking, *not again*.

Tom read out the headline. 'The miracle man. British passenger, sole survivor of fatal plane crash.'

'And, see here,' added Ali, pointing to a paragraph. 'Twenty-one-year-old Thomas Last from Oxford,' he read aloud, 'walked away completely unharmed from the wreckage which took the lives of all others onboard. Tragically, his parents, actress Holly Last and her husband Douglas, were amongst the dead.'

Zoe slid her arm over the table. Finding Tom's hand, she gripped hold of it tightly. 'Tom,' she said, somewhat bemused, 'that's you in the picture.'

Chapter 9
Time Out

'I said, *shut up*, Dad.' Zoe glowered.

One thing Ali knew, all too well, was Zoe inherited her mother's trigger tongue. One false word, he'd get five rounds rapid abuse fired his way. He did as he was told – for now.

Tom struggled to arrange his thoughts. He was distraught, confused and broken. *That's me in the picture. But how?* He couldn't help wondering why he looked exactly the same age as he was now. Reading the article once more, it sunk in: his parents were dead.

Having no memory of them, Tom struggled to come to terms with the loss. *Birthdays, Christmases, holidays, simple things like dinners together, I don't remember any of them*. And now, he would never experience these things again.

Gail entered the room. 'Awfully quiet, you lot. Ali been forcing one of his tricks on you again?'

'No,' replied Zoe.

'It seems,' said Ali, pointing at the tablet, 'our young friend here is suffering some kind of amnesia and wasn't unaware of his parents' death.'

Gail looked down at the screen and scanned the story. 'Oh my,' she said, looking at Tom's face. She held the gaze a few seconds before saying, 'Haven't you aged well.'

'Sure.' Tom sniffed, wiping back a tear.

'Seriously, Mum?' Zoe said with a scowl. 'He's only just learnt his family were killed in a plane crash and your only comment is how young he looks?'

'God, Zoe,' Gail looked hurt by the reproach, 'of course I feel sorry for his loss. But…'

Zoe sat, arms folded at the affront of the woman.

'All I'm saying is he looks exactly the same.' Gail spread

her fingers across the screen, enlarging the image. 'Even his hair-style's the same. His features too. Hang on.' Gail re-read part of the story. 'This means you must be thirty-one now?'

They all stared at Tom, sat in silence looking despondent.

Gail raised a doubtful eyebrow. 'I'm really sorry to hear about all that's happened to you, it's truly unfortunate. But, Zoe has stuff to be getting on with. So if you wouldn't mind...'

Zoe leapt up and fired at her mother, 'How dare you!'

'I... I just feel,' spluttered Gail.

'I know exactly what you "feel", *Mother*,' snapped Zoe, 'but who I choose to spend my time with is none of your business.'

Stepping back, Ali stayed out of this one.

Tom felt his jacket pocket; checking the book was on him, he decided he'd outstayed his welcome. He stood up to leave.

'And where the bloody hell are *you* going?' Zoe aimed an outstretched index finger at him. 'Sit back down.'

Gail stood firm. 'He's eleven years older than you, Zoe.'

'Excuse me? I don't seem to recall introducing Tom as my *boyfriend*.'

'You didn't have to, Zoe, a mother can tell.'

Tom wished he was back in the car wreck. At least it was peaceful there.

Ali had heard enough. 'That is... it,' he bellowed. The room fell silent.

From the shop, came the tinkle of the doorbell.

'Thank the creator,' Ali said, exhaling. 'Saved by the bell. Gail, go deal with that customer. Zoe, stay here and try to chill.'

'And you?' Gail asked, bottling her temper.

'I,' said Ali, 'am going to my office.' He pushed his wife into the shop, then excusing himself headed up the stairs.

Avoiding eye contact, Tom and Zoe sat in silence. They could hear Gail serving a family in the next room who, from the sound of it, were choosing a magic set for their excited daughter's birthday present.

'Do you think it's what caused my amnesia?' muttered Tom, after a while.

'Sorry?'

'The plane crash, do you think that's what caused it?'

Zoe considered this. 'Unlikely,' she answered, stone-faced.

'How so?'

'You mentioned not knowing why you woke up in Penmoor. If your amnesia had been caused by the plane crash, then —'

'I would still remember everything that's happened over the past ten years.'

'Exactly.'

Tom looked at the tablet again. 'I honestly don't know how to process all this.'

'How could you?' Zoe sat close to him. 'How could anyone in your situation? Maybe the answer is not to, for now, at least. The article says you were the only survivor. Do you think, maybe, it was your healing ability that saved you?'

'Seems likely.' He removed the book once more. 'Wish we knew more about this. Maybe we could find something on your tablet?'

'We can try.' Zoe picked up the device from the table. She tapped a few times at the home icon on the screen. 'Sorry, the Internet's a bit patchy sometimes.'

After waiting long enough, Tom asked, 'What about the computer in your dad's office?'

'No use right now. When Dad says he's going "to his office" that's usually his alone time with the bottle of rum he keeps in there.'

'Oh, right.' Tom sighed, feeling dejected.

Zoe considered the situation. Suddenly, her eyes lit up. 'Of course! We can go to the library. It's just down the road.' She stood, urging Tom to do the same. 'The librarian used to be my old schoolteacher, she might be able to help us. Would get us away from here too.'

Tom agreed.

'Miss McCready,' said Zoe. 'That's her, would've defo watched *Dig This*, so we'll have to be careful not to show her that book.'

Tom flicked it open to the first page. 'We might be able to figure out who first signed it. I mean, if it's a thousand years old, maybe it was someone like Merlin?'

'Well, it's more likely to have been someone real, Tom.' She looked at the page, half expecting to see something there. It was, of course, blank to her. 'Can you not read the signature?'

Tom focused on the scribbled writing. 'Not really. The first word starts with an *L*, and I think the last word ends with *son*?'

Zoe looked at the book, then back at Tom. She took a brief moment to absorb everything. 'This is all so... *weird*.'

Tom smiled at her. 'I know. This book, the ability to self-heal, add to that how I look the same now, as I did ten years ago.'

'Maybe your self-healing slows down your ageing?'

Tom considered this. 'Would make sense, I guess? But, if all the people in this book have the same power as me, that could mean they're still alive too. Right?'

Zoe stood up and grabbed a handbag and her car keys from a side cabinet. 'Bring it with you. We can research some of the names when we're at the library.' She checked her watch. 'We should get going.'

Returning the book to his pocket, Tom went over to the back door where Zoe was waiting. 'The Immortal Thomas Last.' He grinned. 'It has a ring to it.'

'If you say so.' Zoe opened the door.

'Sorry. Thomas Last sounds a bit boring, now,' joked Tom. 'Not exactly Lance Goldstorm, is it?'

Zoe swung round. She held up a finger, silencing him. 'Trust me, from what my parents have said about that arsehole, you wouldn't want to be anything like him. Come on, let's go.'

Chapter 10
To the Library

'So how many signatures do you reckon are in that thing?' asked Zoe, as they made their way along the now bustling street.

'Well, there's about twenty to a page,' estimated Tom. 'I'd say there are around fifty pages full, so what's that add up to?'

'A thousand names, give or take a few,' answered Zoe. 'If we *are* assuming all the people in that book have your ability, you'd have thought someone would've noticed them, right?'

'Maybe,' said Tom. 'Although, Lance Goldstorm did flaunt it in public and no one seemed to suspect his ability was anything more than a clever act. Oh, and then there's me, The Miracle Man, remember? That article went on to say how lucky I'd been. I guess when it really comes down to it, no matter how magical it must appear, people will just find a way to rationalise it.'

Zoe caught a glimpse of herself in a passing window; the dispirited child she used to be looked back at her. Bringing herself back, she stopped and pointed towards an old granite building. The tall tower rose high above the leylandii across the street. 'There's the library.'

'Really?' Tom said doubtful, his eyes falling on the building, 'Because y'know, stained-glass windows, big archway for an entrance, steepled tower, I'm no architect, but that looks a lot like a church.'

They walked across a pedestrian crossing to reach the library; Zoe waving politely to a biker on an outlandish-coloured motorbike, who patiently waited for them to pass. 'Originally it was,' she said, 'but they built a fancy new church between here and the next village to cater for more people. The old library burnt down, about nine years ago and, since this building was empty, it became the new one.'

Tom stood on the pavement. He looked through the timber gateway, then up at the bell tower – dwarfing the high-pitched roof of the main building to its right. The spire had an odd-looking kink near its point. 'Looks a bit like a wizard's hat, don't you think?'

'Got struck by lightning about thirty years ago,' said Zoe. 'That's how it ended up crooked. The locals got used to how it looked and just patched up the tiles. It's kinda like a landmark now, s'pose. I used to walk past it every day on my way back from school, pretending my dad was a real wizard, and that one day we'd live here. Sounds silly, doesn't it?'

Tom gazed at Zoe as she stood there looking up. Although she was smiling, her brief silence suggested sadness in the memory.

Looking back at him, she sighed. 'Well, shall we?'

'Yup.'

***

The only sound inside, was that of their footsteps on the polished parquet floor. It echoed around the hall-like space. Zoe wandered over to the help desk on their left, leant over the counter and called, 'Hello?' There was no answer. 'Hello-oo?' A little louder that time. Then lastly, she bellowed, 'Miss McCready, you in here?'

Tom looked around. Down the centre of the space, rows of bookshelves replaced what would've once been pews. At the far end of these, a seating area; four grey sofas and white coffee tables arranged on a raised platform underneath a large round stained-glass window, on which was depicted the image of a man knelt down praying in front of a book on a podium. Beside this area, to the left, there were four computers lined up on a desk.

'Quiet, isn't it?' Tom whispered, joining Zoe.

'It's a library, Tom, of course it's quiet.' She craned over the counter again, trying to peer through the back-office window.

'Doreen must be here, she's the only librarian.' Walking over to a disability lift, Zoe checked it. 'The lift's on this floor, so she can't be upstairs?'

An elderly man tottered out from behind a bookshelf. 'Do you mind keeping it down,' he croaked, leaning on his walking stick.

'Sorry.' Zoe winced. 'Don't suppose you've seen Miss McCready today, have you?'

The old man made his way over to them, the *tap-tap* of his stick reverberating like castanets off the stone walls. 'She was in here a few minutes ago, my love, but she had to pop out,' he said, as he reached them. 'Muttered some nonsense about ruffling her feathers, next minute she'd gone. Not very professional, if you ask me. Still, that's women for you. Always getting distracted by something or other. Isn't that right, young man?' He winked at Tom, who in return cast him a frown.

Peering at the two of them, the elderly man moaned, 'What if something happens here, while she's away, hmm?'

Zoe shrugged, remaining tight-lipped.

'What could possibly happen in here?' asked Tom.

The old man held out a skeletal hand, gesturing to the bookshelves. 'Thieves, lad.'

Tom looked to where he was pointing. 'Huh?'

'They could just waltz on in and steal what they sodding well liked. That's what could happen. The whole place completely looted of knowledge. But oh no, that doesn't bother Doreen as she has somewhere far more important to be. I don't know, no respect.' He pulled a grey flat cap from the back pocket of his trousers, placed it firmly on his head, then shuffled his way past them, grumbling as he made his way towards the doorway.

Tom waited until the elderly man had gone, then turned to Zoe. 'Right then,' he said, clasping his hands together, 'you grab all the non-fiction, I'll swipe the romantic thrillers. We've only got a few minutes to clear the place out, okay? Go.'

Zoe sniggered.

'Okay,' rallied Tom, returning to their mission, 'where

shall we start?'

'We could really do with speaking to Doreen, to be honest, Tom. I wouldn't know where to start. She's probably just gone to the café to grab a cuppa. Her and Beryl are old friends, the town gossips like to suggest something more.' Zoe rolled her eyes at the rumour. 'How about I go take a look, see if she's in there?'

'Okay, I might see if there's a pen and some paper about.'

'Why?'

'I could copy out some signatures and names from the book. When you find Doreen, we can show them to her.'

'Clever thinking.' Zoe placed a hand on Tom's shoulder. 'Try not to look so worried though, Tom. We'll get to the bottom of all this, okay?'

'Thanks, Zoe.'

'Try searching on the computer over by the sofas first. Maybe google the inscription or one of the names, yeah?' Zoe headed out.

Walking over to the help desk, Tom looked for a pen and something to write on. Finding what he needed, he removed the old book from his pocket, opened it to the first page and began copying the first signature. As he was about to copy the next name down, something drew his attention. 'Zoe?' Looking at the entrance, he was certain he'd heard footsteps. 'Miss McCready? Grumpy old man, that you?'

The library was as quiet as, well, a library. Deciding to follow Zoe's suggestion, he hastily shoved the paper in his back trouser pocket then went over to one of the computers situated at the far end.

Pulling in an office chair, Tom found that the screen had been left on. In a matter of seconds, Tom had the search engine's home page on screen. He spent a few minutes fanning through the names and signatures in the book. Pausing at a later entry, Tom thought he heard another sound coming from the opposite side of the room.

After convincing himself he was just being paranoid, he turned back to the book and looked at another signature. The one he picked was William J. Craddock, written in flamboyant handwriting. Tom entered the name into the search box on the screen, then hit *Return*.

A sepia image appeared of a man with a wide handlebar moustache, wearing a dusty bowler hat. His frown was so menacing-looking, it seemed to cut through the computer screen. Tom shivered as he looked at the haunting image. The caption next to it read, 'The Immortal Outlaw, William J. Craddock.'

Tom whispered to himself as he read on, 'Craddock got the nickname "The Immortal Outlaw" due to the reckless disregard for his own life, as well as others. He would often get shot while fleeing bank raids, yet show up in another town, the following day, to steal again.

'The final bank robbery he staged culminated in a four-hour siege on a ranch involving nineteen Lawmen. Eventually, Craddock rode out on horseback, guns blazing. He immediately killed eight men, so the records say. However, when his horse bolted after being hit by bullets, he was thrown to the ground. The remaining Lawmen wrapped a rope around his neck and hanged him there and then. Craddock was buried the same day.

'What makes his story even more intriguing, is that he may have somehow cheated the Lawmen and survived. The date written on the back of this portrait of Craddock means it was taken six months after his burial.'

You sneaky bastard, thought Tom.

A sudden burst of pain exploded in the back of Tom's neck. Lasting only a few seconds, he didn't have time to think before a second blow hit him. Accompanied by a high-pitched tone ringing in his eardrums, Tom slid from the chair then hit his head on the parquet floor.

As his vision blurred, Tom just had enough time to make out a familiar pair of outlandish Cuban-heeled shoes before everything went black.

***

Zoe approached the entrance to the library. She was just about to pass through, when a voice called out, 'Coo-ee, Zoe.'

'There you are, Doreen,' Zoe said, beaming as she spotted the tartan-clad lady wheeling her way up the disabled access ramp. 'I tried to find you in the Copper Kettle.'

Pushing herself closer, Doreen smiled at Zoe. 'Och, well, not to worry, here I am. Sorry I had to leave my post, bit of an emergency, so to speak.'

Zoe gave Doreen a glancing examination. 'Nothing serious, I hope?'

'No, no. I'd completely forgotten to pick up my prescription from the pharmacy, just managed to catch them before they closed,' replied the Hebridean, former schoolteacher, as she reached Zoe. 'It's this blasted stool trouble of mine. I ask you, with the amount of soup I eat, you'd think my jobbies would just slip right on out.'

The image in Zoe's head made her stomach turn, but she did her best to hide it behind a polite smile. 'I can honestly say, I'm shocked to hear that.'

'I know, I'm surprised I haven't popped a vein.' Doreen's soft accent did little to make the comment any less vulgar. 'It's like I'm shitting dry Weetabix.'

'Oh... kay, how about we go inside,' said Zoe, sparing herself further detail. 'I have a friend who needs your expertise.'

Once inside, Doreen steered her wheelchair behind the help desk.

Zoe scanned the bookshelves. 'Tom?' she called out, before looking over to Doreen.

'Try the toilets upstairs,' said Doreen, pointing to the mezzanine balcony above. 'Maybe your friend's up there? They're very well soundproofed.' She watched Zoe sprint up a set of stairs over in the corner. Muttering to herself, Doreen added, 'Lord, I should know.'

He wouldn't have just left, thought Zoe, *would he?* She gave the toilet door a couple of knocks. 'Tom, you in there?' The catch on the door informed her it was vacant, but just to make sure, she opened it and peeked inside. 'Fuuu—' She shuddered, in horror, at the toilet bowl. 'Doreen wasn't lying about her problem.' Reaching to the lever on the toilet, she gave it a double flush.

On the balcony again, Zoe spotted a door at the end marked Bell Tower Access. Staff Only. Walking over, she tried the handle. Locked.

Before returning downstairs, Zoe leaned over the handrail and scanned the main hall. Having to accept Tom had left, she headed back down the staircase and over to Doreen.

Doreen looked up from her desk. 'No luck?'

'Seems odd.' Zoe sighed, confusion in her expression. 'He should be in here. I don't get it?'

'I recognise that look, my girl,' Doreen said, with a wink. 'This lad special to you, is he?'

Zoe broke eye contact, choosing to focus on picking at the beech effect vinyl of the desk instead. 'It's not like that, Doreen. I'm just helping him out with something.'

Doreen's eyebrows bounced up a couple of times, and with a smile said, 'Of course you are, Zoe.'

'We came here to ask you about a book, actually,' said Zoe, changing the topic. 'Don't suppose you know of one from the eleventh century, one that contains a list of names?'

Doreen considered this a couple of seconds. 'Well, only one.'

Zoe's eyes lit up. 'Really? Brilliant.'

'I'm quite surprised that a former star pupil of mine doesn't remember being taught about the *Doomsday Book*.'

Zoe shook her head. 'It's not that one, trust me, this one's different.' *That's an understatement.* 'It's just names, nothing else. Like a register.'

'Not a lot to go on, Zoe.' Doreen pondered, scratching the back of her neck. 'What were the names?'

'Just signatures, mainly.' Zoe saw the vague look on the librarian's face. 'Without seeing them, I couldn't tell you who they belonged to. Tom could, but he's not here.'

'I don't think I can be of any assistance. I'm sorry, Zoe.'

There was the inscription on the inside cover, but Zoe couldn't risk discussing it, just in case Doreen had seen it on *Dig This* the night before.

Doreen gestured towards the computer desk at the far end, 'Have you tried googling it?'

'No, not yet anyway.' Glancing at the entrance, Zoe added, 'I guess I should go find Tom, first.'

Doreen acknowledged this with a warm smile.

***

'What the hell did you hit me with?' Tom gripped the back of his neck, as he sat there on the floor. His eyes struggling to focus on any fixed point. 'Felt like a sledgehammer,' he groaned.

Ali cast Tom an unnerving grin. '*The Wind in the Willows.*' He strutted across the creaky wooden boards in the dusty room. 'Hardback edition. That one had a real thick cardboard sleeve. Not the best thing to stun you with, but was all I could find.' The low plastered ceiling made the big Jamaican seem even more of a giant, as he loomed over Tom. 'You ever read it? My favourite character was always Badger.' Ali's accent seemed thicker now. 'Why, that stripy *Don*, he *tek* no bullshit.'

'Of course I've bloody read it,' snapped Tom. 'What are you doing? Did you follow us here?' He scanned where they were; the grey stone walls of the claustrophobic room feeling like a prison cell.

'Relax.' Ali squatted down in front of Tom. 'I just wanted this.' From inside his pinstriped jacket, Ali produced Tom's book.

Tom attempted to grab it, but his arm got slapped away by Ali's shovel-like hand. The expression on the shop owner's face changed in an instant, like someone flicking a switch to Rottweiler mode. 'Do *not* try that again,' he snarled. Standing up, he towered back over Tom. 'I overheard your little conversation in our kitchen, as I was coming back downstairs. Could it actually be true? I thought. The boy who survived that plane crash and a car crash, now talking about that bastard Goldstorm.' He let out a low growl as he conjured up an image of his rival performing those so-called death-defying tricks. 'How did you get your ability to…' he paused to find a suitable verb, 'regenerate?'

'I don't remember,' replied Tom. 'And, I only found out who Lance Goldstorm was yesterday.'

Walking over to a rotten oak-framed window, Ali jemmied it open. He glanced outside before placing the book down on the sill. Beside the window stood a tall metal shelving unit. He reached down to the bottom shelf and removed something from an open toolbox that lay there. 'Even though you seem to be able to heal yourself,' steeled Ali, 'I'm assuming, Tom, you still feel pain?'

At the sight of Ali's huge fist now gripping a hammer, Tom fidgeted and chose his words carefully. 'Okay, Mister Cassam… sir.' He cowered, pushing himself as far back against the wall as he could. 'You have to believe me!'

Ali raised the hammer.

Tom lifted up his hands. 'Hear me out, please.'

'Go on.' Ali paused. 'Talk.'

'Th-thank you,' stuttered Tom. 'As I said, you have to believe me. Because of the memory loss, I honestly have no idea where my ability came from. But, the other people who signed the book probably will. From what me and Zoe can tell, they have the same power too. They must know something, right?'

Ali was still poised to strike. 'You're the only one who can see what's written on the pages, yes?'

'Yes.'

Ali lowered the hammer. He paced the room, mulling over Tom's words. 'Lance Goldstorm has the power to self-heal?'

'It looks that way,' said Tom, emitting some slight relief.

'And Zoe?' Ali's eyes fixed on Tom's. 'She told you about what he means to us, I suppose?'

Tom nodded. 'She said something about him being responsible for ending your career.'

'They were gonna give us our own telly show.' Ali's shoulders straightened. 'The Saturday primetime slot. Then Goldstorm came along. His illusions, they defied belief, man. Of course, he was an overnight success. The network bosses called our act outdated, they dropped me an' Gail,' he clicked his fingers, 'just like that.'

'So where is he now?'

'Retired, I guess,' huffed Ali. 'Last time I bumped into him was in London, the last night of his sell-out world tour. The *sipple* arsehole was bragging about the million-pound villa he just bought in the Mediterranean. After that night, no one saw him again.'

'That's odd.' Tom scrunched his face. 'Why would he just give it all up?'

'Why not? He'd become the world's number one magician. He'd made his mark, made his fortune, and belittled every traditional magic act along the way. I hate him, no...' Ali slapped the head of the hammer into his palm, '*despise* him.'

'When did all this happen?'

Ali turned away. Moving to the window, he stared outside. 'A little over twenty years ago, now.'

'You've held this resentment for one man all that time? Even though you haven't seen him since that night.'

'Yes.' Ali shifted his stance. 'He stole *my* career.'

'Except he didn't, really,' said Tom, 'did he?'

Ali spun round. 'What do you mean?'

'He didn't forcefully remove it from you.' Massaging the back of his aching neck, Tom winced. 'His magic act was just... better.'

Ali adjusted his grip on the hammer. 'Be careful what you say, Tom.'

Staring into Ali's eyes, Tom had noticed a flicker of hesitation. *There's something not right*, he pondered, *could this all be...* In that brief moment, he saw Ali for who he was. *An act, it's just an act.*

'I don't believe you, Ali,' said Tom, lifting himself up.

'What are you doing?' growled Ali, raising the hammer

above his shoulder.

'You can drop the act now. You're not going to attack me, because I'm not a threat to you. I'm not the person you're angry with.'

'I'm warning you, Tom.'

'This resentment for what happened to you, all those years ago, it's not Lance Goldstorm you're angry with, is it?'

Ali's cheek muscles tensed as he clenched his teeth.

Tom took one step towards the window, the book within his reach. 'You're angry with yourself. You know you weren't as good as Goldstorm. But, it's easier to lay the blame on someone else than face the truth, right?'

'Not exactly.' Ali placed the hammer down onto a wooden box beneath the window, much to Tom's relief. 'I see how she looks at me when I do my magic tricks.' There was a crack in Ali's tone. 'The disappointment in her eyes has been there since she was little.'

'Sorry?'

'You're right, it wasn't Goldstorm's fault. I know that. And yes, I am angry with myself, but for letting Zoe down.'

'Zoe? Hang on a minute. So, you want to be better than Lance Goldstorm… just to impress Zoe?'

'Well, saying it like that,' replied Ali, his accent softening, 'makes it sound crazy.'

Tom flung his hands up. 'It *is* crazy!'

'I just want her to be proud of me. You wouldn't understand, Tom, you're not a dad.'

'No, I'm not. Here's a thought though, instead of assaulting me and making threats, have you tried actually sitting down and opening up to Zoe?'

Ali placed his hands in his trouser pockets. He gazed down at his Cuban heels. 'No,' he muttered. 'I'm no good at all that sensitive stuff, y'know?'

Tom had enough to deal with without standing there playing family counsellor to this idiot. 'Right, well, might I suggest you give it a try.' He turned his attention to the window and tried to reach for his book, only to be stopped by a raven, which had abruptly landed onto the sill.

The charcoal-coloured bird cocked its head to one side. It blinked its cold eyes at the two people in the room, as though trying to assess the situation it found itself in. Lifting its white-tipped wings out, it gave Tom and Ali a loud caw.

'Do something,' whispered Ali, slowly side-stepping away. 'I suffer from ornithophobia.'

'From what?'

'Fear of birds.'

Tom shook his head. 'You have *got* to be joking?'

'Just shoo it away, son.'

'Fine.' Tom approached the raven which had now hopped in front of the book. 'Off you go, little guy,' said Tom, wafting his hands.

The raven drew a foot back, sliding the book closer to the edge of the sill.

'Is it just me,' said Ali, from the far end of the room, 'or is it trying to steal your book?'

Spreading out its wings again, the raven beat down hard; lifting itself up, its toes gripped the edges of the book's cover. Tom made a lunge for it, causing the bird to recoil. 'Get back here,' he ordered, as he leapt onto the wooden box beneath the windowsill.

'Wait!' Ali yelled in horror.

Tom scooped the book back into the room, but stumbled on the hammer sat on the box. The box tipped back, causing Tom to fall forwards. He tried to save himself by grabbing the rotten frame of the window, but just ripped a chunk out as he went head first outside.

'We're in the bell tower,' yelled Ali, but it was too late.

Tom had dived forty-two metres, head first, into the paving below. The speed at which he'd impacted shattered his skull apart. It was, of course, instant death.

Chapter 11
Memory Recall

As the engine from a passing motorbike thundered off down the lane behind the church, Tom's eyes snapped open and air inflated his lungs. Dazed, confused, and trying to suppress another splitting headache, the first thought he assembled was, *The book?*

Looking above him, clouds passed over the oppressing bell tower. His dry throat tickled as he croaked, 'Ali.'

Sitting up, curving his back to one side, he felt his spine crunch back into place. Judging by the lack of any other significant pain, Tom assumed he'd been lying there for some time, long enough for the healing ability to fully do its thing. Giving his limbs a quick flex, he got up off the pavement and took in his surroundings.

The rear of the old church was peaceful, a lawned area with ten or so weather-softened gravestones. He spotted a white van driving along, behind the drystone wall at the far perimeter of the church ground. Reading the logo on the side of it, 'Magic White Linen', the first word brought his mind to one person, Zoe. He hurried around the side of the tower, through the arched doorway, and returned inside to the area that was now the library. Walking up and down the centre, he called out, 'Hello, Zoe?'

'Ah, you must be the mysterious Tom?' said the elderly lady, wheeling herself from the office behind the help desk. She manoeuvred her wheelchair round to arrive in front of Tom.

'Hello, er, yes,' replied Tom, trying not to act as though he'd just returned from the dead. He spotted the assistant librarian badge on the lady's tartan shawl. 'Miss McCready, right?'

'That's me,' she answered. 'Zoe's not here, I'm afraid. She told me to tell you she's gone home. She said you're looking for info on an old book, one with names written inside?'

Tom went to pat his jacket, then remembering what had just occurred, said, 'Yeah, sorry, I've… mislaid it.'

'Oh, that's a shame, m'dear.' Doreen gave him a cheeky wink. 'Still, I expect you'll want to find Zoe, yes?'

'Actually, it's really important I do,' he said. He turned to leave, then halted. Removing a folded piece of paper from his trouser pocket, he turned back to Doreen. 'Um, I copied a signature down on this paper. It was the first name in the book. Don't suppose you recognise it, at all?' He handed it to her.

Doreen's expression piqued as she studied it. 'Do you mind me asking where you got that book from?'

Tom thought fast. 'It's a… family heirloom.'

'How long exactly has this *heirloom* been in your family's possession?' She looked up at him with keen interest.

'Why?'

'Because, I do indeed recognise this signature.' She held the paper up. 'It belongs to the Earl of Kent.'

'Sorry?'

'The Earl of Kent, well, the first one actually,' confirmed Doreen. 'You're probably more familiar with his more famous brother though, King Harold.'

'What? The guy who got poked in the eye by an arrow?'

'Tom,' said Doreen, ignoring his flippant remark, 'that book of yours could be of real historical significance, I do hope you *haven't* lost it?' She moved the wheelchair close to him, 'Because, if so, you really must find it.'

That's not the half of it, Tom thought. 'Trust me, I will.'

'You do that,' insisted Doreen, 'and please, when you do, bring it here so I can see it.'

'Don't worry, I have an idea where it could be. But first, I should catch up with Zoe.'

'Of course.' A slight smile raised the corner of Doreen's lip as she backed the wheelchair from him. 'Love comes first.'

'Oh, erm…' stammered Tom. 'It's, it's not like that.'

'If you say so, my dear.' Doreen turned towards her office.

'Tell Zoe it was nice to see her today, she was always my brightest pupil.'

Tom nodded, thanked her, and left.

***

As he hurried up the street, Tom couldn't shake what Doreen had said to him. *King Harold's brother*, he mused, *he was the first to sign the book?* He tried recalling what he knew about the Battle of Hastings. As it turned out, not much. Apart from the Bayeux tapestry, William the Conqueror, and the aforementioned arrow incident, that was it.

Something drew him from his thoughts. He stopped still on the pavement, and listened. *That song.* It was coming from the open window of the Magic White Linen van, which was now parked next to the kerb. The vehicle's stereo blasted the tune as the driver removed a pile of laundry from the side door. Tom watched the burly man cross in front of him and walk up to a shop front.

'You couldn't get the door for me, could you, pal?' the man asked, heaving the bulky load.

'Er… yep, sure.' Tom grabbed the door to the dry-cleaning shop, opened it, and let him through.

'Thanks,' said the man, heading inside.

Tom's attention returned to the vehicle. *What is it about that song?*

He focused on the lyrics.

'Someone gets excited,
in a chapel yard,
catches a bouquet,' the rock singer crooned.
'Another lays a dozen,
white roses on a grave.'

Every sound around him seemed to die away as the chorus began, 'To be yourself, is all that you can do…'

Wiping the clammy sweat from his forehead, Tom grew agitated. His breathing quickened. Still the lyrics seemed to

86

dominate, pushing themselves deep into his head as though, somehow, they belonged there.

He stumbled, trying to steady himself. Reaching out his hands, he struggled to keep his balance as the pavement started to sway like the deck of a lilting ship. Tom's eyes became transfixed by the crimson spots that had begun to splash onto the pavement. A few specs at first, then becoming larger and more frequent. A strange sensation sloshed within Tom's skull; his brain now seemed to be hearing the song before his ears did. *Uh-oh*, he thought, as everything around him abruptly shifted forty-five degrees, *that's not good.*

The driver stepped out of the shop to the sight of Tom fighting to stay upright. 'Bloody 'ell.' The man gulped as he saw the blood gushing from Tom's nose. 'You need to…'

Tom beat him to it. His knees buckled and he collapsed to the floor.

'Lie down,' the driver finished.

Reality did a pretty good job impersonating a whirling dervish above Tom's eyes, before unconsciousness stuck out its foot and sent reality flying.

***

It was past midnight, he shouldn't still be sat at his desk. But, as usual, Tom had left it to the last minute. The history paper had to be handed in the next morning, first thing. He could hear students in the other dorms, partying, relaxing, not cramming.

'To be yourself, is all that you can do,' he sang, tapping his fingers on the desk in time to the Audioslave tune blasting from his knackered stereo. His other hand clicked the computer mouse.

Scrolling down a webpage, Tom found an article about medieval literature. All he had to do now was find something close enough, copy and paste it, change a few words, then he could finish.

'Huh,' he said, looking at an image of an Old English scripture. He got up, went over to his wardrobe and opened it. Looking down at the suitcase sat at the bottom, he unzipped the smaller one contain-

ing keepsakes from his parents.

Inside, a small jewellery box contained two wedding rings, his mother's favourite bracelet and his father's pocket watch. Removing the box, he pushed some clothes to one side and found a framed photograph of his parents, taken at their last wedding anniversary together. How happy they looked. Tom felt his heart double in weight at the sight of the photo.

It had only been three months since the plane crash. The loss was still very much tearing away inside him. In the photo, his father was wearing the same suit the undertakers had dressed him in, the day of the funeral. The day when his father's true career was no longer kept hidden from Tom.

Douglas Last, professional car thief and getaway driver for a criminal gang. So successful at it, the other gang members had nick-named him 'Fast'.

During the wake, a group of men Tom had never seen before showed up. They arrived outside the pub in a convoy of three black Mercedes cars. A solemn man stepped out from the rear car, then silently made his way over to the entrance, where Tom was stood greeting people. Dressed in an immaculately tailored suit and reeking of too much aftershave, the man handed Tom what he called a 'condolence fund' on behalf of his boss. A gift of twenty-thousand pounds in cash inside a briefcase. Tom looked over to the vehicle. A blacked-out window lowered slightly to reveal the tanned leather face of a man with jet-black hair. A hand appeared holding an envelope, which the solemn gentleman rushed over to obtain before returning to hand it to Tom.

After the wake, Tom found a quiet spot in the pub's beer garden and opened the envelope. It contained a handwritten letter from the man in the car. It expressed sympathy, how much Douglas had meant to their organisation and how much they would all dearly miss him. It commented on how beautiful and caring a woman Holly Last was, then went on to suggest what Tom should, and should not, do with the money. The letter ended with a contact name and telephone number, should he ever feel the need to call in 'a favour'.

Although gained illegally that cash would, at least, allow Tom to go to university, become a teacher and have a more honest career than his father.

Placing the photo back in the case, Tom recounted the words from the letter. 'Don't put the money in a bank, it will be traceable. Find a secure place to stow it instead. To avoid any unwanted suspicion, don't spend it all at once. Trust no one, you'll be fine.' Tom opened the green satchel at the bottom of his dorm room wardrobe, removed a small hand-towel from inside then stared at the remainder of the cash. Still a substantial amount remained.

Turning his attention back to the keepsakes in the suitcase, he rooted around and removed an old book, given to him by his father.

'Here,' Douglas Last had said to his nine-year-old son, 'found this at work today. I know how you like all this old stuff, maybe you could use it as a diary or something? I know I don't see you enough these days, Tom, hope this makes up for it.'

It didn't, of course, but the latest games console that Tom's mother had spoiled him with was an adequate distraction. Tom had placed the book in a bedroom drawer, where it lay doing nothing for twelve years.

The year Tom turned twenty-one was also the year his father was to celebrate turning fifty. Having put a lot of issues behind them – and now being stronger as a family than ever – they were to celebrate both birthdays with a holiday to Malta. As one of the gifts to his father, Tom had sorted out some old family photos, which he planned on collating. The old book he'd been given all those years ago, Tom thought, would make an ideal album to place them in.

During the flight, the plane encountered a freak storm. One of the engines was struck by lightning and burst into flames causing the plane to veer out of control and plummet into a hillside. Everyone on board was killed instantly, with the exception of Tom who had woken up eighty feet away from the wreckage in perfect health.

Lifting that same old book from the suitcase, Tom sat down on his dorm room bed and opened up the first page. He ran a finger over the inscription on the inside cover.

Idly, he flipped the pages, studying family photos he'd tacked inside. But something wasn't right. The pages radiated a shimmering glow. Tom dropped the book on the bed and stood up. 'Late night, plus stress, equals hallucinations,' he mumbled.

A sudden brief flash burst from the pages. All the photos contained within instantly became alight. And, no matter how strong a hallucination is, it doesn't begin singeing your bedsheets.

Tom grabbed a glass of water from his desk and chucked the contents onto the bed. Picking up the book to shake off the water, his eyes widened. 'Where the hell did they come from?' A list of names had miraculously appeared on the pages. Before he could study them further, there was a knock on the door.

'Hold on,' he called, rushing to close the dampened book. He slung it onto his desk. 'Be right with you.'

Chapter 12
Wake Up and Smell the Coffee

'He's coming round,' the delivery driver informed the small crowd of onlookers. 'Give him some room.'

Tom groaned, then opened his eyes. The driver knelt in front of him, eye to eye. 'You okay, pal? You...'

'Blacked out,' Tom interjected. 'I know.' He blinked a couple of times, focusing his eyes on the chubby, unshaven face of the driver, to the sign on the dry-cleaners shop and finally at the gawping faces of the onlookers.

'Yes,' said the driver. 'Happen a lot to you, does it, son?'

'Sort of.' Feeling like street entertainment, Tom sat up and shuddered.

'Whoa, hang on.' The driver placed a hand on Tom's shoulder. 'Don't try and stand. You need a doctor.'

'Trust me,' assured Tom. 'This isn't my first rodeo. I'll be fine.'

The driver scanned Tom. 'I'm not so sure, mate.' Looking first at Tom's nose, then at the pavement, he uttered, 'Hang on, where did your blood go?'

'Umm...' *Bollocks*. Tom's brain struggled for a viable answer, an excuse. Hell, a half-decent distraction would do.

'Qualified first-aider coming through,' came a voice from behind the baffled onlookers.

Thank you, guardian angels. Tom sighed in relief, as the driver turned to face the gap in the front row.

'I'll take over from here. Excuse me, sir, let me through.' It was Zoe.

She winked at Tom. 'Oh, hello, it's you,' she said, tutting and wagging her finger at him, theatrically. 'Don't tell me, you've forgotten your insulin again?'

'Sorry, um... guilty as charged,' admitted Tom, playing

along.

A steady groan rippled amongst the crowd. One by one, realising this wasn't anything worth gossiping about later, they dispersed.

'You'll be all right with him then, will you?' the driver asked Zoe.

'Oh, yes, done this routine a thousand times.'

'He was covered in blood, though,' said the flummoxed driver. 'I don't understand where it's all gone?'

Zoe looked to Tom for help, but getting nothing back, bumbled, 'That'll be... Ah yes, the lack of, erm... glucose.' She mentally high-fived herself. 'Makes the blood super-thin, you see. Especially on a hot day like today, just evaporates away.' She decided it was time they left. Pulling Tom up, she dragged him away.

***

Stepping through the door, Tom and Zoe were greeted by the usual quizzical reaction from the customers of the Copper Kettle. Although less busy than the last time Tom was there, the nattering of the customers soon continued to fill the quaintly decorated room. Tom saw the table where he'd met Leonard was vacant.

'We can sit there, if you want me to grab it?'

'Yep, go for it,' said Zoe. 'I'll go order.'

Tom did so, and sat down.

'Hello there, Zoe, m'lovely.' Beryl beamed, wiping the soap suds off her hands with her salmon pink apron. Spotting Tom sat waiting, she added, 'And what can I get you *both*?'

Zoe ordered an espresso for Tom, raspberry milkshake for herself.

'Some of my memory has come back,' said Tom, once Zoe had sat down. 'Cool, huh?'

Holding off her questioning for the moment, she simply answered with a, 'Sure.'

'I remember being at uni, seeing how the names within the book first appeared to me.' He looked around the room, checking he wasn't talking too loudly. 'It was my dad who gave me the book, when I was a kid. Turns out he worked for some criminal gang. At my parents' wake, I now remember the boss of the gang showing up and giving me a load of cash.'

'That's a lot to take in,' said Zoe, astonished. 'No surprise you had a nosebleed. I wonder how your dad got hold of the book?'

'I think it's safe to assume it was stolen.'

Zoe, distracted by a loud family that had just entered the café, turned her attention back to Tom. 'Anyway, you haven't explained what happened to you, back at the library?'

'Oh, right.' Tom faltered. 'Sorry.' He glanced outside, allowing time to consider how to explain Ali's actions.

Zoe knocked on the table, prompting him for a response.

'Well…' began Tom, 'it's all a little crazy.'

'I've kind of grown used to crazy since meeting you, Tom.'

He took a deep breath. 'I… erm, sort of fell out of the library tower.'

'The bell tower? You being serious?' Zoe stared at him, her eyes fixed on his. 'How?'

'A bird tried to steal the book.'

Despite the look of disbelief on Zoe's face, Tom continued, 'I managed to stop it, but ended up on the pavement below.'

'What the fu—' Zoe, realising where she was, leant in closer to Tom, then whispered, 'Why were you up there in the first place?'

'I was…'

'Go on?'

Think, Tom, think. 'I…' Luckily for him, Beryl arrived with their order. He took advantage of the moment to work on a convincing lie.

Once Beryl had finished serving them, Zoe pressed Tom some more. 'So, you were about to tell me what you were doing in the tower?'

'I was just being nosey, that's all.' Tom took a sip from his cup.

'Right,' said Zoe, not buying his excuse, 'but, you still have the book, yeah?'

'It was left on the windowsill. By the time I'd recovered from the fall, then gone back up the tower, it had vanished.'

'Do you think Doreen might've found it?'

'I doubt it,' said Tom, avoiding eye contact.

'How so?'

'I bumped into her as I was leaving. She didn't know anything about it.' Tom recalled what the librarian had told him. 'Doreen did, at least, recognise the signature I copied out though.'

'Which one?'

'It was the first person to sign the book.' Tom saw Zoe's eyes widen. 'None other than the first Earl of Kent, King Harold's brother.'

Zoe raised an eyebrow at him. 'What, Harold as in, arrow-in-the-eye King Harold?'

'Yep, apparently so,' replied Tom, 'which confirms the book's as old as the *Dig This* team said it was.'

'Definitely,' agreed Zoe. 'I bet this Earl of Kent had the same ability as you?'

'Probably.' Tom mentioned how he'd searched on the computer too. 'I found another name from the book. Some outlaw from the Wild West called William J. Craddock. From what I read, he came back from the dead after being hanged for robbing a load of banks.'

'I'd say the book is definitely a list of names of people with the same ability, then,' deduced Zoe. 'Any more idea when you may have signed it?'

'No.' Tom sighed. 'Just that my dad gave it to me when I was a kid.'

'What if the underground crime gang, your dad worked for were actually part of some secret order of immortals,' said Zoe. 'Maybe your dad inducted you into it, some time before the plane crash?'

Tom gave her a doubting look. 'Seems a bit, y'know... *Da Vinci Code*, to be honest.'

Zoe sipped her milkshake through its paper straw. 'I think it's safe to assume anything is possible, right now. Think about it, what if King Harold's brother discovers a way to cheat death. He then sets up a secret society and enlists others to join him. To keep everyone in check, they have to sign that book like um...'

'To swear allegiance?'

'Yes.' Zoe clicked her fingers as a thought popped into her head. 'Maybe the book was supposed to remain in some secret headquarters too, but got stolen?'

'Hmm? What if you're half right,' said Tom, 'and the book was taken from that headquarters by someone in a criminal gang, like my dad?'

They both paused for a moment, allowing their minds to cool off from the speculations. Tom blew on his espresso, then downed it.

The sound of Zoe's mobile phone ringing meant they'd have to return to the theories later. Removing the phone from her handbag, she sighed. 'Oh joy, it's Mum.' Rolling her eyes, she answered it. 'Hello, you okay?'

Tom watched, with growing concern, the crease between Zoe's eyebrows deepening. 'Just calm down, Mum,' she responded. 'Huh? I'm sat in the café, why?'

'What's going on?' whispered Tom.

Zoe flapped her hand at him to shut up. 'You and dad always row, Mum. Why do *I* need to be there?' The confusion on her face, as she listened to what Gail was telling her, eventually changed to distrust. 'Sorry, Mum, what did you say dad was holding?'

Tom moved back from Zoe as she ended the phone call.

'So,' she said, 'tell me again what happened in the library. Only this time, you can include the part where my dad ends up with the book.'

**

'I'm so sorry,' concluded Tom, cautious not to trigger Zoe's detonate switch. 'It's just, I didn't want to upset you.'

'Oh, I'm upset all right,' Zoe said, fuming. Her eyes darted around the café, aware the other customers might be eavesdropping. 'But not with you.'

'Thank God for that,' eased Tom.

'Don't get me wrong, Tom, I'm disappointed you hid the truth from me. But, I guess I can understand why you did. What I don't understand is what the hell Dad thought he'd achieve by stalking you and acting the way he did?'

'Yeah.' Tom winced, rubbing the back of his neck. 'I know, he really lost it for a while. I'm glad he saw sense when he did.'

'You know, when I was a kid my dad would insist on being the entertainment at my birthday parties, but he'd always end up ruining them.' Zoe paused for a second, taking a sip of her drink. 'I can't remember how many times he'd stuff up a magic trick, get annoyed with himself, shout and throw things, scare the other kids away. But this, Tom, this is something else.'

Tom shook his head. 'Sorry. Look, he had his reasons for acting the way he did in the tower. You should ask him why yourself though.'

'Well.' Zoe tapped the screen of her phone. Checking the time, she huffed, 'No time like the present. Mum wants me back home to speak to him.'

'I'll come with you,' offered Tom, trying to be of some help. 'He does have *my* book, after all.'

'I don't think that's a good idea. If anyone's going to get through that thick Jamaican skull of his, it's me. I think you should go back to the prof's and chill out for a bit. You've been through a lot today.' She stood up. 'I'll get your book back, don't you worry.'

There was no point arguing about it. Tom could see in her eyes he would only lose. 'All right,' he sighed, 'but give me your phone number first.'

'Bit forward of you.' Zoe grinned, picking up a napkin. 'Technically we've only just met.'

Tom smiled as Zoe walked over to the till. She paid Beryl for their order, and asked to borrow a pen. 'Here you go,' she said, handing him the napkin with her mobile number on.

Tom thanked her. 'I don't seem to own a mobile. Well, maybe I do, but...' he pointed towards his forehead, 'don't recall owning one. But, there's a house phone where I'm staying. I can give you a call later.'

'Sure.' Zoe stood. 'Come on, I'll give you a lift back to the prof's house.'

Chapter 13
A Puff of Smoke

All was quiet as Tom entered the lodge, shut the door and re-moved his jacket. He looked over towards the sofa area to his right, then the kitchen to his left. Stepping forward to the stair-case, he yelled out 'Hello? Ed?' There was no answer.

Walking over to the kitchen, he rummaged through the cupboards, found a bag of crisps to snack on, then made his way over to the sofa. Clutching the napkin Zoe had given him with her phone number on, he placed it beside him then allowed the moment of calmness to envelope him; peace at last. With so many questions still vying for his mind's attention, any hope of relaxation was soon lost.

Half an hour went by. He finished off the last bits of salty crisps and placed the scrunched-up empty packet on the coffee table. Grabbing the napkin, he got up and strode over to a small wicker table by the front door. *Right*, he thought, picking up the handset from a telephone sat there. *Hopefully, she'll be back by now*. Tom tapped Zoe's number into the keypad. *Great*, as the phone beeped back at his ear, *voicemail*.

'Hi, Zoe. So, um… yeah, it's Tom. I'm just calling to give you this number.' He read out the telephone number written on a sticker on the phone. 'Hope everything goes all right with your dad. Okay, um… bye.' He returned the handset and stood staring at the telephone like a complete numpty.

Looking out through the tiny round window in the door, Tom could see thick black smoke billowing from a crooked metal flue on the roof of Leonard's workshop.

'Shit,' he gasped.

The door to the workshop flung open. Ed stepped out wearing lab goggles, coughing and spluttering as he waved his hand about in front of his face. Stood gawping at the almost comical sight, Tom watched as Ed removed the goggles to reveal a patch of clean skin on his otherwise sooted face. Tom winced, as Ed then leaned against the cottage wall and vomited into a drain.

Leonard appeared from the workshop. He tugged open a stubborn window, then wiped blackened sweat from his head with the green apron he was wearing. Tom grabbed his jacket, and opened the door.

'For Christ's sake, Ed, how many more times,' boomed Leonard, as Tom hurried across the courtyard to them. 'Leave the welding to me.'

'What happened?' Tom alternated between looking at the workshop, Leonard and a coughing Ed.

'Ah, Thomas, my lad,' Leonard said, beaming as he placed his arm around Tom's to deflect his attention from the scene. 'Nothing to fret about. Ed, here, was just attempting to burn down my workshop.'

Ed retched, wiping sweet and sour bile off his lips. 'You're welcome.'

'Shit, you both okay?'

'Yes, yes. A minor hiccup involving an oil can and a welding torch,' said Leonard. 'I promise you, it's all under control now. I've put the fire out.'

Tom turned to look at the workshop. By now the smoke had dispersed. 'Well, as long as no one was hurt, I guess.'

'Oh, good Lord, no,' chuckled Leonard, marching himself and Tom away from the smell of Ed's sick. 'So, how's your day been? Any update on the old…' Leonard gave Tom a gentle tap on the forehead, 'memory problem?'

Tom avoided chatting about Ali and the library. 'Well, actually, I've had some memories come back.'

'Really?' said Leonard, keen to hear more.

Tom nodded. 'I now know my parents are dead.'

Leonard placed his hand on Tom's back. 'Gosh, I'm very sorry to hear that, Tom. How awful.'

'Thanks.' Tom gave Leonard a smile, pausing to compose

his memories again. 'They died in a plane crash. Somehow, I survived it. I remember being at their funeral, the wake.'

Ed broke the conversation with another retch. 'Urgh. Sorry.'

'Where do you begin to process all this?' Leonard sighed. 'Is that all you can remember?'

'No. I know my dad was involved in some criminal gang. Oh, and that I went to uni.'

Leonard removed his hand from Tom's back. 'Oh, Tom, my dear lad. This is such hard news to hear. What triggered the return of these memories?'

'I fainted on the pavement in the village. When I came round, there they all were.'

Ed chipped in, 'That'll be your brain's coping mechanism for the influx of data. It basically crashed, from the sound of it.'

Leonard tutted. 'Yes, thank you, Ed.' He turned back to Tom, and leant in close. 'Right,' he whispered, 'I know what will make you feel better, my lad, a stiff drink.'

'Bu—' began Tom.

Leonard took hold of Tom's arm. 'Come on. I won't take *no* for an answer.'

'But, I'm waiting for…' Tom pointed towards the lodge.

'Whatever it is, you can still be waiting with a glass of sherry in your hand.' Leonard pulled Tom to the rear door of the cottage. Glancing back to Ed, he said, 'If you've finished yakking, go switch everything off in the workshop. And, might I suggest a shower, Ed?'

Apologising, Ed bowed his head like a scolded schoolboy. 'Yes, Prof,' he said, before walking over to the workshop door.

***

A mismatch of cupboards in various states of disrepair surrounded Leonard's kitchen walls. Tom was distracted by the vintage washing machine, clattering away under a cream tiled work surface. Pots, pans and cooking utensils, piled on the worktop, rattled in unison to the old turquoise washer.

'Well?' Leonard repeated, louder this time.

'Sorry, what was that?' Tom's eyes darted back to Leonard, who was stood in a doorway leading into the front of the cottage.

'Your car, Tom. I said, "It's not on the driveway".'

'Ah, yeah,' replied Tom. 'Had some trouble with it earlier.'

'My, my, things really aren't going your way at all. Well, luckily for you, there's a bloody good mechanic in the village. I'd be happy to give him a call? I'm sure if there's any parts you need, he'll source them.'

'I think he'd be sourcing them for a long time, to be honest. Although, he'd find a load of the parts for a Triumph GT6 scattered about near Penmoor. It's totalled.'

'Oh my.' Leonard's eyebrows shot up so quick they looked as though they'd been electrocuted. 'Sherry. Yes, that's what's called for now. Then, tell me everything.' He directed Tom towards the door. 'Shall we?'

'Just a quick one though.' Tom followed the professor through to his study. 'I'm expecting a phone call.'

'Yes, of course.' Leonard waved, not really listening.

Stepping through to the study, Tom was immediately drawn to the shelves of books to his left, which almost completely blocked out the drab green flock wallpaper. 'Like to read then, Leonard?'

'Whatever gave you that impression,' chuckled Leonard, heading over to a large globe nestled on a wooden stand opposite Tom. Lifting up the northern hemisphere to reveal various bottles within, he selected one of them and sat it on a nearby sideboard. 'You read much, Tom?' he asked, picking up two sherry glasses from a silver tray.

'Not really,' replied Tom. 'Although, it appears I have an interest in ancient literature.'

'Feel free to browse.' Leonard gestured to the shelves. 'There's a lot of historical ones on there. Well, no surprise, I guess, since I used to teach history. I think there's a few fiction titles at the far end, if you'd prefer also?'

Tom peered along the shelves. Resembling a mini library, the room sent a shiver down his spine as he recalled the incident with Ali.

'Here you go,' said Leonard, handing him a glass.

'Thanks.'

Holding up his own glass, Leonard toasted, 'To health and happiness.'

'Health and happiness,' repeated Tom, before taking a sip. 'Bloody hell fire,' he wheezed, after swallowing the sweet, fiery tipple, 'that's got a kick to it.'

'It's a sly one, for sure.' Leonard winked, knocking back his own. 'Come, take a seat.'

Tom settled into a high-backed leather chair between the kitchen door and a small beige-tiled fireplace. Leonard retuned to the globe, closed the lid, and flicked a small brass catch down from Columbia to Peru. 'Can I get you something to eat?'

'I'm fine, thanks.' Tom nodded, daring another sip. 'I really can't stay long.'

Being a persistent host, Leonard continued regardless. 'I'll go grab the cheese and crackers, just in case. Anyway, you must tell me what happened to your car?'

'Really, I...' Tom gave up. Leonard had already pottered off into the kitchen. The old professor's eagerness suggested to Tom that he didn't get many guests. And, by how Leonard ordered Ed about the place, that didn't really surprise him. Tom now felt a sense of obligation to stay a while longer.

Chapter 14
Ring, Ring

When Zoe had returned home, she found the kitchen empty. The shop had been closed early. Usually, around this time, Ali would be neatening the stock, sweeping the floor; Gail, hovering around the oven preparing dinner, but not today.

Making her way upstairs, Zoe entered the living room. Her mother was cleaning the hell out of everything; ornaments polished so vigorously, if you picked one up it would feel as hot as her temper. The surfaces of the bookshelf, the sideboard, all fifty square inches of the television screen – gleaming. Given enough time, Zoe was in no doubt her mother would've washed the purple floral print off the wallpaper.

Without even turning to greet her daughter, Gail spoke, coldly, 'Your dad's sulking in his office.'

'You mentioned on the phone he'd brought up the past again?' Zoe chanced.

'Yes.' Gail's dust cloth hovered above a small brass shire-horse's back, which sat pride-of-place on the lustrous surface of the dark wooden sideboard. 'When he got in, I asked him what was wrong. At first he wouldn't say, then after I demanded, he opened up. Started rambling on about Lance Goldstorm, of all people. You know what happens whenever that name crops up.' Gail slung the dust cloth onto the cushion of a cream leather sofa, then faced her daughter. 'I've heard it a million times, Zoe, how *that yankee stole my limelight*. I didn't need to hear it again.'

'And…' Zoe braced herself, 'the book you said he was holding?'

'That old thing,' flared Gail. 'I hit him with it.'

'What?'

'He was acting like the past didn't matter any more. I don't need to tell *you* how much he used to obsess about performing again. But then he starts going on about Lance belonging to some group of people with special powers. He then went on to say that book of Tom's has all their names hidden inside it. Anyway, I snatched the bloody thing right off him, and bounced it off his head.'

'Mum!'

'Don't act so shocked, Zoe. He's had it coming for years. Anyway, once he'd calmed down, he did the whole "I'm going to change, put family first" routine.'

'I wasn't aware there *was* a routine?'

Gail pointed to the door. 'Look, Zoe, just go and speak to him. I'm too tired and annoyed with myself for believing things will be different this time. Maybe you can get through to him.' Swiping the can of polish off the glass coffee table, she aimed it at a wedding photo on the sideboard. 'And Zoe?'

'Yes?'

'Tell him his apology gift needs to be something really special this time.'

'Right.'

Zoe approached the office door and waited. Inside, it sounded like her father was sobbing.

'Dad? Can I come in?'

The sobbing stopped. After a few seconds, Ali answered, 'Yes.'

Sat facing away from her in his high-back swivel chair, as she entered, Ali appeared to be staring at two objects in front of the computer keyboard on his desk. The room felt smaller than usual, Zoe thought. With cluttered shelves full of binders and folders, along with other documents for the shop's admin in two large filing cabinets, there wasn't much space for two people anyway, but right now Ali's woeful mood had shrunk it more so.

'The book you've got there, Dad,' said Zoe, as she stood beside him, 'I promised Tom I'd give it back to him later.'

Without hesitation Ali leant forward, picked up the book and handed it to her.

'Thank you.' She pointed to the other object on the desk:

an award. The grey die-cast hand clutching a gold-coloured ticket looked tarnished with age. 'Is that what I think it is?'

'Our *Golden Ticket* award. I don't want it in our home any more.' Ali lifted up the heavy object. 'Doesn't feel welcome here.' The wastepaper bin clanged as he dropped the trophy inside.

'You can't just throw it away.' Zoe stooped down and fished it out. 'You came first place in a national TV show to win this. Here, take it.'

Ali refused. 'I don't need some stupid piece of junk reminding me I'm a failure, Zoe.'

Thumping the trophy on the desk, Zoe glared at her father. 'Tell me what's going on, Dad. I know you overheard Tom and me earlier, and that you assaulted him in the library. His ability to heal is incredible, but to try to obtain it by bullying him, it's just not like you.'

Ali remained silent.

'What did you want it for anyway? Are you thinking of returning to the stage?'

'Yes, but it wasn't about that.' Ali's eyes quivered as the most important person in his life viewed him with such disappointment. He wiped away a tear. 'I wanted to impress you.'

Broadsided, Zoe spurted, 'You're kidding, right?'

'I know you think my magic tricks are a joke, I see how you look at me. If I had the same ability as Tom and Lance, I thought I could become a success. Then you wouldn't feel embarrassed by me.'

Zoe looked shocked. 'What? Is that what you honestly think?'

'You mean the world to me, Zoe. Do you remember how you would tell everyone I was secretly a great wizard?'

'Of course,' her eyes looked to the carpet as the thoughts of her childhood returned, 'but I was five years old. I just wanted to impress my friends.'

'It made me feel special, though. I decided whatever those fools in television had thought about our magic act didn't matter, because my girl believed in me. Then over the years, even you stopped believing.'

'Oh my God, you're serious, aren't you?' Zoe knelt down beside him. 'I adore you, Dad. But the reason I stopped believing in your tricks was because you own a bloody magic shop, and I would see you testing the tricks out. Add to that, you and Mum arguing whenever one of you mentioned your shows, that kind of shit has repercussions for a kid.'

Zoe perched on her father's lap and cradled into him. Holding each other there, nothing more needed to be said about it. This moment was all that mattered.

Eventually, Ali opened up to her about the shop's financial situation. They were barely breaking even.

'How about I pour you a glass of rum,' offered Zoe. 'I'll take a look at the figures before we break the news to Mum.'

'Yeah, mon.' Ali smiled, with some sense of relief. 'That's my girl.'

Zoe stood, kissed her father on top of his bald head, then said, 'Just let me make a phone call first.'

***

Ed made his way down the spiral stairs of the lodge. In a clean set of white jogging clothes and feeling much cleaner, he wandered into the kitchen area. Opening the fridge, he removed a beer bottle. He flicked the cap off and sighed. 'Man, have I been looking forward to this.' Before he had a chance to take a swig, he was interrupted by the house phone. 'Oh, come on,' he moaned, plonking the bottle down on the kitchen work surface.

'All right, I'm coming,' he mumbled, before picking up the receiver and answering with a sharp, 'Hello?'

'Hi, Tom?'

'Nope, it's Ed. Who's this?'

'It's Zoe from Cassam's Magic Emporium. Can I speak to him?'

'Oh, hey, Zoe.' Ed recognised her voice now. 'He's over in the cottage swanning it up with Lord Muck. How do *you* know

Tom?'

There was a brief pause before her reply. 'Never mind that. Can you let him know I've got the book,' quickly adding, 'in stock, I mean. If you could get him to call me back, I can arrange to give it him.'

'I might,' huffed Ed. 'I might not. Depends.'

'Excuse me?' snapped Zoe, loudly.

Ed rattled his little finger inside his ear before bringing the earpiece back to it. 'Sorry, just winding you up.'

'Listen,' said Zoe, 'I haven't forgotten that forty quid you owe me from poker night in the pub.'

Bollocks, he thought, *that girl's relentless*. Backtracking, he replied, 'Sorry. Sure, I'll let Tom know you rang.'

'Right. Thank you. The book's important to him. Don't forget.'

'Yup, important book, call him back,' relayed Ed. 'Got it.'

After ending the call, Ed returned to his beer. *At last.*

When he eventually drained the last drop from the bottle, he tossed it into the bin, then heaved a long slow sigh as the phone rang again.

Chapter 15
That's the Spirit, Tom

'So, let me get this straight.' Leonard paused, drew on his pipe, then sent a smoke ring sailing across the room. 'You were dive-bombed by a kamikaze buzzard?'

Tom nodded before taking another sip of painfully addictive sherry.

Leonard leaned forward in his chair. 'It's amazing you weren't killed. Don't you agree?'

'Just lucky, I suppose.' Tom decided to change the topic, 'It's a beautiful place though, the Penmoor.'

'Well, actually,' Leonard eagerly tapped the ash from his pipe, 'some suggest Penmoor and the village of Penworthy have connections to the name Pendragon, as in Arthur Pendragon.'

'Oh, right,' said Tom, feigning interest, 'and is there any evidence for this?'

'Not conclusive, but, there is the...'

'The...?'

'The... A-hole.'

Tom choked on his drink. Patting his chest, his wheezy cough concealed the laughter. 'Sorry, the what now?'

'Un... believable,' huffed Leonard, shaking his head. 'Ed reacted the exact same way when I mentioned it to him. It's a perfectly befitting name. A triangular-shaped sacred stone, it has a four-inch slit through its upper half like the letter *A*.'

'Okay,' smirked Tom.

'There are those who believe it's the stone King Arthur pulled Excalibur from.'

'Really though, Leonard, who decided to call it that?'

'I don't understand why people find the name funny.' Leonard looked almost offended.

Tom explained why the name was amusing. He even stood

to show Leonard which part of the anatomy he was referring to.

Leonard fumbled with his pipe, spilling the ash down onto his brown corduroys. 'Good grief,' he exclaimed, flicking the grey residue away. 'Does it? Well, that explains a lot, I must say.'

'The locals should really think about renaming it.'

'Indeed.' Leonard took a pinch of fresh tobacco and pressed it into the bowl of his pipe. 'No wonder Dotty Perkins's niece once slapped me when I offered to take her up there?'

Tom's mouth dropped.

'Of course, I was just being friendly.' Leonard tutted. 'Her niece was staying for the summer, and Dotty mentioned how bored the poor teenager was. So, when I next bumped into them, I offered to show it to her. Thought she might be interested in learning about the myth. I see now why she was so irate.'

'That's so funny,' chuckled Tom. He finished off the last of his sherry and placed the glass down. His eyelids felt heavy. 'Think I'll make that one my last.'

'Oh my,' Leonard saw the time on his watch, 'I must apologise for detaining you.'

'It's okay,' said Tom. He went to stand but struggled to lift himself from the chair. 'I think I'm a bit of a lightweight when it comes to sherry.' His arm muscles felt like rubber as he slunk back down.

'I'll go grab you a glass of water.' Excusing himself, Leonard headed out of the room to the kitchen.

'Ugh.' Tom peeled his tongue off the roof of his mouth. His eyes blinked, trying to stop the room from spinning. *Maybe I'll just stay here a few more minutes*, he thought, letting out a big yawn, *sleep it off…*

Chapter 16
A Rabbit in a Hat Trick

As the evening went on, Zoe's concern for Tom grew. It had been hours since she'd left the message with Ed. Her continual glares at her mobile phone had not gone unnoticed.

'He survived a plane crash, car crash and falling from the library tower,' Ali had told her. 'Relax.'

Sitting down together, the two of them had tried to find more information on Tom's mysterious book. Typing the inscription into Zoe's tablet had only displayed a translation in the search results. And, of course, no mention of the book came up when they typed in 'Lance Goldstorm' or the 'first Earl of Kent'. They did, however, discover the latter's name. Zoe had made a mental note to ask Tom if it fitted the first signature in the book.

After trying one last time to call Tom, Zoe conceded it was time to call it a night. *Dad's right*, she thought, *Tom will be okay, he's bloody immortal.*

Ali, not wanting to leave a full glass of rum, stayed up to finish it off.

***

It was 2:30 a.m.

All was quiet at Cassam's Magic Emporium. A white rabbit rose from the large black top hat, in the dimly lit shop window. It looked to where the mechanical rabbit, now hidden under a velvet display cloth, lay with its robotic neck twisted apart. Sniffing the air, and with a look of intent in its pink eyes, the white rabbit leapt down from the hat, hurried through the curtain and into the shop.

Checking the coast was clear, it ran across the shop floor, weaving around the glass cabinet, sales counter, then through the door to the kitchen.

With nostrils flaring, it sniffed a second time. *Carrot*, it thought, *I smell carrot*. Hopping over to a vegetable rack beneath the sink, it saw what it craved. *Food*. It sprang up onto the bottom shelf of the rack, helped itself to a carrot, then another.

As it sat there nibbling, its ears pricked up. *Growling? No, not a dog. Man snoring. Safe to proceed.*

Crossing to the stairs, this furry intruder hopped up every step until it reached the top. Peering around a wall, it checked the landing was clear then lifted its head up, sniffing some more. The scent was strongest from a room up ahead. *There, yes, that way*.

A quick sprint and it was inside the room, but not alone. *What to do? What? What?* Its heart quickened as it stared at the giant of a man lying asleep on the sofa.

The rabbit spotted the fluffy slippers on Ali's feet and panicked. *Try not to get mistaken for footwear*. Creeping up to him, the smell of rum hit the back of the rabbit's nostrils. It hopped up onto the sofa, but was unable to locate its quarry. *It's here, I know it is*.

Turning to hop back down, it spotted what it had come for. Jumping onto a glass coffee table, the rabbit slid across and head butted the book onto the floor. *Got you*.

Checking the big guy was fast asleep, the rabbit continued nudging the book along the carpet towards the door.

'Aww, hello there, little fella,' cooed Gail, stepping into the living room. 'Aren't you just the cutest.'

Unhand me, thought the rabbit, its hind legs flailing as Gail picked it up.

'As far as making-up presents go, Ali's really outdone himself with you.' She looked at her husband snoring away. 'Still got the magic touch, eh,' she whispered. 'I think we'll leave him to sleep that rum off.' She gave the rabbit a tickle under its chin. 'I think I'll call you Snowball. Let's go find you somewhere to sleep.'

The rabbit tried to escape Gail's cuddle as she carried it out of the room.

'It's a good job I saw Ali had left the living room light on,' purred Gail, making her way downstairs, 'or who knows where you would've ended up.'

I am on a mission, twitched the rabbit. *Put, me, down.*

After finding a large plastic box, lining it with scrunched-up newspaper, and placing a few torn-up lettuce leaves inside, Gail just needed to add the final touch.

Watching from on top of the kitchen table in complete and utter fury, the rabbit needed this woman out of the way, sharpish.

'Right,' said Gail, placing a small bowl of water into the box, 'let's get you in this, then I can pop you safely under the stairs for the night.'

What? There was no way the rabbit was going in there. It looked at the pantry door, then to Gail. *Think, Snowball, think. Oh no, I called myself Snowball. Damn you.* It watched Gail carry the box into the pantry. This was its chance.

Readying itself, the rabbit sized up the distance from the dining chair to the pantry door. Taking a deep breath, it ran. Like a plane taking off, it bounded along the table then leapt. Its forelegs hooked the back of the dining chair, causing it to tip over against the pantry door, swinging it shut. With a clatter, the chair toppled to the floor causing the rabbit to somersault onto the tiles. *No time to lose.* It set off around to the bottom of the stairs and headed back up.

'Hello?' came the muffled voice of Gail from inside the pantry. 'I can't open the door from in here.' She banged her fist against it. 'If this is some kind of joke, Ali, it's not funny, okay?'

On the landing, the rabbit slid the book over the edge of the stairs. It waited for it to tumble to the bottom before it hopped down. Along the kitchen floor, completely ignoring Gail thumping at the pantry door, the rabbit continued to push the book towards the shop.

Shunting the book up against the front door, the rabbit left it on the doormat and made its way over to the shop window. With a big hop, it then sneaked between the curtain and up to the glass.

Tap-tap, its nails wrapped, *tap-tap-tap*.

A shadowy silhouette darkened the doorway. The figure of a man in a jet-black suit and top hat stooped down and looked at the large letterbox on the bottom of the door. His white gloved hand slipped through and carefully lifted the book off the mat. 'The Eternus, returned at last,' he murmured. After sliding out the old artefact, he breathed in the familiar scent of the leather cover.

Standing up, he checked the quiet street for onlookers. The flap of the letterbox rattled as the rabbit finally squeezed through.

'You have done well.' The man grinned, hoisting the animal up by its ears. 'Let's fly.'

Straightening his top hat, the figure casually strode down the moonlit street. The pavement was bathed in silver light; the man's attire repelling the lunar glow as though its very fabric was woven from a black hole. After passing several shops, the figure turned down a narrow alleyway and stopped. The rabbit caught up with its master, shivered, then braced itself for what was coming next.

The man clapped his hands together, causing a brilliant white flash to light up the alleyway. When the flash vanished, so had the man; now replaced by an enormous Andean condor. Beating its white-tipped wings down hard, it grabbed the rabbit in its talons then soared up into the clear night sky. Shutting its eyes tight, the rabbit clung on to the book with all four limbs, praying not to drop its master's precious object.

***

Gail pressed her back against the wall of the pantry. She lifted her feet up against the door and started to push. Buckling under the force, the small latch on the other side snapped clean off, sending the door flying open and Gail falling to the floor with a bump. She was *not* impressed.

'Where are you? Get down here… Now,' enraged Gail, from the bottom of the staircase. 'Both of you, here this minute.'

Zoe and Ali arrived at the top of the stairs and looked down at Gail. Panting heavily and with her hair trussed up in rollers, she resembled the winner of a psycho-mother-of-the-year award.

Delicately dangling the words, Zoe asked, 'Okay there?'

Through gritted teeth, Gail hissed, 'I have just been trapped in the sodding pantry, Zoe. You know I hate confined spaces, do I look like I'm "okay"?'

This was something that Zoe always found odd, considering her mother used to be a magician's assistant. She decided now was not the best time to bring up the subject, instead choosing to say, 'We'll be right down.'

Ali muttered something in Jamaican as he trundled down the stairs behind Zoe.

'Don't give me that Jamaican bullshit, Ali,' spat Gail, as they arrived. 'Which one of you trapped me in there?'

'Huh?' replied Ali and Zoe in unison.

'Don't give me *Huh*.'

'But, I've been upstairs all night, sugar,' Ali ventured.

Arriving at the kitchen, Zoe noticed the fallen chair. Walking over to pick it up, she spotted the plastic box and its contents. 'What's that for?'

'Sorry?' Gail looked to see what Zoe was pointing at. 'It's for the rabbit your dad got me.'

'Rabbit? I didn't get you a rabbit,' said Ali, 'and, I didn't lock you up either.'

'So who did?' Gail placed a defiant hand on her hip. 'A ghost? The wind? Well?'

Confused, Ali looked in the pantry for a rabbit. 'So where is this damned rabbit, then?'

Here we go again, thought Zoe, *Ding, Ding, round four thousand*. Blocking out the arguing, she looked down at the floor, scanning for any sign of her mother's mysterious new pet. After checking in the cupboards, and underneath them, she decided to have a quick look in the shop. Flicking on the light switch, she scanned the room. Before leaving to rejoin the argument in the kitchen, Zoe realised she hadn't checked the shop window.

Quietly approaching it, just in case the animal was behind the curtain, Zoe held out a nervous hand. She paused briefly, then slowly drew back the red curtain.

'Dad,' she called out, 'you need to come see this.'

'See what?' shouted Ali, from the argument in the kitchen.

'Someone's maimed Roger.'

Both Ali and Gail entered. With the display curtains drawn back, the decommissioned robotic bunny lay on the velvet cloth like some bizarre corpse in a tiny stage production. The moment Ali caught sight of it, his eyes welled. He rushed over and picked up its head. 'This has been the centrepiece since the day we opened. Who did this? Why?'

Gail, still broiling about being trapped in the pantry, sneered, 'It's plastic, Ali. We can get a new one. Where's my Snowball?'

Zoe raised an eyebrow. 'Who?'

'The real rabbit your dad got me. I named it Snowball.'

Ali dropped the broken plastic head back on the velvet cloth. 'For the last time, Gail,' he grunted, 'I didn't buy you a bloody rabbit.'

'Can you both please just stop bickering for one minute?' snapped Zoe. 'Something really weird is going on.'

Her parents stared at her blankly, awaiting an explanation.

Zoe stood firm. 'Mum, you got locked in the pantry, not by me or Dad. Roger here, has been vandalised by someone. And somehow, a real rabbit has appeared, but has now disappeared.'

Her parents nodded in agreement.

'So might I suggest we try and figure out what these all have in common?'

'Suppose so,' they both replied, reluctantly.

'Great.' Zoe adopted the role of detective. 'Mum, where did you first see the rab… Snowball?'

Gail pointed a finger upwards. 'Well, it was in the living room. Just sat there on the carpet, when I saw your father was asleep.'

'Good, now we're getting somewhere. And did you notice anything else unusual?'

'Well, not really,' said Gail, recalling the scene in her mind. 'I mean, there was that book of Tom's lying on the floor beside the rabbit, but apart from that everything in the room was as normal.'

Ali shot Zoe a worried glance. 'The book.'

'Hey,' cried Gail, as Zoe and Ali darted out of the shop. 'What's so important about that crappy old thing?'

Returning to the living room, their eyes widened. 'It can't have gone,' said Ali, checking under the coffee table, then by the sofa.

'But, according to Mum, you were fast asleep. It's possible, Dad, that someone could've broken in and stolen it without any of us knowing.'

Gail raised an eyebrow. 'You should probably try calling your new friend, Zoe, see what he knows.'

Zoe retorted, 'I don't think Tom is the sort of person to break in, vandalise Roger, steal his book then leave a rabbit as some kind of consolation gift?'

Ali scratched the back of his head. Shrugging his shoulders, he offered, 'Maybe it was payback for me threatening him in the library?'

'Unbelievable,' she groaned. 'I'm going to call him, right now. But to check he's okay.' As she stormed off, she had a bad feeling Tom was in serious trouble.

Chapter 17
Mind Reading

'All right, enough,' croaked Tom. 'I'm awake, shut up now.'

The clock clanged again.

Seriously, I get it, he thought, easing his eyes open. The darkened unfamiliar room was, at least, more kind to his eyesight. Feeling groggy, Tom ran his tongue around his dry mouth. *That's the last time I'm drinking sherry.* He squinted up at the grey wooden-slatted ceiling. *Where the hell am I? And what is that smell?* He took another long sniff. *Burnt metal?*

More aware of his position, Tom could feel the softness of the chaise longue underneath his back. Unable to move his hands apart, he soon figured out why. *I've been tied up.*

'Leonard?'

His call went unanswered.

'Professor?'

Struggling, he lurched to one side but his wrists weren't the only things bound together. Dropping onto the cold quarry-tiled floor, Tom writhed about like a fish on a deck, trying unsuccessfully to loosen the rope from his ankles.

He pulled his knees to his chest and grabbed hold. Rocking on his back, he managed to upright himself. Feeling his heart pumping with adrenaline, he clawed at the rope around his ankles, all the time frantically looking around him. Shelving, cupboards and cabinets, shadows and dark shapes, in the low light of the room.

Occupying the centre of the floor stood a long workbench.

Shifting onto his feet, he carefully lifted himself up and gazed at an array of odd-looking machinery, cluttering the surface of the bench. A wooden box ticked away as a copper cylinder revolved on top of it. Beside that, a tall glass bell-jar containing a series of brass cogs turned slowly as steel pistons moved up and down. Tom watched as every few seconds tiny sparks danced along the inside of the glass.

At the far end of the bench, Tom's eyes were drawn to something unnerving. Attached to a metal stand, wired into a pulsing oscilloscope, the object – part gun, part trumpet – consisted of a large dull-steel barrel, fluted at its muzzle and decorated with a dragon carving. Apart from the modifications to its body, the weapon looked antique.

Bolted on one side of the gun, the oblong of spiralled brass pipework housed a tangle of coloured wiring, criss-crossing each other. On a variety of small metal boxes, around the body of the weapon, sat flashing LED displays, dials and switches. Tom had no intention of hanging around long enough to see this contraption being used.

Seeing a broken hacksaw blade, gripped in a vice on the side of the bench, Tom quickly shuffled over. He began to rub the rope, that bound his wrists together, against the saw's teeth. 'Bollocks,' he whispered, frozen to the spot. *Was that footsteps?* Working faster now, Tom could definitely hear someone approaching from a door over at the far corner of the room. *Why isn't this stupid thing cutting?* A closer inspection revealed the teeth to be blunt. 'Shit.' With no time for a better plan, Tom ducked down behind the bench and prayed.

Someone had entered the room.

The stranger strode over to the bench and placed something on it. At the opposite side, Tom was attempting to unpick the rope from his ankles while staring at the person's unfamiliar black trousers and polished black shoes.

A white rabbit appeared beside the stranger's feet. The curious creature was in no doubt about who *it* was staring at. Cocking its head to one side, raising up onto its hind legs, it wagged a foot at Tom.

What the hell? Tom stared back at the rabbit. *Is it waving... at me?*

The rabbit continued to attract Tom's attention.

Still unsure as to what he was witnessing, Tom blinked

and focused his eyes as he continued to watch the animal's surreal behaviour.

The rabbit wiggled its head, then gave Tom another little wave.

Reciprocating, Tom nodded back as the rabbit stopped then scuttled off to the corner of the room. Completely transfixed by this, he leant to one side to see what it was up to. He responded, silently, by mouthing the word 'Hello?'

The rabbit shook its head, then froze as it appeared to be staring above where Tom was crouched.

Feeling something hard and sharp press into his neck, Tom's internal monologue announced, *I believe it was trying to tell you I'm stood right here.* Surprised by his own mind's statement, Tom let out a loud, 'Holy shit.'

Get up, continued Tom's mind, *now*. Whatever was poking into his neck started burning the skin.

'Okay, okay.' Tom did as his mind told him. Clutching the bench, he got up onto his feet. He now realised it was the stranger pressing the implement against his neck. 'Are you talking to me through my own thoughts?'

A simple psychic connection. It also allows me to read your thoughts, so don't try anything stupid.

In front of where Tom's hands lay on the bench, he noticed a mallet. *If I could just grab it quick enough*, he thought, *maybe I could…* The excruciating pain in Tom's neck was only brief, but enough to halt his plan. 'All right, point proven. You can read my thoughts, I get it.'

If you try something like that again, ordered the voice in his head, *take it from me, your healing power won't prevent you from screaming in agony. Now, slowly, move away from the bench and sit down.*

'Maybe you could untie my legs first?'

Now!

Shuffling his feet, Tom moved to the chaise longue, and sat. Only now, was he able to get a better look at his captor; dressed in a black suit, top hat and white gloves like some sort of magician. An appropriate assessment given that the man was holding a golden wand from which a green spark glowed intensely at the tip.

'Why can't I focus on your face?'

By manipulating the neurons in your temporal lobe, I can confuse your brain. A perk of the psychic connection, you could say.

Having assumed his headache was just from the sherry, Tom now figured otherwise.

And please, save the term 'magician' for your new friend Ali. You can refer to me as Conjuror.

'Okay then, *Conjuror*, what have you done with Leonard?'

The man ignored Tom and produced the book from his jacket. *Now that I have this, I'm afraid I must end your existence.*

'But you've seen inside my mind,' said Tom, 'so you must know I can't be killed.'

That's not true. The Conjuror, keeping the wand aimed at Tom, placed the book on the bench. Sitting down on a tall stool, he added, *This is the book of Eternus. Once signed, it grants you extended life. Your body can heal all wounds, but you still age, albeit at a vastly slower rate than everyone else. Slow enough to outlive all those who you hold dearest, regretfully.*

'That's how I got my ability? By signing that thing?' His brain struggled to comprehend the revelation. With some of his memory returned, Tom was now able to recall the day he signed the book. The Conjuror, seeing the same memory, laughed inside Tom's mind. *You were making a birthday gift for your father, how quaint. But turning the book into a family photo album, a rather cheap gift, no?* The Conjuror could see the memory of Tom writing a birthday message inside the book. *So that's how you signed it?*

'My dad gave the book to me, when I was a kid,' replied Tom. 'He always loved how I would sign my name whenever I wrote to him, back then. I figured making the book into an album, and signing it would bring back happy memories for him. How was I to know it would give me these powers?'

The Conjuror didn't respond.

'But, since then, I've survived at least three fatal accidents.' Tom tried again to focus on the face of his captor, with no luck. 'What makes *you* so sure you can finish me off?'

Because I know how the Eternus works. The Conjuror flicked the book open and thumbed to the last entry. *Your signature is the only thing binding the power of the curse to you.* Able to see Tom's signature, the man pointed to it.

'I don't understand?' Tom felt something soft nudge up to his ankles. Undeterred, he asked, 'Why do you want to kill me? What have I done to you?'

The Conjuror, unaware of what his rabbit was up to, continued, *I too signed the book. But for me to be free of the curse, I must erase the names of all that have followed me. I'm sure you see by now, Thomas Last, that includes you.*

Tom stood up, forgetting his situation. 'Now wait a minute,' he yelled. 'You can't just go around killing people because *you* don't want to be alive any more. It's not fair.'

A bolt of pure green lightning arced from the Conjuror's wand, impacting into Tom's ribcage. Flung backwards by the force, he smacked against the wall before tumbling forward to the floor.

Stay down.

Gasping for air, Tom rolled over and cowered into the corner of the room. The smell of baked blood filled his nostrils as he patted the hole in his shirt and chest. 'You b-bastard.' Wheezing, Tom raised his red-soaked hands up in front to protect himself. 'No, stop. Not again.'

The Conjuror lowered the wand. *Remain still, enjoy one last heal from the Eternus.*

Winded, Tom felt the now familiar healing process begin.

Now, the Conjuror turned his attention to the work bench, *if I can find a knife, we can begin.*

Making sure it wasn't seen, the rabbit made its way over to Tom and tapped a foot beside him to gain his attention. Tom raised his knees up, as the rabbit started gnawing through the rope.

Over at the bench, the Conjuror had found what he was looking for. *I just need some blood, Thomas*, he held out a scalpel, *and with a simple swipe of it across your signature, your connection to the Eternus will be severed and you will cease to exist. Try not to worry, the effect will be instantaneous.*

The rabbit yanked the now severed rope away, then leapt into Tom's hands. The action happened so quick; instinct took control as Tom launched the rabbit straight at the Conjuror's head.

The Conjuror, caught off guard, let out a cry as he stumbled backwards and slipped onto the floor.

Tom's face turned white. *What? It can't be?* His feet now free to move, he sprinted over to the desk and snatched the book. With the psychic connection severed, Tom glowered at the face of the man lying on the floor. 'Leonard?'

The shock of seeing the man who'd been so kind to him from the start lasted only seconds. Leonard, still gripping the wand, swung his arm up and released a full discharge of green energy from the tip. Another direct hit into Tom's chest, but this time the blast incinerated his betrayed heart.

Chapter 18
Escapology

The yellow Mini turned off the road and crept up next to the entrance of the driveway. With the headlights off, there was only the brief red glow of the brake lights as the car stopped.

Zoe, dressed in a black hooded top and navy jogging trousers, Ali in black trousers and his darkest green velvet tailcoat, got out and stepped over to the shadows of a high brick wall next to the entrance.

'Stay here, child,' whispered Ali, beefing up his chest. 'I'll handle this.'

'Do you even have a plan? And really, Dad, why have you brought that thing with you?'

He held up the cane he was clutching. 'I know you've got a knack of predicting when people are in trouble. I figured this'd be good to belt someone with.' He pointed at the cane's elaborate top. 'The skull's solid crystal, y'know.' He sucked his teeth in response to the dubious look from his daughter.

'Guess it's better than a library book,' She sighed. 'And, your plan?'

Peering around the wall, Ali viewed the house ahead. 'I'll walk up to the door and knock, see if the professor's home. I doubt he'd appreciate being woken up this time of the night though. Stay here.'

'What the hell?' hissed Zoe, grabbing his arm. 'What was the point of me switching off the car's headlights and parking here, for you to just swagger over, bang on the front door and say "hello"?'

Ali shrugged his shoulders. 'Element of surprise?'

'How is that the element of surprise?' retorted Zoe, now regretting bringing him. 'Look, never mind.'

'Well, we can't go breaking into people's homes, Zoe, if

that's what you're thinking.'

'No, of course not,' replied Zoe, 'but, we could have a quiet nosey around, though. Look through a few windows?'

'Kind of rude though, honey. Don't you think?'

Zoe trudged off through the entrance to the drive, keeping to the left in the shadows. 'Just come on,' she beckoned.

Reaching the cottage, they could see all the curtains downstairs were drawn. All the lights were off, aside from a flickering bulb in the arched porch way.

Ali sidled up to Zoe. 'Nothing unusual so far.'

'We'll try round the back. Tom said he was staying in a separate building behind the main house.' She followed the path round the left of the cottage with Ali creeping, almost comically, in tow.

At the rear of the property, the two of them edged along the wall of the cottage. 'That must be where Tom's at, yes?' whispered Ali, pointing across the courtyard to the converted barn. 'All quiet there too, from the look of it. He's probably asleep.' Ali checked the time on his watch. 'Three in the morning. Maybe we should just... Wait.' Ali pressed his hand onto Zoe's shoulder, pushing her back against the wall of the cottage. 'Something just flashed from inside that window there.'

'Where?' Zoe scanned the dark courtyard. 'I can't see anything?'

'From in that old wooden shack.' As Ali pointed, there came an unsettling noise from inside Leonard's workshop. 'Sounds like someone's injured.'

'Tom.' Zoe went to run, but Ali stopped her.

'Whoa there, Wonder Woman, just wait. You can't just go bursting in. Even if it is Tom, you don't know what's happened.'

'Dad, it's fine.' She pushed his arm away. 'Peeking through windows, remember?'

Ali nodded. 'All right, but just a look, nothing else. If it's anything serious, we call 999.' He stepped ahead of Zoe. 'And, I'm going first.'

'Fine.'

Taking care to be silent, they approached the wooden-clad wall of the workshop. Standing either side of a small window, they both leant in to take a cautious peek.

'Who is that?' Ali used his finger to wipe a small bit of dirt from his section of window. With a clearer view inside the dimly lit room, he now made out the person stood inside. 'Professor Goodwin?'

'Er… Dad?' Her finger trembling, Zoe pointed to the corner of the room. 'Look down there. Something's happened to Tom, he's hurt.'

They both stared in disbelief as Tom jumped up and threw a rabbit at the professor's head, sending him tumbling behind the workbench. A thick green streak of electricity arced across the room. Watching in horror, they saw the blast impact into Tom's chest, sending him flying against the nearside wall.

Zoe's fingers gripped the windowsill like vices. 'NO—'

Her scream was cut short by Ali's hand over her mouth as he pulled her with him away from view.

Ali risked another peek and saw the rabbit re-emerge from behind the work bench. Looking dazed, the rabbit shook its head. Spotting the face of the man it had stolen the book from peering in through the window, the rabbit quickly ran from the workshop and into the cottage. Within seconds, the rabbit came out of an old cat-flap in the kitchen door and was now on the courtyard.

Hearing the clatter of the flap, Zoe turned and spotted the creature. She lunged towards it, but it gave her the slip.

'Hey,' huffed Ali, trying to coral the tiny creature.

The rabbit gained some considerable distance then skidded around and halted. Narrowing its pink eyes, for just a split second, it regarded both Ali and Zoe as allies. Taking a couple of heavy breaths into its tiny chest, the rabbit ran straight towards them. After covering a couple of metres, it leapt high into the air and clapped both its forelegs together mid-air. A metallic ping echoed within the courtyard as a flash of pure white light engulfed the creature, illuminating Zoe and Ali's bewildered faces.

When their pupils adjusted to the darkness again, they saw Ed, sat on the ground.

Dressed in white clothes, he brushed himself down. He spat out some fur, with a 'pah.' Looking at Zoe and Ali's shocked expressions, he greeted them. 'Morning.'

Standing up, he juddered to shake the remnants of shape-shifting magic away, then focused on the present situation. 'Get Tom the hell out of there,' he ordered Ali. 'Right now!'

Ali stood still, partly amazed, partly in shock. 'What have you done with that rabbit?' he jabbered, scanning the courtyard as Ed rushed over.

'Hell-oo, right here, mate,' replied Ed. Swinging his hands towards the workshop, he shouted, 'Look, there's no time for this. Leonard is about to erase Tom from existence, right this minute, unless you stop him.'

Zoe, baffled at what she'd just witnessed, blurted, 'Bu… but, how were you a rabbit a few seconds ago?'

'Once more, no time to explain.' Ed gestured towards the workshop, 'Go inside, get that book off Leonard. NOW.'

'Right,' said Ali, resting his cane against his leg. He tilted his head from side to side and pulled on the cuffs of his shirt, exposing them from his velvet jacket. Straightening the lapels, he cleared his throat and announced, 'Showtime.'

'Dad?'

'Zoe, remember what you asked me on the journey up here?' Ali handed his cane to her, to hold for a moment. 'You asked me why I'd chosen this jacket?'

'Of course.' Zoe looked into her father's eyes. 'You replied by saying, "A magician should always be ready".'

Placing his right hand behind his back, Ali winked at Ed. Bringing his hand back in sight, he was now holding three throwing knives. 'Like I said, showtime.' He fanned out the knives, the contoured wooden handles facing outwards.

'What the…' gasped Zoe.

'Just stay back, Zoe,' ordered Ali, taking the cane from her with his free hand. He strode up to the door of the workshop.

With one mighty boot, he kicked the door open and stepped in.

'Don't move, Prof...'

A bolt of green lightning hurtled past Ali's head from the opposite end of the room. He raised the cane up in front of him, deflecting the second blast. The crystal skull vibrated as it absorbed all of the energy, before shattering to dust.

Ali launched the cane like a spear, striking Leonard's hand and sending the wand skidding across the workshop floor. 'What did I just say?' he boomed, readying a throwing knife.

'You're in over your head, Magician.' cried Leonard, as he dived behind some metal drawers below the bench. 'This isn't your fight.'

'Be careful, Dad.' Zoe peered into the room. She saw Tom lying unconscious on the floor, his hands covering his glowing chest. 'He's alive,' she called out, 'and healing.'

There was a moment of calm. Ali side-stepped over to guard Tom. 'I should warn you, Professor, I'm a professional. I can clip a ponytail on a revolving wheel from ten metres with these.'

'Okay, okay,' answered Leonard, from behind the bench. The tone of his voice became placid. 'I'm getting up.'

Tom stirred as Zoe rushed in to help him.

'Ed,' shouted Ali, 'get in here and help Zoe.' He turned back to Leonard, holding firm like a centurion. 'I'm waiting, Professor.'

A gloved hand reached up onto the bench.

'Don't try anything stupid.' Ali adjusted his grip on the blade of the knife. Behind him, Zoe and Ed were dragging Tom across the floor to the doorway.

'The book, Ali,' heaved Ed. 'Get the book. It's on the bench.'

Taking advantage of Ali's brief lapse, Leonard swung his other hand onto the bench and aimed a pistol at him. Without hesitation, he pulled the trigger.

Ali felt the tip of his right earlobe explode. 'Go, Zoe,' he cried. 'Get out.' With force, he sent the knife spinning across the room. The eight-inch blade embedded into Leonard's shoulder.

Switching the pistol to his other hand, Leonard pulled the trigger. Being an outdated weapon, the mechanism jammed.

Ali jumped forward and grabbed the book off the bench. 'Ed,' he shouted, throwing it towards the doorway, 'take it.'

Ed picked the book up off the ground, then together with Zoe they hoisted Tom up onto his feet.

'Where?' murmured Tom.

'Don't worry, it's me Zoe. We're getting you to safety.' She gave a quick glance back, then continued to help Ed drag him further away from the workshop.

'Not safe...' uttered Tom. 'Leonard is immor—'

'It's okay.' Zoe felt Tom's weight begin to lighten as he found his footing. 'That's it, Tom, move those legs. Help us.'

Like a zombie, Tom began to scrape one foot in front of the other.

'Good,' said Zoe. 'Keep going.' She turned back to look into the workshop. 'Dad, hurry.'

The sound of another shot rang out from the workshop.

Ali's head jerked back, recoiling from the force of the bullet. His arms fell to his side, the remaining knives clattered to the floor.

Dad? Releasing her grip on Tom, Zoe turned and froze. In that infinitesimal moment, the world shrank to just herself and her father as he collapsed like a crumpled chimney stack in the doorway. 'No. No,' she screamed. Ignoring the risk to her own life, she rushed over to him.

'Zoe,' cried Ed, struggling to steady Tom. 'Bollocks.'

Tom could only look on.

Another gunshot fired, this time the bullet scuffed the ground in front of Ed's feet.

As though snuffed out, everything fell silent.

'One move, she dies,' ordered Leonard, stood over Zoe.

'Murderer,' she sobbed, feeling the pistol press into the back of her head as she knelt beside her father.

'I am so sorry, my dear,' said Leonard, eerily calm. 'I honestly never intended for anyone else to get hurt. But, I simply cannot allow Tom to survive.'

'He can't be killed, you know,' hissed Zoe. 'So this was all a waste of time.'

'I know about Tom's ability.' Leonard sighed. 'Takes one to know one, as the saying goes.' Looking over to Ed, Leonard barked, 'Come now, don't be silly. Bring me the book, or you know what the repercussions will be.'

'Give him what he wants,' croaked Tom. 'Just save Zoe.'

Ed removed something metallic from the front pocket of his hooded top. 'I'll give him what he wants, all right,' he spat. Thrusting his hand forward, Ed was holding the wand that Leonard had dropped earlier. 'Missing something, Prof?' he shouted.

Ed's magical prowess lacked the ferocity of his master's. Instead of a blast, the wand merely fired a succession of small pink bolts that splatted against the workshop wall like paint-balls.

Ed's arm lowered. 'Bugger.'

Leonard stood, unperturbed by this feeble assault. 'I expected better, lad. Even from a level one like yo—' Leonard's jaw was forced shut. He gurgled as blood filled his throat.

Twisting one of her father's throwing knives deeper into Leonard's chin, Zoe's eyes burned with pure vengeance. Letting go of the knife, she took the pistol from Leonard's hand as he fell to the floor. Only then did she realise what she'd done. Disgusted with herself, she burst into tears and collapsed to hug her father.

'We have to go,' said Ed, rushing to her. 'Leonard will begin to heal any second.'

'No, I can't leave Dad.'

'There's no time.' Ed pulled Zoe off Ali's motionless body. 'We must get Tom and the book away.'

Zoe, giving her father a final look, dragged herself away and over to Tom. Together, she and Ed helped him around the side of the cottage.

'Wait here,' said Zoe, once they reached the driveway. Adrenaline coursed within her, as she wiped the tears from her eyes. 'I'll go get my car.'

In less than a minute, the Mini's headlights illuminated Ed – who was acting as a crutch for Tom.

'Come on,' Zoe called out, beeping the horn. 'Let's go.'

Ed helped Tom onto the backseat, before getting into the passenger side.

Torn apart by the guilt of leaving her father behind, Zoe slammed her foot down hard on the accelerator pedal. As the car skidded across the driveway, the tyres fired chippings into the front wall of the cottage, smashing the bulb in the porch way.

Journal of a Sorcerer
I I

'Although being from the same bloodline, I am not immune from the king's dominance, nor his disregard for life. This I discovered, so callously, today as I sat with my dear brother and handed him the Eternus book.

'He wanted proof of its accursed power. As the tip of a blade pressed against my spine, I hastily signed the page. No sooner had I placed the quill down onto the table, Harold's sword plunged through my torso.

'I believe it was my fate to experience death. The seething pain throughout my body, the terror of my last breath ebbing away. Surely, God's punishment for sacrificing that innocent girl's life?

'As the Eternus resurrected my body, I awoke to the sickening laughter of my brother. In his hands, he held the book, and thus, the power to raise an army of immortal men.

'My payment for giving him such a gift is that I am the first. I am forever.'

Chapter 19
The Magician's Assistant

'A rabbit. A sodding white rabbit,' Zoe said, fuming, as she navigated the winding road. '*You* can change into a rabbit? How the bloody hell can you do that?'

'Yeeeah, so... I can shape-shift.'

'What?' yelled Zoe. 'So was that you in our house earlier?'

'Um... yeah.'

Flinging her arm over, she slapped the side of his head with her palm.

'Ow. Bloody hell.' Ed winced. 'I was trying to save Tom.'

Slapping him again, Zoe cursed. 'How is stealing that book for that psycho professor saving Tom?'

'Okay, okay.' Ed shook a finger at the road ahead. 'Please don't do that while you're driving. We're not out of danger yet. Leonard will be right behind us.'

Tightening her grip on the steering wheel, Zoe looked away from him in disgust.

'Look,' Ed started to explain. 'I've been secretly helping Tom out from the start. For example, Leonard ordered me to tie Tom up, so I chose rope I knew I could easily chew through in rabbit form. I couldn't risk Leonard finding out what I was up to, of course, so I had to make it look like I was going along with his plan.

'It was me that woke Tom up after his fall in Penmoor. I wanted him to get away before Leonard found him. How was I supposed to know he would drive into Penworthy, bump into Leonard in the Copper Kettle, then end up bloody staying with us?

'When Tom saw the letters appear in the book, I tried to convince him he was imagining it, so he wouldn't do something stupid, like actually go and *steal* the bloody thing. That was my plan. I wanted to hide the book from Leonard and stop him from ever finding it again.'

Tom leant forward from the back of the Mini. 'Everything,' he groaned, the wound to his chest practically healed. 'I want to know everything.'

'Sorry, mate, I thought you were asleep back there.'

Tom repeated his demand. 'Tell me, now.'

Ed turned to him. 'Okay. That book, it belongs to Leonard, he created it. He was the first person to ever sign it, *The Prime Eternee*, he used to call himself. But it's a privilege that came with conditions.' Ed checked in the side mirror of the Mini for any sign they were being followed.

'So he's King Harold's brother?' Zoe asked.

'Yes. His real name is Leofwine Godwinson. Not only that, but he's probably the most powerful sorcerer… like, ever.'

'So why does he want Tom dead?' demanded Zoe.

'He said something about wanting to be free of the curse?' Tom added.

'When you sign your name in that book,' replied Ed, 'you become bound to it, the ability to heal forever.'

'Yes, I know that now, thanks.' Tom rubbed the skin of his chest through the hole in his shirt.

'After being alive for a thousand years, Leofwine, I mean, Leonard, wants out.'

'Out?' quizzed Zoe.

'To die.'

'But he can't, because of the curse, right?' Tom sat back in his seat. 'He told me the only way to break the curse was to erase the names of all those who signed it after him.'

Ed nodded. 'Yep, which is everyone in the book. Except him, of course.'

'Or he'll just carry on living?' asked Zoe.

'Ageing,' corrected Ed. 'But as he's the first, who knows how many more years he has left. A hundred? Another thousand possibly?'

'Is this what I've got to look forward to then?' Tom could

feel the blood drain from his face. 'Living for an eternity until I go insane?'

'Pretty much, mate, sorry. But hey, at least you have one thing going for you that he doesn't.'

'Yeah? What's that?'

'You're not an arsehole.'

Tom looked out through the side window and half smiled. 'Thanks.'

'I can't believe it's the book that gave you that power, Tom,' said Zoe, shaking her head. 'And, all this time we thought it was some sort of secret society list.'

'Really?' Ed laughed. 'What, like masonic immortals?' He spotted the glare Zoe cast his way, and shut up.

'So what do we do right now?' Zoe asked, slowing the Mini down as she approached a junction.

'You have to get that book as far away from Leonard as possible.'

'What? That's ridiculous,' said Zoe. 'Surely Leonard has to be stopped.'

'That's just it, though, he can't be.'

As the Mini idled at the junction, allowing a lorry to pass by, Zoe looked in the rear-view mirror. 'You okay, Tom?'

Tom was staring through the glass; the view outside was beginning to sway. He could feel his nostrils tingling. Rubbing his nose with a thumb and forefinger, he felt something warm and wet. 'Shi-it,' he stuttered.

'Tom?' Zoe turned to look at him. 'Your nose is bleeding.'

'It's vortex-lag,' said Ed.

'What's vortex-lag?' asked Zoe, unclipping her seatbelt and reaching over to steady Tom's now jerking legs.

'Like jet-lag,' explained Ed, 'only for time travellers.'

Tom stared at Ed. 'Ti-ti-time travel?' His head loped to one side and hit the glass of the window with a thud.

Zoe shook Tom's knee 'Wake up.'

'His memory is realigning.' Ed reached into his pocket and took out his mobile phone. He set the stopwatch function to start, then looking at Zoe, said, 'He should be okay within ten minutes, hopefully.'

Zoe looked at Ed in utter bewilderment. 'You said "time travel". You *are* joking, right?'

'Tom fell through time,' said Ed, 'from ten years ago. It was how he originally escaped Leonard.'

'Okay. So, magic is real. Shape-shifting people are real, and now so is time travel. What next, aliens?'

Ed checked the mirrors again. 'I'll explain more later. Right now, we have to keep going.'

The sound of a Harley-Davidson motorbike thundered past them. The bike's rear tyre squealed as it skidded round on the road to face them.

'Oh, joy. Here we go.' Zoe gripped one hand on the handbrake, her other on the steering wheel, readying herself for a fast getaway. 'Can Leonard ride a motorbike?'

'Not as far as I'm aware,' replied Ed, feeling the adrenaline pumping through his chest as he spotted something attached to the front forks of the bike. 'Zoe, please tell me that isn't what I think it is? Look.'

Zoe watched the biker, dressed in blue leathers, dismount, the stranger's face hidden by the helmet's black visor. Unclipping a long-barrelled gun from a holster on the bike's forks, the person stood facing towards the car.

'Okay, get ready,' ordered Zoe, revving the engine. 'I'm going to force him out of the way.'

The biker swung the shotgun up, pumped it, then opened fire at them.

'Go!' screamed Ed.

'He missed,' answered Zoe. Dropping the handbrake lever, she slammed the gearstick into drive. A loud thud came from the Mini's roof. Something huge, dark and feathery bounced onto the bonnet then tumbled onto the road.

'Why are we still here, Zoe?' cried Ed. 'Drive.'

'I think that biker just shot a bird out of the air?'

'Bollocks, this is bad,' Ed said, panicking as he looked at the black-and-white Andean condor lying motionless on the road. 'That bird, it's Leonard.'

'What?'

'Yep, he's a shape-shifter too.'

Another shot rang out as the biker fired the gun into the bird.

Zoe, transfixed at the event happening ahead, stared open-mouthed. 'Whoever that is,' she whispered, 'they really have it in for Leonard.'

'Either that,' stammered Ed, 'or they enjoy making road-kill.'

Zoe glanced back at Tom. 'He's still out for the count back there.'

'Oh, come on.' Ed gulped. 'The guy's got a machete now.'

Zoe looked at the biker, who'd placed the shotgun down and had now produced a large knife. 'I've had enough guns and knives for one day.' She watched as the biker knelt with one boot on the bird's body and began hacking through the white-collared neck.

'I think I'm going to vom,' said Ed, clutching a hand over his mouth.

The biker threw the bird's head against the side of the road, turned to the Mini, then made a peace sign with one hand before picking the shotgun back up off the road.

Confused by this strange act of friendship, Ed looked at Zoe. 'What do we do now?'

'Just try to stay calm,' Zoe insisted, taking a long deep breath. 'I don't think he's going to harm us.'

The biker walked back to the Harley-Davidson, reloaded the shotgun before dropping it back into the holster, then started unclipping the strap on the helmet.

'I think,' said Zoe, as she watched the long loose curls of blonde hair unravel, 'he, is a she.'

Placing the helmet on the handlebars, the face of a woman in her thirties smiled towards Zoe and Ed. Flicking her hair over her shoulders, she casually marched over to the car.

'I don't believe it,' gasped Ed, recognising the famous face. 'That's Aquaria Redhart.'

'Who the bloody hell is that?' Zoe glared at the woman, who was now nearly at their car.

'She used to be Lance Goldstorm's assistant.'

'Oh, great.' Zoe sighed. 'That's all we need.'

Chapter 20
Blundering Blunderbuss

Zoe lowered her side window. Forming an opinion based on Aquaria's pouting red smile and flawless fake-tanned skin, she greeted the woman with simple, 'Hi.'

Aquaria looked back to the feathery mess on the road, then to Zoe and Ed. 'You guys okay? What about the young man in the back?' In her Texan accent, and how she was leaning on the car, she could almost have been a highway patrol officer.

'We're great, thanks,' spluttered Ed, seemingly star-struck. 'And you?'

'Nice shooting,' said Zoe, saving Ed further embarrassment. 'Suppose being American, you're used to gunning down wildlife, right?'

'Let's get back to your magic store.' Aquaria pointed to the headless remains of the condor, 'I take it you know who that bird really is?'

Both Zoe and Ed nodded.

'Cool. I'll have more time to explain once we get back, okay?'

'We were already heading back there, actually.' Zoe felt Ed nudge her, but continued, 'Who said you were invited?'

'Your mother. She's waiting for you.' Aquaria smiled, straightening herself. 'I told her I'd get you back safely. Where's Alister?'

Zoe's knuckles whitened, squeezing the steering wheel hard. 'Don't call him that, he hated being called that.'

'Sure.'

'He's dead.' Zoe forced back her tears. 'That bastard lying in the road shot him.'

Aquaria took a second to process this. 'Your father was a good man. I know he and Lance didn't see eye to eye, but I always tried to stay out of their rivalry.' For a moment the stoic American seemed genuinely shaken by the news, but switched back to a more authoritative tone. 'We should be getting on. Time's ticking and there's a lot to prepare.'

Zoe buckled up her seatbelt. 'Prepare? For what?'

Aquaria gave Zoe a sweet wink. 'We're going to stop Leonard and save the lives of everyone in his book.'

'Right,' muttered Zoe. 'Of course we are.'

Aquaria started to head back to her bike.

'Shouldn't we do something about what's left of Leonard there?' Zoe cried out. 'Like bury the body or something?'

Aquaria stopped. Without turning round, she answered loudly, 'Wouldn't stop him. Don't want to right now either.' She continued to walk. 'Like I said,' she called out, 'we gotta get back and prepare.' With that, she went back to her bike and mounted it.

'Why are you being so rude to her?' said Ed. 'She just saved us from Leonard.'

'Sure, because in the form of a bird, he would've done what exactly?'

'Well, he managed to knock Tom's car off the road.'

'Hmm...' conceded Zoe. 'I just don't trust her, that's all.'

Zoe steered the Mini out of the junction and drove on. Aquaria tailed closely behind.

***

'I wonder why my parents never mentioned her to me?' said Zoe.

Ed could see she was still in shock over her father's death. He did his best to divert the conversation away from mentioning Ali, which was proving difficult.

He heard a groan from the back seat. 'I think Tom's coming round.'

'From his... what was it again?' asked Zoe.

'Time-lag,' replied Ed, after checking the stopwatch on his phone.

'You're serious, aren't you?'

Ed nodded.

'Okay.' Zoe heaved a sigh. 'Go on. Don't miss anything out.'

'Ten years ago,' Ed began, 'Tom activated a vortex-gun. It opens tunnels through time. Leonard and I invented it. Only, we hadn't properly tested it out, y'know, fixed any bugs. Somehow, Tom fell through a time vortex trying to escape Leonard.'

'So, Tom and Leonard already knew each other? Why doesn't he now?'

'We aren't exactly sure,' said Ed, rubbing his temple. 'We think his memory loss is due to the vortex not being stable when he passed through it. As I'm sure you can imagine, there's a whole bunch of calculations to be made when messing around with time travel. We hadn't ironed everything out, including time-lag.'

'Right.' Zoe nodded, trying to keep up. 'So what you're saying is his memory got left behind?'

'Well, yeah,' said Ed, surprised at her understanding. 'That's pretty much what we figured. So, basically, Tom got spewed out the other end into the present day. We knew which day he'd appear, from the readings on the time-gun. By the way, I dubbed it the Chronos Blunderbuss. Cool, huh?'

Zoe humoured him with a smile. 'How did you know *where* to find him though?'

'Easy. The entrance and exit of every vortex is always at the same location. So—'

'If you enter in Penmoor, you exit in Penmoor,' interjected Zoe.

'Er... right again. Give or take a metre or two.'

Tom stirred. 'The difference between standing on top of a cliff,' he said, sitting up, 'and falling down one, yeah?' His body shivered.

'Thank God you're okay.' Zoe smiled, relieved to see him looking back at her in the rear-view mirror.

'What Ed's telling you,' Tom stuttered, 'is the truth.'

'You heard us?' said Zoe.

'Yep. And, I think some more of my memory's back.' He looked behind, out of the rear window at the headlight of the motorbike. 'What's that moron's problem? Any closer they'll be sat on the back seat.'

'That, is our new ally.' Ed grinned. 'You'll never guess who it is.'

Tom, feeling like he'd slept through an entire party, just shrugged.

'While you were napping,' Ed explained, 'we had a run in with Leonard.'

'He's a shape-shifter like Ed,' interrupted Zoe.

'Yes, thank you, Zoe.' Ed continued, 'He was in his favourite form, an Andean condor.'

Tom shrugged again. 'A what?'

'A big bloody bird,' said Zoe.

'Yes, thanks.' Ed shook his head. 'Anyway, as I was saying, before he had chance to attack, that biker showed up. Turned out it was Aquaria Redhart.'

'Who?'

'She used to be Lance Goldstorm's assistant, Tom,' Ed replied. 'She totally kicked Leonard's feathery arse, a few minutes back.'

'Just not permanently, though.' Zoe slowed the car and took a right turn. 'So, long story short, she knows about the book, how Leonard can shape-shift and seems to know how to stop him.'

Tom considered all this. 'And, you're cool with this, Zoe? Given how much your dad disliked Lance.'

'I'll give her a chance.' She glanced at Ed. 'After all, she did just save us from Leonard.'

'And what about you, Ed?' said Tom, leaning forward. 'I take it, you're on our side now, right?'

'Yes.' Ed looked away. 'I'm doing the best I can. It's not been easy, though.'

'Listen, I'm not judging you.' Tom placed a hand on his shoulder. 'I'm guessing Leonard's got some sort of hold on you. I mean, you're not exactly the evil sidekick type?'

Ed shut his eyes in silence.

'Back at the workshop, Leonard said there'd be repercussions for you.' Zoe gave Ed a brief look. 'What exactly did he mean by that?'

'I used to stay at my nan's bungalow in Penworthy during the summer holidays, when I was a kid,' Ed began. 'My parents would tell me how it was important to get the country air inside my lungs. In truth, they both worked for huge corporations in London and had little time to look after a stroppy kid who loved taking gadgets apart.

'Nan was good friends with Leonard. They got on well. After she passed away, my parents thought it would be good for me to continue coming here every summer, so they asked Leonard if I could stay with him. I was twelve at that time. Honestly, I think he liked having me around. Like I was the grandson he never had, I guess.

'Being something of a smart-arsed kid though, I soon discovered his workshop. Leonard decided to let me help him out with his inventions, as long as I kept it a secret. I agreed. This went on for a couple of years, and then…' Ed's voice cracked. He cleared his throat.

'Take your time, Ed,' said Zoe. She glanced at him, then back at the road. 'It's all right.'

'He told me he'd figured out how to move between periods in history, actual time travel. Of course, I didn't believe him at first, but then he showed me the equations, the schematics. It was absolute genius. A particle accelerator that was portable yet powerful enough to smash atoms together at an insane velocity.' He took a deep breath. 'Basically, a sort of mini-cannon that blasts holes in time.'

'The Chronos Blunderbuss,' said Zoe.

Ed smiled at her for using the name.

'So how does it work?' asked Tom. 'Because all I can remember, so far, is firing the thing off in Penmoor. I swiped it out of Leonard's Land Rover thinking it was a weapon.'

'Why did you go there in the first place?' asked Zoe.

'From what I can recall,' said Tom, scratching his head, 'I'd gone up there to bury the book. But, shortly afterwards Leonard found me. It's still a bit blurry.'

Ed looked at Tom. 'And that's when you fell through the vortex, right?'

'Yeah, I don't remember too much after that.'

'Hang on.' Zoe looked at Tom in the rear-view mirror. 'So, that explains why you look so young, how you look the same age now as you did in that newspaper article?'

'Yes,' replied Tom. 'But, having this power to heal helps too, I guess. Right, Ed?'

'Indeed.' Ed saw the expression on Zoe's face. 'I know, it's a lot to take in. Sorry.'

'Just tell us as much as you know, Ed,' said Zoe, 'before we get back to my place. 'Time travel, you were saying…'

'Right. Think of time as a groove on a record,' enthused Ed, 'but where the centre is the start, and it plays outwards in an infinite spiral.'

'Okay,' replied Tom.

'If you draw a straight line from the centre, crossing over the grooves, you can skip back and forth across time.'

'Like lifting up the needle and moving it to another part of the song?' suggested Zoe.

'Yes, that's it. Except the Chronos Blunderbuss rips a hole through the grooves, for the needle to pass through.'

'So where's the Chronos…' Tom frowned, 'thingy now?'

'Blunderbuss. Leonard retrieved it, ten years ago, when you, y'know,' Ed's hand mimicked Tom diving, 'took a header into the vortex.'

'Did you manage to test it again?' Zoe asked. 'I mean, could we not put it to use now?'

'There's the problem,' replied Ed. 'So that Leonard couldn't use it again, I had to make him think it was busted. It's been sat on the workbench in his workshop for the past few years. Every now and then a couple of components,' he made speech mark gestures with his fingers, 'would *accidentally* get damaged.'

'And if we could keep Leonard away long enough for you to fix it?' asked Zoe.

Ed gave a cautious grin. 'I could get it working in a couple of hours.'

'What?' Zoe slowed the car. The sound of Aquaria's Harley-Davidson roared up close behind them. 'Then shouldn't we go back to the cottage and get it up and running?' she said, excitedly. 'We can go back in time and put an end to this.'

'Hold on, it's not that simple,' said Ed. 'Remember, Leonard's a bloody powerful sorcerer. He has been for centuries. We shouldn't rush into anything that would get us killed.'

'So, how *can* we stop him?' asked Tom.

Ed looked back, out of the rear window of the car, at Aquaria. 'I say we wait and see what trick the magician's assistant has up her sleeve first. Then decide what to do.'

Chapter 21
The First Encounter

'Carry on, Ed.'

Zoe saw the familiar road sign for Penworthy up ahead. Along the journey, the topic had returned to the hold Leonard had over Ed.

'One night, I could hear Leonard cursing loudly outside my bedroom window. He was stood out in the courtyard, pacing around angrily. He clapped his hands together, there was a flash, and suddenly he was an owl. *Obviously*, it scared the shit out of me. I grabbed my things and tried to make a run for it. But, with no idea where I was going, I soon got lost on the moors. That was when I saw the same owl fly down at me. Another flash, and there he was.'

'So what did you do?' asked Tom.

'What do you think? I froze. Leonard was furious with me. I'd discovered his secret. He told me he was a sorcerer, and that if I told anyone about what I'd seen, he would fly straight to London and kill my parents.'

'God, that's awful,' said Zoe. 'So what happened when it was time for you to go back home? Did you keep quiet?'

'Of course,' replied Ed. 'However, something weird had happened to my parents. My dad had become really aggressive towards my mum. He would hit her. It was like he was a different man. Mum, normally a strong confident woman, became withdrawn. Then one day Dad went too far, began beating the crap out of her. I tried to stop him, but he threw me down the stairs. I managed to get out of the house and told one of the neighbours. In short, Dad got sent to prison for serious assault, and his career was ruined. Mum, she had a complete breakdown, ended up in care. As for me, guess where I got sent?'

'Back with Leonard?' said Tom.

'Yup. He even came to London to collect me. So anyway, he got me working on the Chronos Blunderbuss. And, to show his gratitude, he taught me how to shape-shift. His threats to kill my dad had ceased, since the guy was now in prison. But the prof wasn't so generous towards my mum, should I not do what he asked.'

'He made you his servant,' said Zoe. 'What a bastard.'

'And then,' sighed Ed, 'that's where you come into the story, Tom.'

Tom looked at him, remorse in his eyes.

'It was on the morning that we were going to field test the blunderbuss. We had it all loaded up in his Land Rover.' Ed shuffled on his seat. 'Leonard was sat having breakfast, when he picked up his morning newspaper. Suddenly he leapt up and began ranting about someone being the sole survivor of a plane crash. What happened to your family had made the front page. Obviously, Leonard had his suspicions that you'd signed that book, or at least knew of its whereabouts, so off he went. He was gone for days. I contemplated doing a runner, but all I could think about was Mum's safety, so I stuck around.

'Eventually, he returned. He was absolutely livid, ranting about how you'd stolen *his* book, used the Chronos Blunderbuss, and in doing so had busted the time matrix decoders which had taken us years to perfect. All he knew of your whereabouts was your location and when you'd return in the future.'

Tom felt the half-reloaded memory sting his brain. 'It was him that came knocking on my door at uni. I remember now.'

'This is heavy,' said Zoe. By now, they'd reached Penworthy. 'Let's just hope Aquaria really can stop him.'

'If not,' said Ed, tears welling up, 'it won't just be our lives in danger, but also my mum's.'

'It won't come to that, Ed.' Zoe placed a reassuring hand on his knee. 'Let's stay positive and work together.'

As the Mini pulled into the car park behind Zoe's shop, she tried to convince herself there was hope.

Chapter 22
Therianthropy

Zoe parked the Mini round the back of Cassam's Magic Emporium and switched off the engine. The roar of the Harley-Davidson could be heard reverberating around the private car park as Aquaria parked beside a white Ford Transit van. Dismounting the bike, she removed her helmet and placed it on the handlebars. She unstrapped the shotgun, then rushed over to the Mini.

'C'mon, get inside, quickly,' she announced, as the others got out of the car. Checking up at the clear starry sky, she scanned around. 'It'll be getting light in an hour or so. We've a lot to do before then. Leonard could be here any minute.'

'You okay there, kid?' asked Aquaria, looking at Tom.

'I guess,' he replied, massaging his forehead. 'Just an overload of memories forcing themselves back into my mind.'

'Sure. I understand y'all must be shattered, but try to stay focused.' Aquaria walked off, disinterested in anything else Tom had to say.

'Charming,' tutted Zoe, walking up to Tom. 'Let's just do as she says, for now.'

'I don't know about you two,' said Ed, gawping at Aquaria, 'but I'm going to stick close to her. She's got a gun, and guts to match.' He hurried across the tarmac to join her by the rear of the shop.

'Okay then,' said Aquaria as they all stood outside the kitchen door. The rear of the old building was silent, except for the sound of a clattering extractor fan that had been crudely mortared into the three-hundred-year-old brick wall, between the door and window. 'You should know, shortly after you and Ali left, I turned up here. I explained to your mom about Leonard and the book. Naturally, she was worried for you both.'

'Okay?' said Zoe, shivering as she wrapped her arms into

her hooded top.

'I'm sorry I wasn't quick enough to stop Leonard from killing Ali.'

Zoe, taken aback by Aquaria's bluntness, just nodded and stepped past her. She unlocked the door and entered the dark kitchen.

No sooner had the fluorescent tube light blinked on than Gail came running down the stairs. Having changed from her nightwear into a cream cashmere sweater and tight pink leggings, the softness of her sweater provided extra comfort to Zoe as they embraced.

'Zoe, my angel,' she said, ecstatic to see she was safe. 'Thank God you're all right.'

'Mum,' said Zoe, clinging to Gail.

The others entered, their eyes adjusting to the brightly lit room. Ed scanned the kitchen, the yellow doors of the cupboards conjuring images of his nan's house; a welcome distraction from his anxiousness.

'Please,' said Gail, releasing herself from her daughter. 'Everyone help yourselves to tea, coffee, whatever you want.'

Gail turned to Zoe again. 'I've been so worried. Aquaria thinks Professor Goodwin stole that book belonging to Tom. She told me he's some sort of powerful sorcerer, or something. I can't get my head around it; he's always been so polite. Your dad won't be happy, I imagine he gave him a piece of his mind, right?' She snorted a tearful laugh, then wiped her nose with her hand. 'Where is your father, anyway?'

Zoe burst into tears.

Standing in the middle of the chequered tiled floor, like the last remaining pieces on a chessboard, Aquaria hinted for Tom and Ed to give the Cassams some time alone.

'I'll stay with you,' said Tom, placing his hand on Zoe's back.

Zoe sniffed and took a couple of short breaths. 'It's fine,' she replied, struggling to speak. 'Go upstairs.'

Without question, Tom obliged. 'If you need us, just say.'

Walking past Zoe, Ed calmly said, 'He died a hero. You should be proud of him.'

Aquaria pushed him towards the stairs. 'Dude!'

'Oh, er, right,' blathered Ed. 'Sorry.'

As they ascended the stairs, they heard Gail cry out, 'Why are you saying this? It's not true.' She let out a howl. 'No, not my Ali.'

No one spoke as Aquaria, Tom and Ed entered the living room. Downstairs, they could hear Zoe trying to recount the events that led to her father dying.

'Look,' said Aquaria after a few minutes. 'As awful as this is, we must carry on getting ready.'

'Firstly, Aquaria,' said Tom, as he sat down on the sofa, 'I think you need to explain your involvement with Leonard.'

Aquaria nodded, then replied, 'Sure, I'll brief you.' She checked the time on her watch. 'He used to be my lecturer when I was at university, over here. One day, I discovered that he could change into bird form. Instead of being angry, the professor chose to mentor me in the art of therianthropy, and how to perform it.'

'Sounds familiar,' snorted Ed, picking up a white porcelain hare from off the sideboard and frowning at it.

'Sorry,' interrupted Tom. 'Theri-what?'

'She means shape-shifting,' added Ed.

'Correct.' Aquaria paced the middle of the room. 'I hear you're something of an earth elemental, right, Ed?'

'Indeed I am,' he answered. 'Passed level one with flying colours. I'm guessing from your name you chose water?'

'Level seven,' Aquaria responded, giving him a wink.

'Oh.' Ed sighed. He stepped across the room and casually selected a book from a shelf. 'I guess you've been practising the art a lot longer than me.'

'But hey,' said Aquaria, 'level one's pretty good, darling. A rabbit has its uses.'

'Damned right it does.' Ed straightened his back. 'I'd like to see a fish break into a shop.'

Tom, interrupting their little game of 'who's better', asked, 'I don't understand. What do you both mean by level one and level seven?'

Aquaria smiled. 'All therianthropists transform into creatures based around one chosen element – that's just how the magic works. Shifting can become muddled, so to speak, if you attempt creatures from different elements; you could become a bird with scales, or a cat with gills, for example. But, you can learn to change into a variety of creatures based within the same element. The more creatures, the—'

'Higher the level?' said Tom.

'Correct.' Aquaria placed a hand on her chest. 'For me, I can change into seven water creatures.' She pointed to Ed. 'For Bugs here, it's one earth creature.'

'All right, love,' snorted Ed, slamming the book back onto the shelf. 'I'll have you know a rabbit's a complex animal to perfect for level one earth.' He turned to Tom. 'It's all the fur, you see, difficult to concentrate on.' Looking back at Aquaria, a hint of indignation in his stare, he asked, 'What was your level one, a goldfish?'

'Octopus.'

'Ah,' said Ed, deflated. 'Bloody marvellous.'

'Thank you,' said Aquaria, giving him a smug grin.

'So how does it work?' asked Tom, 'I mean, a rabbit is smaller than you, Ed. Leonard can change into a bird? How does...' he mimicked scrunching up something with his hands, 'everything fit in?'

'Did you never hear,' said Aquaria, 'how the entire human race can be compressed into the volume of a sugar cube?'

'Really?' Tom doubted that was true. 'How is that even possible?'

Aquaria moved over to the window. She pulled back a white chenille curtain and checked outside for any sign of Leonard. 'Look,' she said, turning her attention back to Tom. 'In short, there's a whole lot of nothing inside us. If you squeeze out the space, then you can easily become smaller. And, with a little magic,' she held up her hands showing Tom two identical rings, one on each of her middle fingers, 'you can manipulate and control the structure of atoms.'

Tom looked at Ed's hands, realising the same two rings were on his fingers also.

'They were created by Leonard,' said Aquaria. 'There's only, like, twenty pairs of these rings in the whole world. The metal is supposed to have been forged from a mystical sword, apparently.'

'Pretty awesome, huh?' Ed chipped in.

'But where do your clothes...' began Tom. 'Actually, don't answer that.'

Aquaria and Ed, with pursed lips, stared at each.

Tom pointed to Aquaria. 'So, you're a water therianthingy,' and then to Ed, 'and you're an earth one.'

'Yes,' they both replied.

'Leonard's what, air, I take it?'

'Uh-huh,' said Ed.

Tom remembered there were meant to be four elements. 'So, what creatures are fire, then?'

'Fire element therianthropists don't exist,' said Aquaria, 'end of story.'

'I know what you're thinking, Tom,' said Ed, joining him on the sofa. 'But dragons are just the stuff of fairy tales.'

'Of course.' Tom blushed at his own naivety. 'Although, I suppose people would say the same thing about sorcerers.'

'Well, that's true,' agreed Aquaria. 'Seriously though, a dragon is a cross-element creature anyway. Fire and air. It's way too difficult to attempt.'

'A fire-breathing bird with scales,' said Tom.

'Exactly.'

'Do you really think you can stop Leonard?' Zoe entered the living room, her cheeks red, sore from tears.

Tom rushed straight to her.

'How's Gail doing?' asked Aquaria.

'We'll survive, thanks.' Zoe straightened her back. 'Let's

just finish this.'

'Good,' said Aquaria.

Zoe looked at Ed. 'You're right. My dad was a hero.'

Aquaria went over to her. 'Leonard can be stopped. You have my word.' Taking hold of Zoe's hand, she added, 'I just need you and Gail to be strong for a while. Can you do that?'

'Whatever it takes.' Zoe squeezed Aquaria's hand. 'I'm not letting Dad's death be for nothing.'

Aquaria gave her a reassuring smile. 'That's what I want to hear.' She addressed them all. 'Okay, I'll need a tool kit.'

'What's the plan?' enquired Tom, standing ready.

'I'm gonna need a few minutes with the guillotine in the shop downstairs. You have the book on you, Tom?'

'Yes,' he replied, removing it from his jacket.

Aquaria rubbed her hands together. 'Then, let's get to work.' With that, she waved Tom and Zoe through the door, then followed them.

Ed stood in the empty living room. 'Don't let me stop you,' he called, feeling excluded. 'Was only me looking out for Tom in the first place.'

'Quit whingeing, Bugs,' yelled Aquaria, from the bottom of the stairs.

'What*ever*, fishy... gill... woman,' he called back. Reluctantly heading off to join them, he mumbled to himself, 'Great comeback, Ed.'

Journal of a Sorcerer
III

'Knights of the Eternal Order, my brother named them. I looked upon the banquet hall at those men sat before me. They groped and pawed the serving women, beating the manservants for amusement. Greedily, they tore at the food to fill their bloated bellies with meat and mead. A more fitting name for these soldiers would be savages.

'Nonetheless, the king's speech successfully seduced every single one of them and I was soon witness to their allegiance. This, of course, came by way of a humble signature in the Eternus.

'After the banquet I questioned the king on the evening's deceit. Why gift the power of immortality to such animals? His reply was twofold. Firstly, seeing them as nothing more than dogs of war, he told me they were to be sent into battle first, as a means of levelling the field. And lastly, for daring to question him, I was imprisoned.

'Torture, such a simple word, does nothing to describe the evil I suffered. During those weeks within the dungeon, I truly understood the curse of the Eternus. Men who begged for death had their prayers answered. I shall never know such peaceful release.'

Chapter 23
The Guillotine

After removing two rubber flaps – disguised as part of the wooden base – from under the head-hole on the guillotine, Aquaria unscrewed a hidden panel from above. Next, she lifted out the fake plastic blade stowed inside. 'Zoe, if you could hand me that ratchet set?'

Tom and Ed leant against the shop counter, watching with intrigue to see the prop's illusion being dispelled, as it was dismantled. Taking the ratchet, Aquaria began unbolting one of two hidden steel blocks either side of the hole.

'Do you want me to work on the other one?' Zoe offered, holding a spanner ready.

Dropping a bolt to the wooden floor, Aquaria nodded.

'So, that's how it's done.' Ed smiled, the trick now exposed. 'The blade is stopped by the blocks and the magician can safely slide his head down between those flaps. The fake blade drops down, covering the hole and creating the illusion of the real blade landing. It's so simple.'

'You'd be surprised how many magic tricks are,' said Zoe, removing the steel block from her side. Looking up, she gestured towards the array of products on sale within the shop.

After clearing the spare parts off the floor, Aquaria climbed up to reach the top of the guillotine's frame. She began adjusting the rope to allow the real blade to fully drop down.

Ed stared at Aquaria. It was a look of being star-struck, tinged with confusion. 'Dude,' he whispered to Tom, 'can I have a private word?'

'Sure, mate.' They excused themselves, then went into the kitchen.

'Listen,' said Ed, perching his bottom on the kitchen table. 'There's something not right about Aquaria.'

'Okay.' Tom raised an eyebrow, then quietly pushed the shop door to. 'Go on?'

'So, as you know, I used to love watching the Lance Gold-storm shows, when I was a kid.'

'Yeah?'

'I'm twenty-six now, and those shows I saw back then were repeats.'

Tom moved in closer. 'Your point is?'

'Think about it, Tom. How old does she look to you?'

Tom gave a quick look to the door, then back. 'You think she's like me?' he answered, in a low voice. 'She has the same power, I mean?'

'Well, duh. I mean, she can't look much older than thirty.'

'Wait here.' Tom slipped back into the shop, and back to the counter. Grabbing the book from where he'd left it, he returned to the kitchen.

'Do you think Aquaria's her real name?' asked Ed, watching Tom flick through the pages.

'Doubt it.' Finding Lance's name in the book, Tom scanned the other names on the page. 'I can't see a woman's name on here, or any kind of signature that might match.'

'Check the previous page,' said Ed, in hushed tones.

Tom ran his finger down the page. 'Nothing, from what I can see?'

Shaking his head, Ed insisted he checked again.

'Look, I'm telling you there's nothing there.'

'But she's got to be around the same age as Gail, right? In her early fifties?'

Tom placed the book down on the table. 'From what you and Zoe have said, she was a big celebrity at the time. Maybe she's just had surgery done?' he suggested.

Ed stood and peeked through the gap in the door. In the shop, Aquaria was testing out the guillotine; the blade dropped straight through the head-hole, clunking hard into the wooden trough below.

'Listen,' said Tom, waving him away from the door, 'does it

really matter, right now?'

'I guess not,' said Ed, turning his attention to the shotgun on the table. 'All I'm saying is, maybe I was being a little hasty to trust her? I mean, both of us put our trust in Leonard.'

'You're overthinking things.' Tom walked back to the shop door. 'Come on, let's just carry on for now. Okay?'

Ed nodded and followed Tom back through.

'This should work fine,' said Aquaria, patting the frame of the guillotine.

'So you're going to chop his head off, again,' said Ed. 'But, what then?'

Zoe looked at Ed. 'I don't understand. If decapitating him in bird form wouldn't stop him, how will chopping his head off in human form be different?'

'I wasn't trying to stop him back there, just stall him. When he arrives here, which he will, we knock him out and restrain his arms.' Aquaria walked up to the front door of the shop, where Gail was stood. 'Any sign of Leonard or a bird out there?' she asked.

'Nothing,' replied Gail, her eyes fixed to the sky outside. 'I'll keep watching though.'

'Thanks, you're doing great.'

'Sorry,' said Tom, interrupting her. 'Just a quick thought, while we're on the subject. What would happen to me, if someone chopped my head off? Can my body simply pick my head up and pop it back on again?'

'No, you'll be unconscious until someone *else* sticks your head back on, then your healing power will kick in,' replied Aquaria. 'Leonard, however, not only can his mind stay conscious, but he can also still control what his body does.'

'You do know the prof can control other people's minds too?' Ed wiggled his fingers like a bad hypnotist, much to Aquaria's annoyance. 'How are you going to stay one step ahead of him?'

'His psychic abilities don't work on me. Trust me.'

'That's convenient,' said Gail, stepping away from the

door.

'Excuse me?' Aquaria felt all eyes judging her. 'Hey, I'm not the bad guy here. I'm trying to stop Leonard, and help save your asses.'

'Funny how both you and the professor have the same knack for looking younger than your years, though?' Gail stood, arms crossed. 'I know Tom's the same, but he's just the innocent victim in all this.' She looked towards Zoe. 'Right?'

Zoe nodded.

Ed gave Tom a nudge. 'She's got a point, eh?' he whispered.

'I haven't signed the book, if that's what you're suggesting.' Aquaria mirrored Gail's stance, but stretched herself up a little taller. 'If you must know, I've always looked younger than I should. It's part of the reason Lance employed me as his assistant. Some of us just age better than others, honey. That, and the fact I can change into a shark whenever I want to, helped a lot.'

'No way,' gasped Ed, cutting through the tension. 'Lance's water tank trick, when he was bitten in two by a shark?'

'Yep,' acknowledged Aquaria, 'that was me in the tank. And before you say it, Lance really was attacked. But of course, he healed when the curtains dropped.'

'Epic.'

'That's cheating,' tutted Gail. 'Illusions aren't illusions if the magic is real. Where's the skill in that?'

'Okay,' Tom interjected, 'let's keep things friendly. We're all feeling tired and stressed here. Bickering isn't going to help us.'

'Look,' said Aquaria, walking over to the central glass cabinet and inspecting the tat on the hexagonal shelves. 'I haven't been completely honest with you.'

'Go on,' said Gail, 'spill the beans, *honey*.'

'I *can* heal faster than most. I mean, not like you, Tom. But way faster than a normal person should.'

'Oh, come on,' chuckled Ed. 'And you're honestly telling us you've not signed that book?'

'I swear,' said Aquaria, holding up her hands. 'God's honest truth. I've just always been able to. In fact, it wasn't until the final night of our European tour that I knew Lance's healing power was because of that book. He'd never let on as to how he got his ability. It was only when Leonard showed up demanding the book back that I found out the truth.'

'So what did you do?' asked Zoe.

'What *could* I do? Leonard used his psychic ability on Lance. Made him reveal where he kept the book. He manipulated the poor guy into placing his neck into our own guillotine. He forced me to go fetch the book from Lance's Ferrari, but when I got to the parking lot, someone had stolen his car.'

'But Lance would be able to heal from being decapitated though, right?' asked Ed.

'Sadly, he didn't get the chance to.'

'I think she's telling the truth,' said Tom, looking pale. 'I can remember my dad giving me the book when I was a kid. Turns out he was a car thief for some criminal gang.' Tom looked at Aquaria, then to the floor. 'I'm guessing he must've stolen Lance's car, and the book too?'

'What?' Aquaria, rocked by this revelation, scowled at him. 'So it's your dad's fault Leonard took his anger out on my Lance.'

'Sorry,' said Tom.

'Look.' Aquaria calmed herself. 'I don't mean to snap.' She heaved a sigh. 'It's just been really tough, y'know?'

'So, what did Leonard do to Lance?' asked Gail.

'When I returned, empty-handed, Leonard fired his wand at me. I don't know how long I was unconscious for, but when I came round...' she paused, feeling the pain of the memory, 'the blade of the guillotine had dropped. All that remained was Lance's head. His body had been taken.'

The whole room was in shock. Gail broke the silence. 'Ali and I thought you'd both retired.' She looked mortified. 'Gosh, I'm so sorry.'

'Yeah, well,' Aquaria stiffened her back, 'I swore I'd get re-venge on Leonard. This is it. Speaking of which, we should get a move on. Tom, you got the book?'

'It's in the kitchen,' he replied. 'On the table.'

Zoe gave her mother a worried glance. 'You look shattered, Mum.'

'It's all so much to take in, angel.' Trying to stay positive for her daughter, Gail forced a smile. 'I'll be all right.'

'How about I go make you a hot chocolate?' Zoe kissed her mother's cheek, then turned to Tom. 'I'll bring your book in, when I come back.'

'Okay.' Tom smiled. 'Thanks.'

'Not to sound like a bitch,' added Aquaria, 'but please, do hurry.'

***

'By luring Leonard inside,' explained Aquaria to the others in the shop, 'and as I'm immune to Leonard's psychic ability, I'll be the one to restrain him and place him into the guillotine, okay?'

Tom and Ed nodded in agreement. Gail just looked white as a sheet.

Aquaria continued. 'Using your Zig-Zag cabinet, Gail, you can lock his body in there while I get his head as far away from here as possible.'

'Well, that's grim,' said Ed. 'Plausible, but grim.'

'What will you do with his head?' said Gail, wincing at the thought.

'I figured I'd set it in concrete, then dump it in the middle of the Atlantic.'

'Yup,' said Ed, 'equally grim.'

Looking over to the corner of the shop, at the tall garish Zig-Zag cabinet, Tom asked Aquaria, 'And, the body?'

'With the bolts across the cabinet, it'll basically just be like a coffin. If you have no objections to me borrowing that van of yours parked out back, Gail? I'll do the same for the body. Well, bury it somewhere instead.'

'You've really thought this through,' said Gail. 'Done this

sort of thing before, have you?'

'No.' Aquaria avoided eye contact. 'I've had... time to consider what would truly stop him.'

Zoe entered the room, holding a mug of hot chocolate in one hand, the book in the other. 'I can't believe we're actually going through with this? It's barbaric.'

From upstairs, there came the sound of something flapping. Everyone froze. In a matter of seconds, the same sound was in the kitchen.

'Shit,' spat Aquaria, stepping to the centre of the room. 'I thought we'd have more ti—'

A flash of light came from the kitchen door, followed by Leonard. 'You know, if you're going to try to stop me,' he aimed Aquaria's shotgun at Zoe's head, 'don't leave windows open upstairs.' He looked over at Aquaria. 'Hello, Miss Redhart. Thanks for the loan of this gun. Lance doing okay?'

'Leave my daughter out of this,' screamed Gail, stopped from launching at him by Aquaria. 'You bastard!'

'Please,' tutted Leonard, tightening his grip on the shotgun, 'you wouldn't want to lose your daughter, as well as your husband in the same night, now, would you?'

Chapter 24
Encore

'Let her go, Leonard,' pleaded Tom. 'It's the book you want, not her.'

Zoe carefully placed the mug down, then gripped the book in both hands, her eyes looking at everyone for answers.

'Zoe is going to carry the book to her car for me.' Leonard nudged the barrel of the shotgun against her temple. 'Isn't that right, my dear?'

Remaining tight-lipped, Zoe gave her mother a reassuring glance.

'Now everyone, just stay where you are.' Leonard nudged the barrel once more.

The others remained stock-still.

'Tell me what you've done with Lance's body,' growled Aquaria, 'or I swear I will make you suffer.'

Leonard roared with laughter. 'By the time you find me, Aquaria, it will be too late. I'll have wiped all the names from the book, including Goldstorm's, and I'll be free.'

He backed Zoe from the room and through to the kitchen. 'Be a good assistant, my dear, and fetch your car keys.'

Zoe did as he said.

'Try to stop me,' Leonard called out, 'and Zoe dies.'

As soon as they could, the others ran into the kitchen. Unable to do anything to stop him, they watched helpless as Leonard pushed Zoe across the car park towards her Mini.

Gail grabbed Aquaria's arm. 'Please, don't let him kill her.' She watched Leonard shove Zoe to the car.

Aquaria looked defeated, as she turned to Gail. 'I don't know how to. I'm so sorry.'

Arriving at the Mini, Zoe's hand was shaking as she passed the key fob to Leonard. 'You have what you need. Please let me go.'

The old sorcerer's sick smile confirmed his intentions, as he opened the door. 'You're driving. Now, get in.'

From inside the kitchen, Ed slid Leonard's wand from his hoodie. Rolling it in his nervous hands, he glanced over to Gail, on her knees weeping with fear.

Aquaria looked through the window and slammed her fist down on the draining board of the sink. 'Damn you Leonard,' she screamed.

Outside, Leonard turned to face her. His eyes locked onto hers as he made his way round to the passenger side.

Tom stood at the kitchen door, his hands clenched. 'I hope I'm quick enough,' he muttered, rocking from foot to foot. He exhaled, then dashed out onto the car park. Barely halfway across, a shot blew his skull open, spinning him sideways into the tarmac. Leonard reached into his jacket pocket. Taking out a handful of cartridges, he began to reload the gun.

With Tom down, it was up to Ed now. Backing into the shop, his heart thumped inside his chest like a drum roll. Focusing, he remembered the words Aquaria had said to him: *A rabbit has its uses.*

Clapping his hands together, the burst of white light enveloped him. When Gail turned round to look, a familiar creature was on the floor. 'Snowball?'

The white furry hero hotfooted it outside, carrying the metal wand between its teeth. Accelerating, the rabbit didn't stop until it reached where Tom lay healing. It skidded to a halt, taking cover behind Tom's shoulder. *Get ready*, it thought. *Timing. All about timing.*

Leonard gave Aquaria a final glance, unaware of Ed's position.

Go. The rabbit leapt over Tom and rushed towards the car. *Must get inside*, it thought as it hid under the Mini.

Leonard scanned the area. He saw Tom lying on the ground, the others seemingly still in the kitchen. The sound of the shotgun had made a couple of bedroom lights come on in the distance. Opening the passenger door, he aimed the weapon over at Zoe. 'Start the engine, we need to be going. Try anything, I will redecorate the seat covers claret. Got it?'

Zoe nodded.

The rabbit peeped its head out from below the sill of the door. With Leonard's attention on Zoe, maybe this was its chance. It crept out and jumped up.

The butt of the shotgun swung so hard against the side of the rabbit's head it sent the creature hurtling across the car park. The wand clattered under the car.

'You.' Leonard took aim at the rabbit. 'Foolish imbecile. Did you really expect to get the better of *me*?'

Zoe, seizing her chance, flung her door open.

'Stay where you are,' cried Leonard.

On the cold tarmac, the rabbit shook its head in pain.

'After I've erased all the names from the book,' raged Leonard at the rabbit, 'I will kill your mother. You squirming, pathetic, little shit bag.' He fired the shotgun.

The rabbit spun on the spot. A spiral of blood splattered the tarmac, as its left foot exploded. Cries of protest came from the kitchen as Aquaria and Gail looked on in horror.

'I've never been one for killing defenceless animals,' snarled Leonard, taking aim, 'but you are the exception.'

All the rabbit could do was close its little eyes and pray for a miracle.

Leonard eyed the rabbit's head in the gun's sights. 'Goodbye, Master White,' he said, calmly. The shotgun, however, didn't fire. Instead, the only sound to be heard was that of Leonard crying out in agony. The weapon fell to the ground as he grasped at the throwing knife, that had impaled his hand.

Yanking the knife out, he swung around to see the silhouette of a tall man, stood on the fence behind the Mini. 'No,' gasped Leonard, his face dropped as the realisation hit. 'You? But… but it can't be?'

Another knife found its mark, piercing Leonard's throat. Quivering, the stunned sorcerer focused on the blood dripping from his hand, but then something else caught his eye.

Zoe had placed the book down on the passenger seat. Leonard had just seconds to act. He dropped to his knees, leant forward and snatched the book. Tearing it open, he began smearing as many pages with blood as he could.

Realising her error, Zoe swung her leg over the gearstick and kicked out hard at the crazed old man. As he fell backwards onto the ground, the last image he saw before his heart stopped was Ali Cassam standing over him.

'Dad.' Zoe's entire body shook. 'Is it really you? Am I dreaming?' Her chin trembled as she spoke. 'Is this some kind of trick?' She rushed out of the car and straight into his arms.

'Of course it is,' replied Ali. His smile widened like a Cheshire cat.

Where his silver tooth once sat, Zoe now saw a gaping hole. 'Did you...'

Ali placed his hand into his trouser pocket and produced a bullet. 'Best trick I've ever performed.'

The elated reunion was suddenly interrupted by Aquaria screaming out, 'Tom!'

Zoe turned to see the American stood looking in horror at a cloud of ash drifting across the car park, like petals in a gentle breeze. 'Where is he?' shouted Zoe, striding over. 'Where's Tom?'

Aquaria tried pushing Zoe back from the remaining pyre on the ground. 'I'm sorry. There was nothing I could do.'

'What do you mean?' cried Zoe. 'Where's he gone?'

'He jus... just vanished in a plume of ash.' Aquaria fought back the panic in her voice. 'He's dead. Leonard must've erased his signature.'

Collapsing to the ground, Zoe ran her hands over where some of the ash had fallen. 'This isn't right.' She turned to her father. 'This isn't what's supposed to happen.'

Journal of a Sorcerer
I V

'I am to remain at the castle while the king and his armies defend the northern borders from invading Norsemen.

'In the period of my imprisonment, I convinced my brother of my absolute allegiance. So much, that he has declared me steward. His arrogance will betray him, that I am certain.'

*

'Word from the battlefield is that the outnumbered Knights of the Eternal Order have succeeded in slaying their attackers. The people of our land are already calling the king's men Warriors of God. This idolatry must end.

'Tomorrow, I shall make the journey north to the ancient temple, the source of all magic. There, I will beg for the sacred elders to undo the Eternus spell.'

Chapter 25
Footloose

Aquaria stepped away from Leonard, her knuckles reddened and sore from venting her rage. The old man's head slumped forward on the chair he was bound to, his face soaked in blood.

Catching her breath, Aquaria paced the shop floor allowing her temper to cool.

Ali entered. 'Ed's in trouble.' He looked at Leonard's face, and choosing not to say anything, continued, 'He's back in human form, but is losing too much blood.'

'What he did back there took some courage.' Aquaria wiped Leonard's blood off her hands with a nearby cloth. 'I'll come right through.' She checked the ropes around Leonard's hands and feet, then walked over to Ali. 'Did you check if any of your neighbours saw what happened outside?'

'Yes, straight after we dragged Leonard in here,' replied Ali. 'The Tanners, next door, are away on holiday. Everywhere else seems quiet enough.'

'At least that's something. Can't have the cops showing up.' Pointing to the unconscious professor, she ordered, 'Guard him. If he stirs, you know what to do.'

'Sure,' said Ali, cracking his knuckles.

'If you start to feel like your thoughts aren't your own,' warned Aquaria, 'get out of here immediately. Oh, and Ali?'

The Jamaican gave her a stoic look. 'Yes?'

'I'm glad you're okay.'

Entering the kitchen, Aquaria felt as though she'd walked into a hospital operating theatre. The kitchen table, where Ed lay unconscious, was red from blood, the floor beneath also.

Gail was in pieces. A trembling mess, she was covered in Ed's blood. She'd used a tea towel to make a tourniquet around Ed's left shin. However, it wasn't enough to stop the blood dripping out from the splintered mess of bone, sinew and gaping flesh that was once Ed's ankle.

Zoe checked his pulse, her quivering fingers resting on Ed's wrist. 'I… I can barely find a beat,' she stuttered, through tears.

Aquaria reached out a hand to rest it on Zoe's shoulder.

'Get away from me,' snapped Zoe, batting her hand away.

Aquaria obliged.

'It's your fault Tom's dead.' Zoe's eyes, like ice picks, turned on her. 'Why couldn't you do something?'

'Zoe,' cried Gail. 'It was an impossible situation. Aquaria isn't to blame.'

Aquaria's shoulders dropped. 'It's okay, Gail. Zoe's right, I should've done more.' She looked away; the image of Tom's death stabbed at her soul. She'd seen him get up off the tarmac after the healing had finished. He had looked over to Zoe, just as Leonard was attacking the pages of the book. Before he had time to react, it was as if Tom had spun into the ground, before exploding into ash. She shook the thought from her mind, as Ed groaned.

'Oh no,' said Gail, as Ed convulsed in front of her. 'We have to get an ambulance here, now.'

'There's no time,' said Aquaria, as Ed's body went still.

Zoe checked his pulse again, looked towards where the book was sat, then back at Aquaria.

'We'll need a pen,' Aquaria said. 'Quick.'

Zoe rushed over and grabbed what they needed. She turned her attention first to Ed, then back to Aquaria. 'Tom died because of this thing,' she said, thrusting the book and a biro at her. 'Don't let that happen to Ed.'

'He's still breathing,' said Gail, holding an ear to Ed's mouth. 'It's shallow, but still there.'

'Good,' said Aquaria, placing the open book on his chest. She lifted up his hand and wrapped his fingers around the pen. 'God, this better work.'

'Ed?' Zoe tapped his cheek. 'You have to sign Tom's book. Can you hear me?' She stood trembling as no reply came. 'Ed? Please,' she begged, 'you're going to die.'

Aquaria tried. 'Hey, hero,' Still no response.

Gail checked his breath again. 'He's holding on. Keep trying.'

'Hey,' Aquaria shouted. 'Fluffy.'

Zoe saw the pen twitch slightly in his feeble grip. 'I think he heard you. Keep going.'

'Oi, Snowball.'

Ed closed his fingers into a fist.

Aquaria saw his eyelids flickering. 'C'mon, Bugs. Show me what you're made of.'

Gail returned to check his breathing. 'I think he's trying to say something.'

Zoe and Aquaria watched as Ed's lips quivered. 'Well?' they both said in unison.

'It sounds like...' Craning in closer to him, Gail began to relay his faint whisper. 'He says, don't...'

'Yes?' replied Zoe.

'Call...'

'Go on,' Aquaria urged.

'Me...'

Aquaria smiled at him. 'Bugs?'

'Hero,' replied Gail. 'He said, "Don't call me hero".'

Ed opened his eyes, just slightly, but enough to scowl at Aquaria.

Aquaria placed her hand on his shoulder. 'Can you move your hand?'

Ed gave a slow nod.

'You have to sign the book,' insisted Aquaria. 'Do it now.'

He mustered all the strength he had left. His entire arm trembled as he began to scribble across the page of the book.

'Good,' said Zoe. 'You got this.'

As the nib of the pen dragged the final letter of his signature across the vellum, Ed's hand dropped. The biro fell to the floor.

'Ed?' Gail leant in to check his breathing again. 'I can't feel anything.'

'Ed.' Aquaria slapped his cheeks. 'Wake up.'

Zoe searched for a pulse. 'Bollocks,' she cried, pressing her fingers on the veins of his wrists. 'There's nothing.'

The three of them looked at each other, then back to the still body on the table. The seconds became a minute, then two minutes. Still, no response came from Ed.

Aquaria kicked one of the kitchen chairs away in anger. 'Shit. Shit. Shi—'

'Wait.' Gail's eyes widened as she stared at the blood on the table. 'Is that steam?'

Zoe let out a cry of relief. 'It's the healing.'

Aquaria stepped back from the table and allowed her fists to relax. 'It's working.'

***

Ali was now face to face with Leonard. He studied the old man's eyelids, as they gave the slightest hint of a flicker.

'Oh no you don't,' he growled. Bolstered by pure resentment, Ali's right hook slammed so hard into Leonard's head that the professor's whole body toppled backwards. The chair hit the floor of the shop with a clack. 'And, stay down,' rumbled Ali.

He walked over to the door and poked his head through to the kitchen. Looking on in astonishment, Ali gawped as steam rose from the table and floor surrounding Ed. The tourniquet around Ed's leg caught fire, as the healing lit up his wound in a brilliant white glow. This was accompanied by an eery sizzling sound.

'This is some straight up *voodoo* shit,' gasped Ali, taken aback by the magical sight.

Zoe turned to her father and smiled. 'It's the book at work, Dad. The power comes from signing it.'

Ali sucked his teeth, then tutted. 'Well, I'll be…'

Aquaria gently flicked the now charred remains of the tourniquet off Ed's leg. Her eyes widened at the sight of what was revealed.

'What is it?' asked Gail. 'What's wrong?'

'I hoped this wasn't going to happen.'

Everyone watched as the glow faded from the end of Ed's leg. Aquaria blinked slowly, then looked at everyone. 'We couldn't save his foot.'

The healing power had knitted the skin together over what was now a stump.

'He'll live, though?' said Gail.

Aquaria nodded. 'I reckon so.'

'What about the boy?' asked Ali, from the doorway. 'Is there any way to bring him back?'

'No,' replied Aquaria.

Zoe caressed Ed's forehead, then looking at Aquaria through steeled eyes, said, 'Go do what you have to with Leonard. We'll take over in here.'

'Understood,' said Aquaria. She stepped past Ali and entered the shop.

'Need a hand?' Ali offered, following her in.

'The magician becomes the assistant, huh?'

'Something like that, yeah.' Ali helped her lift the chair up, with Leonard still unconscious and bound. They dragged it over to the guillotine. Together, they tipped him forward and rested the old sorcerer's neck in place.

'Don't worry,' said Aquaria, seeing the apprehensive stare in Ali's eyes. 'This doesn't make you a murderer, if that's what's worrying you. We're not actually killing him.'

'Just do it,' replied Ali, wiping the cold sweat from his brow.

***

Ed had woken up. He blinked, then looked at Gail and Zoe leaning over him.

'What happened,' he said, his voice raspy, dry. 'Did we stop Leonard?'

From the next room, the sound of the guillotine blade

striking the wooden base could be heard. This was immediately followed by the sound of puking.

'Okay.' He gave Zoe a confused look. 'Did I just hear your *dad* throw up?'

'Leonard didn't kill him,' said Zoe, helping Gail lift him up. 'He showed up just in time too.'

Ed noticed how Gail kept looking at his leg. 'Why can't I feel my foot?' he asked. Tilting his head down, his expression dropped. 'Oh. I see.'

'I'm so sorry,' said Zoe. 'Leonard completely destroyed your foot when he shot you.' She gripped his hand. 'There was nothing left.'

'Hey, look,' he faked a smile, 'I'll be fine.'

He heard the others speaking in the next room. 'How's Tom? I guess he must be feeling relieved, yeah?'

Seeing the tears form in Zoe's eyes, Ed's heart filled with anguish. 'He's healed, right?'

'You were a real hero today, okay?' Zoe cupped his hand. 'But, Tom's gone. Leonard smeared blood on his signature.'

Ed's eyes narrowed in frustration. 'If only I'd taken more care sneaking into the car. If I could do it all again, I'd make sure Leonard wouldn't see me. Tom might still be alive.' He cursed his incompetence. 'I screwed up. I rushed in like a dickhead.'

'It's okay, Ed. It's not your fault.' Zoe gave him a hug. 'There just wasn't enough time.'

Time. The word was like a klaxon going off in Ed's mind. *Time.* He broke away from the hug, then froze as sparks in his brain ignited.

'You all right?' Zoe gave him a concerned look. 'You're kinda blanking there.'

'Time,' he blurted out, startling Zoe and Gail. 'Of course.' Grinning from ear to ear, he swung his legs round on the table. 'It'll take me a while,' he jabbered excitedly, 'and we'll need to get back to Leonard's workshop. But trust me, maybe I can make everything okay.'

With that, he jumped off the table. Forgetting his left leg

was minus a foot, he fell flat onto the kitchen floor.

Chapter 26
Spares & Repairs

Zoe's Mini drove up to the front of Leonard's cottage. Last time she looked upon the six-hundred-year-old building, it was through the rear-view mirror with eyes full of hatred as she sped away. This time, with a renewed sense of purpose, she allowed herself a moment to take in the setting. The ivy growing up the wall, the grey thatched roof, it actually seemed peaceful. Idyllic, almost.

Ed drummed his fingers on the dashboard, as Zoe finally switched the engine off.

'You sure about this, Ed?' Zoe asked.

'It's our best shot.'

'So,' said Aquaria, helping him out of the car, 'you and the prof built a time machine. An actual fully working time machine, just like in *Back To The Future*?'

'That's right.' Ed wobbled on his right foot, before finding his balance. 'Well, except it's not a Delorean, it's a gun.'

Aquaria took hold of Ed's arm, supporting him as they headed off around the cottage. 'And, Tom stole it then used it to travel here from ten years ago?'

'Sort of.'

'Sort of?'

'It's a long story, but the short version, it wasn't calibrated properly when Tom used it. Also, he didn't know it was a time machine. From what we now know, he thought it was a regular gun, accidentally activating it when he was in Penmoor after a run-in with Leonard.'

Cornering the back of the building, Ed looked towards the old wooden workshop. He was finally free of Leonard's grip. As long as Ali and Gail stuck to their part of the plan.

Before they'd left the Cassam's place, Aquaria had stowed

Leonard's decapitated head in a lockable chest she found in the shop. She moved it out of the building and into the back of Ali's van. As long as Ali made sure no one went near the vehicle, Leonard couldn't latch onto anyone's mind with his psychic connection.

Next, Aquaria and Ali placed Leonard's body into the Zig-Zag cabinet and locked that up also. That was to be kept in its place in the shop. Gail had needed some persuading to stand guard. Both Ali and Gail were under strict instructions not to deviate from this plan. If they could all pull off what Ed had planned, then Leonard could be given the death he wanted, without anyone else being killed. And, just possibly, Tom could come out of this alive and well… maybe.

Ed opened the door to the workshop. He, Zoe and Aquaria entered.

With the small grimy windowpanes offering little of the early morning sun through, Ed made his way over to the light switch. Waiting by the door, Aquaria became aware of the smell; a mix of welding fumes, oil and grease, reminding her of the mechanics garage where her Harley-Davidson was serviced. Her eyes were drawn to something glinting on the floor as Ed flicked on the lights. She bent down and picked up a small silver-capped tooth. Frowning, she handed it to Zoe.

'Thanks.' Zoe held it up to the light, studying the dent to the side. 'I can't believe Dad actually caught a speeding bullet.'

'I know, right?' Aquaria grinned in amazement. 'The best god-damned trick he ever performed and no one will ever know.'

'Except me, Tom and Ed, of course.' Zoe pocketed the keepsake. 'Oh, and Leonard too, I guess.'

Aquaria walked around, looking at various tools and random mechanical parts littering the workbench and shelved walls. 'All this stuff, Leonard was quite the mad inventor, huh?'

'You don't know the half of it,' answered Ed, hopping over to join her at the work bench.

Zoe looked at some of the strange contraptions on the bench. 'What do you do with all these?'

Pointing to a couple of the inventions, Ed replied, 'That one's a capacitor for storing magical energy. And, the glass jar thingy, that counts the expansion rate of the Universe.'

Aquaria watched a spark dance across the glass, inside the jar, 'If you say so, honey.' She turned to look at a rectangular stainless-steel box, twice the size of a microwave. 'And, that one?'

'Oh, yes.' Ed smiled. He hopped over and started fiddling with the contraption's dials and switches. 'This, is one of my best inventions.' The whole thing hummed before a pipe at the side of the steel box jettisoned steam out into the room. Wafting the cloud away, Ed opened a small circular hatch from the lower part of the box. 'Magic,' he said, taking out a small espresso cup.

'It makes coffee?' said Aquaria, unimpressed.

'Not just any coffee,' replied Ed, urging her to try some.

Aquaria took the cup and sniffed the heady aroma of the steaming liquid. 'Whoa.' Her head felt like it had suddenly been spring-cleaned. She took a small sip and swallowed. The instant affect was like having her brain removed, thrown into an Icelandic waterfall while a chorus of angels had an orgy in her skull. 'Jesus,' she gasped, 'that shit kicks like a mule.'

Zoe giggled at Aquaria's facial muscles, twisting like the winner of a gurning competition.

Aquaria's vision sharpened. 'I gotta have me some more of tha—'

'Noooo.' Ed snatched the cup from her. 'I haven't perfected it yet. More than one sip will most likely turn your mind to mush.'

'And on that note,' signalled Zoe, 'the mission?'

'Right, yes.' Ed shifted around the work bench to where the Chronos Blunderbuss sat. He unscrewed a small, concealed panel on its side, then set to work. As he twiddled with the knobs on the nearby oscilloscope, he said, 'This will take a while.'

Aquaria marvelled at the strange gun. 'Why did the prof want to travel through time?'

Still fiddling with the oscilloscope, Ed answered, 'Why

not? Also, I guess Leonard was hoping he could do a do-over.'

Aquaria looked confused. 'How so?'

'Well, y'now, not sign the book. But, the laws of time travel don't work that way. There's paradoxes.'

'Huh?'

Ed paused what he was doing and turned to Aquaria. 'Sorry, but can I just continue with getting this thing operational?'

'Sure.' Studying the room, Aquaria spotted the chaise longue in the corner. She walked over, knelt down and examined the shape of its carved wooden feet. Looking over at Ed's stump, her super-caffeine brain had an idea. 'Ed, you got a hacksaw in here?'

'In the drawer of that cabinet over there,' said Ed, waving. He looked away from reading a tiny LED display panel attached to the side of the time-gun, then turned to Zoe. 'You okay to go find that journal from Leonard's study, as we planned on the drive here?'

Zoe nodded in agreement. 'Is it really his?' she asked.

'Uh-huh,' replied Ed. 'The text needs translating from Old English for us to understand it. But, we just need the map inside it, for now.' He took a soldering iron and began welding a wire into the Chronos Blunderbuss. 'Remember, it's hidden with the dustcover of a book called *The Fall Of Arthur* around it.' He gave the soldered connection a quick blow to cool it, then ushered her out.

***

Zoe entered the study. Feeling stuffy with stale air, the first thing she did was wander over to the window, throw back the curtain then jiggle the frame open. The freshness permeated the room, causing dust to glisten like a galaxy of microscopic stars disturbed by the light breeze. This didn't do anything to revitalise the dark interior; any section of the forest-green wallpaper that hadn't been hidden by bookshelves and paintings seemed to neutralise the early morning light shining through the small window.

Next, her attention moved to the globe. She spun it round, stopping on America. Flicking the latch, she lifted up the northern hemisphere. As she picked up the various-sized decanters and bottles, she noticed a small blue medicine bottle hidden at the back. Reading the label, her eyes widened. 'Rohypnol? Bloody hell, Leonard.' Shaking her head, she figured it may come in handy so pocketed the bottle in her trousers.

Moving over to rows of books on the shelves, she sidestepped along. Her head tilted, as she read a few of the titles. Books varying in topic, but mostly about history. It wasn't long before she found a title that made her snort with contempt. '*The Bayeux Tapestry*,' she read out loud, as she slid it from the shelf. 'Let's have a look at you in action then, Leofwine.'

Leafing through the pages, she saw that Leofwine Goodwinson had died on the battlefield along with his brothers Harold and Gyrth. 'You must be the first example,' she jibed, 'of someone faking their own death.'

Closing the book, she returned it to the shelf. It wasn't long before she found what she came for. As she slid the title out, she noted the author's name. 'Tolkien? Doesn't surprise me.'

Discarding the dust cover, she held the ancient journal up to the light. As she did so, a folded parchment dropped out. Picking it up, she opened it out to reveal what appeared to be a map of a coastline. Studying the detailed drawing, Zoe spotted an X with the words, 'Wandwich Castrum' written above it. In the top left-hand corner of the map was an unusual symbol: three different-shaped leaves were entwined together, forming a triangular pattern. She felt a shiver run down her spine, as though someone had crept up and placed an invisible cloak over her. Looking around the room, it now seemed stuffier than before. She folded up the map and replaced it inside the journal, before joining the others.

Entering the workshop, Zoe saw sparks dancing from the metal box on the side of the blunderbuss, as Ed was busy welding. The protective goggles he wore made him look like a World War I fighter pilot.

Aquaria was stood over at the opposite end of the work bench. The sawn-off chaise longue's foot was held tight in a vice, as she finished filing smooth the roughly cut side. She called Zoe over to help her. 'See those galoshes over there by the door?'

'Um,' replied Zoe, 'the green wellies?'

'Sorry.' Aquaria corrected herself, 'Yeah, I mean the wellies. Would you mind fetching the left boot over?'

'Are you doing what I think you're doing?'

'Uh-huh.' Aquaria winked. 'Ed's been so into that blunderbuss, I don't think he's noticed what I'm up to.'

Zoe placed the journal down on the bench, then fetched the wellington boot for Aquaria. 'Will it work?' she asked, as Aquaria loosened the vice then slid the wooden foot inside the boot.

'Don't see why not?' said Aquaria. 'Could you help me find something to pad it out with?'

By the time Ed had finished his work, Aquaria had finished hers. Ed unhooked the Chronos Blunderbuss from the stand, detached wires and held the gun up. He let out a huge sigh of relief, then said, 'I've actually done it.' Mimicking shooting the device, he added, 'Up yours, Leonard.'

Zoe and Aquaria both congratulated him as he placed the contraption back down on the bench. Only then, did Ed spot the boot sat on the table, and a wonky chaise longue in the corner of the room. 'What's going on?'

'Tah-dah.' Aquaria held both hands out at the boot.

Ed tried to look anything but unimpressed by the old wellington boot. 'It's a wellie,' he said, in a flat tone.

'Just shut up,' demanded Aquaria, 'and try it on.'

Ed hopped over, took the boot and slid his leg inside it. He felt the softness of a microfibre wash-mitt cushion his stump. 'Huh?' Allowing it to take his weight, he stood straight with perfect balance.

'You'll probably need to wrap this duct-tape around the

top to stop it from falling off,' said Aquaria, holding up a grey roll. 'But hey, it'll do for now, right?'

Ed took the tape and bound it tightly around the boot, as Aquaria had suggested, then did a little tap dance to illustrate how well it worked. 'It's bloody brilliant.'

'Will your plan work?' said Zoe. 'Can we actually bring Tom back?'

'Right, yeah.' Ed lifted the blunderbuss from the bench. He flicked the device on, checking it powered up. 'So, time follows a very strict set of rules.' He fiddled with the controls. 'Everything we do when travelling back to the past, if we're not super careful, could potentially cause catastrophic repercussions that might smash down the very building blocks of the known Universe.' He saw the blank expressions on both Zoe and Aquaria's faces. 'Only joking. Worst-case scenario, we'd just completely rewrite the history books and in doing so write ourselves out of it.'

Zoe and Aquaria glanced nervously at each other.

'How about I give you two a little demonstration of what this bad boy can do?'

'Um… sure?' said Aquaria.

Ed gripped the Chronos Blunderbuss with both hands as it began to whir. 'Zoe, could you make some space on the bench, please?'

Unsure what was about to happen, Zoe did as he asked, lifting some of the gadgets and tools away from the centre, keeping a close eye on the time-gun as she did so.

'Okay,' said Ed, taking a deep breath. He checked the time on a wall clock, then tapped his finger on a few tiny buttons on the side of the gun. 'Check this out.'

As they watched, the surface of the bench appeared to move in a circle. Slowly, at first, but then becoming faster. It was as if the wooden bench was melting into a swirling brown liquid.

'How the hell are you doing that?' gasped Aquaria. 'You haven't even fired that thing at the bench yet?'

Shushing her, Ed replied, 'Keep watching the vortex.'

There was now a hole inside the bench. As Zoe and

Aquaria peered in, they could see the floor of the workshop through the centre of the hole. Within seconds, the vortex snapped shut. A clunking sound came from underneath the bench.

'Yes,' cried Ed. 'Aquaria, could you reach under and retrieve the wellington boot from there?'

Aquaria's brow wrinkled as she stooped down. 'I... I don't believe it.' When she stood up, she was holding a boot exactly like the one that remained by the door. 'Neat trick.' She smiled. 'You've made a copy.'

'Nope,' said Ed. 'It's the same one.'

Zoe looked bewildered. 'But it can't be? It's still sat on the floor over there.'

'Correction,' Ed said, with a wink. 'I haven't used it, *yet*.' With that, Ed lifted up the blunderbuss and took aim at the space on the bench where the vortex had appeared before. He gently placed his right hand under the barrel and placed his index finger on the trigger.

As he squeezed the trigger there was an almighty boom. An inch-thick beam of pure neon blue light blasted from the fluted muzzle. Holding the vibrating device steady, Ed slid his left hand along the stock of the gun to a set of dials. Zoe and Aquaria took a step back. As he turned one of the dials, just a few tiny amounts, the beam grew wider. On the surface of the bench, a vortex had begun to emerge. When it reached the same size as the previous one, Ed called to Zoe over the loud rumbling noise. 'Grab the wellie, the one still by the door.'

Zoe obliged.

'Cool,' said Ed, holding firm. 'When I give the signal, I want you to throw it into the vortex. Got it?'

'Yep.'

Still clutching her version of the boot, Aquaria looked on, open-mouthed.

Ed released the trigger, causing the beam to vanish in an instant. 'Okay, Zoe?' The vortex continued to spin on the bench. 'Wang it.'

'Huh?'

'Wang it.'

'Oh,' sniggered Zoe, 'sounded like you said—'

'Bloody throw it in.' Ed flapped a hand at the vortex. 'NOW.'

Zoe lobbed the boot inside it, like a pro-basketball player. The vortex snapped shut, and the room fell quiet.

They all took a moment to breathe.

'Um,' Aquaria placed her wellington boot down on the floor, 'explanation, please?'

Ed gave the Chronos Blunderbuss a once-over. He deactivated it and placed it back on its stand. 'I just sent that wellie back in time,' he said, looking pleased with himself. Seeing the baffled expression on Aquaria's face, he elaborated. 'So, just then, when Zoe threw it into the vortex, the wellie travelled backwards in time and arrived, here, a couple of minutes before.'

'When we saw that first vortex open up, right?' added Zoe, keeping up. 'And the boot fell out under the bench.'

'Spot on.'

'Okay,' said Aquaria, 'but why were there two in the same place, at the same time?'

'Because,' answered Ed, 'when the *future* wellie arrived in the past, that exact same one hadn't yet been thrown into the vortex.'

'I think I need another cup of your magic coffee,' replied Aquaria. 'This is heavy.'

Zoe rubbed her forehead. 'So, what if the same thing happened with people?'

'You would, essentially, end up bumping into yourself.' Ed frowned at the idea. 'But that would be bad.'

'Dunno,' said Aquaria. 'Be kinda fun, wouldn't it?'

'No.' Ed glowered at her. 'You could seriously mess up your own timeline. For example, what if your future self did something to prevent the past version of yourself from wanting to go back in time? You would, literally, talk yourself out of existence.'

'Oh,' muttered Aquaria. 'So, no bumping into yourself. Got

it.'

Zoe picked up the journal from the bench. 'But that's unlikely, where we're going. Yeah?'

'Let's just make sure we only alter what we need to.' Ed took the journal from her and opened it up. He removed the map from inside and spread it out on the work bench. 'Okay. One night, when I was younger, Leonard and I were sat outside when we saw a bright shooting star streak across the sky. He said that he'd created his magical book, the Eternus, the same night that a comet had passed over. And that his brother had thought it a good omen. In truth, it was actually Halley's comet.'

'April 1066,' said Zoe. 'I just read about it in Leonard's study.'

'Right before the Battle of Hastings.' Ed nodded. 'It was in that battle that Harold was killed by an arrow in the head, and when Leonard faked his own death.'

'I saw that too,' acknowledged Zoe. 'Well, obviously it showed Leonard, or Leofwine, had been killed.' Returning to the map, she asked, 'So, is this a map of Hastings then?'

'Nope,' said Ed. 'This is a map showing the location of Wandwich Castle.'

Zoe and Aquaria both craned in to have a better look. 'Can't say I've ever heard of it,' said Zoe.

'That's no surprise,' said Ed. 'Hardly anyone has. Those that have, though, think it's a myth.'

'How so?' asked Aquaria.

'Well, the castle had once been impenetrable. Supposedly protected from invasion by a magic spell.' Ed looked at Aquaria, 'But the sorcerer, whose power created that spell, had betrayed the king. The spell was broken, which led to the castle being invaded, and ultimately destroyed. Since no one's ever found the ruins of Wandwich Castle, it remains a myth.'

'You're saying that the sorcerer was Leonard?' said Aquaria, her eyes widening.

'Yup,' said Ed. 'And not only is this map proof that it was real, but from the entries written in Leonard's journal, I'm pretty sure it's where he created the book and first signed it.'

'Awesome.' Aquaria smiled. She slapped her hands on the work bench, then stepped back. 'Then, let's go kick some medieval ass.'

'There's just one slight problem,' said Ed, pointing to the map. 'I'm not exactly sure where this coastline is.'

'You're kidding, right?' Aquaria shook her head.

'Hey,' snapped Ed. 'I don't know everything.'

'So, how are we going to find it?' said Aquaria. She folded her arms, awaiting his response.

'Well, we'd need an expert on geographical history for that.' Ed folded up the map and slipped it back inside the journal.

Zoe stared into his eyes. 'You know someone, don't you?'

'Might do.' He made his way over to the Chronos Blunderbuss and picked it up. 'Do you trust me?'

'Is there a reason why we shouldn't?' asked Aquaria.

Ed opened a drawer, removed what looked like a guitar strap and clipped it onto the Chronos Blunderbuss. The other two watched as he slung the time-gun over his shoulder, swiped the journal off the bench, then walked over to the door. 'You coming then?' he asked.

'Lead on,' replied Zoe.

Chapter 27
Field Trip

'Should be in for another fine day, guys,' chirped Toby Johnson, stretching his arms. He strode over to a couple of fold-out picnic benches, arranged end to end. His full English breakfast was, of course, already waiting for him at the head of the table. The crew did their best to ignore his moans of satisfaction, as they sat there spooning lukewarm soggy cereal from their polystyrene bowls.

Sat at the other end of the table, Jeremy Huxley trowelled some marmalade onto a doorstop-sized slice of toast. 'Reckon we've got as much as we can out of that last trench, Toby,' he called over. 'Best if the team finish checking through the others, eh? What do you all think?'

One of the archaeology students amongst the crew chipped in. 'As long as I'm paid, I'll dig wherever you tell me to, mate.'

Toby sat fiddling with his clip-on microphone. 'That's the spirit, Danny,' he grumbled, without taking his eyes off what he was doing.

Danny pointed over to the far gate. 'Looks like we've got three helpers heading over.'

Zoe, Ed and Aquaria were making their way along the dew-damp field towards the *Dig This* crew.

'Blimey,' muttered one of the other students, as the trio arrived at the tables. He gulped at Aquaria, dressed in her tight blue leathers. 'You're... erm, a bit overdressed for a dig, miss?'

'Calm down, son,' she purred, then gave everyone a well-rehearsed, pouted smile. 'How y'all doing, this fine morning?'

The male students stopped eating and tried to act cool, no easy feat when sat at picnic tables eating soggy cereal. The female crew just tutted and rolled their eyes.

Toby stood, ran his right hand over his dyed black hair, then extended it to greet Aquaria. 'Good morning, my love,' he said, giving her a slow wink. 'I'm Toby Johnson. But, of course, I'm sure you already know that. And, you are?'

'Here to speak to Miss Jenkins, not you,' she replied.

Toby's professional smile vanished at the mention of *that* woman's name. 'Well, I'm afraid she's no longer working on this project.' He dropped his hand. 'I can't say I'm disappoint—'

Aquaria ignored his prattling and moved on. Walking to the other end of the table, she joined Zoe and Ed beside Jeremy.

'Hello there,' said Jeremy with a kind smile. 'I was just asking your friends here if I could be of some assistance?'

'I hope so,' said Zoe. 'This is Ed and Aquaria. And, my name's Zoe.'

'Aquaria?' replied the white-haired beardy historian. 'Did you know, there's a Nordic myth regarding a mermaid by that name?'

'How interesting.' Aquaria smiled. 'Please, Jeremy, do continue.'

Toby's jealous glare from the opposite end of the table evaporated as it hit Jeremy's warm, jovial expression.

'Really?' said Jeremy, somewhat surprised. 'Gosh, normally no one wants to hear my tales of old.' He gave a little excitable chuckle. 'Well, you see, Aquaria fell in love with a young Viking man she once saw sailing onboard a long boat, returning to shore. After that day, whenever a boat would sail past, it was said that Aquaria would use magic to calm the rough sea, in the hope that the young fellow would be onboard, thank her and fall in love with her. Rather sweet, isn't it?'

'Sounds like you know your mythology, sir?' asked Zoe. 'It's funny, really. That's partly why we wanted to speak to Jane. We're trying to find the location of—'

'That tale sounds a bit fishy to me,' joked Toby, as he approached them. 'Get it? Tale? Tail?' Seeing he was the only one laughing, Toby shook his head and tutted. 'Anyway, the producer's on her way, Jez. Time for anyone not associated with filming to leave.' He gave Aquaria an arrogant grin. 'Off you pop, then.'

'Oh, don't be so rude, Toby,' said Jeremy. He turned to the three visitors, 'Sorry. Look, I'll tell you what, how about I walk across the field with you, then I'll see if I can help?'

'Thanks,' said Ed, turning to leave. 'Don't suppose you've heard about the myth of Wandwich Castle, have you?'

Jeremy stood to face him. 'Oh, that old chestnut,' he chortled. 'Yes, I'm familiar with the legend.'

Ed held up the folded parchment. 'How about its location?'

Jeremy raised an eyebrow. 'Let's walk. Shall we?'

***

Jeremy had listened intently to Ed as they approached the gate at the far end of the field.

'Well, sadly, most of the maps that claim to show the whereabouts of Wandwich Castle turn out to be false.'

'Oh, I have pretty good evidence,' said Ed, 'that this is the real deal.' He handed the map to Jeremy, who opened it out on a drystone wall beside the gate out of the field.

'My, my?' Balancing his half-spectacles on the edge of his nose, Jeremy gave the bristles of his beard a good thought-inducing scratch. 'This *is* something special. Seems you're lucky to have bumped into me, I'd say. You see, I know the myth very well indeed. It was the reason I wanted to be a historian, all those years ago.

'My father told me how the legend of King Arthur had borrowed a lot from the story of Wandwich. A young servant boy from the castle supposedly found a sword embedded in a stone while out exploring one day. Sound familiar?' His eyes twinkled before continuing. 'Anyway, I can tell you straight away that the age of this map is eleventh century. Also, this symbol here, the three leaves entwined, is an ancient Druid protection symbol.'

'That makes sense,' said Ed. 'So, you convinced yet?'

'Well, who really knows? But, there is one thing I can tell

you.' Jeremy tapped his finger on the lower half of the map. 'That coastline isn't Cornwall. Which *is* interesting, since every speculation suggested the settlement of Wandwich may have been somewhere between Pentire Point and Tintagel.'

'S… Sorry?' sputtered Ed. 'Say that last bit again.'

'The map isn't anywhere in Cornwall.'

'How can you be so sure, Jeremy?' asked Aquaria.

'Well, it's obvious. See?' Jeremy's finger traced around the coast. 'Because of the distinct shape of it.'

'Okay,' said Zoe. 'So, you recognise it. Yes?'

'Indeed. This is a map of Portland, a tied island off the south coast of Dorset. I know it very well.' Jeremy pointed to where Wandwich Castle was marked on the map. 'There's actually a castle stood on that very spot, today. I should know because we've filmed there.'

Their eyes lit up at the news. 'But, I thought nothing remained of Wandwich Castle?' asked Ed.

'Well, no,' said Jeremy. 'The castle, that's there today, is called Rufus Castle and was built around the late fifteenth century. Little is known about what lay there before, but evidence hints that Rufus Castle sits on the ruin of another, built in the twelfth century. But, prior to that, the history gets sketchy, to say the least. Maybe, there was another one before that? Improbable, but not impossible.' Jeremy scratched the back of his head. 'Look, I can't confirm this map is a hundred per cent real, without proper analysis of course. But, if by some miracle what you have here is real, it would certainly pooh-pooh one myth that suggests the servant boy of Wandwich pulled his sword out of the A-hole of Penmoor.'

'How so?' asked Aquaria, ignoring the smirking from Ed and Zoe.

'Well.' Jeremy shrugged. 'I mean, to come across the A-hole so far away from Wandwich Castle, doesn't really sound plausible, does it?'

'Ah, sure.' Aquaria nudged her elbow into Ed's rib, silencing him. 'No, I get your point, Jeremy.'

A member of the crew called over to them from the trenches. Jeremy waved back, then apologised for having to leave. 'I'd be happy to get that map dated and checked for you. Seems you may have something wonderful in your possession.'

'Ah, sorry,' replied Ed. 'We need to hold on to it for a while.'

'Oh well. Should you change your minds, though, we'll be here until this evening.'

'Thank you for taking the time to speak with us.' Aquaria extended her hand.

Jeremy shook it, then reaching into his trouser pocket, he produced a scrap of paper. Finding a pen, he asked, 'Um... I don't suppose I could trouble you for an autograph?'

'Oh, you recognised me? You should've said so.' Aquaria smiled. She took the pen and paper and signed her autograph.

'I didn't want to make a fuss in front of the others. My eldest daughter loved your show as a teenager. I can't wait to tell her I've met you.' He took the pen and paper back, smiled at it, then bid them a farewell before heading off.

'Suppose you get that a lot?' asked Ed, as the three of them headed back towards Zoe's car.

'Not so much these days,' replied Aquaria. 'You and Jeremy are the only two people in the last four years. Still, it's always a nice feeling, y'know?'

When they were finally sat back inside the Mini, Zoe tapped Portland into her sat-nav. 'It's going to take us two hours, forty minutes.' She sighed.

'Don't worry,' said Ed, from the back seat. He lifted up the Chronos Blunderbuss. 'When we're leaving the eleventh century, I'll set this so we can arrive back with plenty of time to spare.'

Chapter 28
A Leap of Faith

They arrived at a sand-swept car park. Surveying their surroundings, to the right they saw a young couple walking their dog along moss-like grass. To their left, a group of elderly women stood staring at a menu board outside a white timber-clad restaurant.

Zoe looked up at the tall white and red lighthouse ahead of them. With the clear blue sky behind it, the structure stood like a rocket, awaiting lift-off. 'Prepare to launch, eh?' She sighed.

Ed seemed distracted as he slid Leofwine's journal inside a polythene bag, then tied a knot, making it waterproof.

'So why can't we use the blunderbuss next to Rufus Castle, instead of having to come right down to here?' asked Aquaria, as she watched what Ed was doing.

'There's no records showing the exact layout of Wandwich,' replied Ed, as they got out of the car. 'We could emerge from the vortex into a busy marketplace, a hall full of people. Worse still, we could pop out next to a bunch of soldiers. Not good if we're trying to be inconspicuous. The ocean is our best entry point.' He grabbed the Chronos Blunderbuss off the back seat, then slid it over his shoulder.

'I'm no fan of being in the sea,' said Zoe, hearing the sound of waves in the distance. 'The way the saltwater stings your sinuses.' She did her best to stay focused on saving Tom, and stopping Leonard.

'Doubt we'll be in the water long,' added Aquaria. She saw the look on Zoe's face and sensed there was a deeper worry.

'It's all right for you,' snorted Zoe. 'You'll be a bloody shark.'

'Well, that's true.'

Zoe spotted a signpost to the right-hand corner of the car

park. 'Pulpit Rock's that way.' She stowed her car keys behind the front driver's side wheel. 'You're sure everything will be as we left it when we get back here?'

'If we stick to the rules,' replied Ed. Realising he'd forgot to place his phone in the polythene bag, he untied it and dropped the device inside.

His action hadn't gone unnoticed by Aquaria. 'And, how is taking a cell phone back to the eleventh century sticking to the rules?'

'I've loaded an Old English translator app onto it. Just in case.'

'Let's hope it doesn't come to that,' said Zoe. She recalled how, on the journey to Portland, Ed had calculated the numbers for the blunderbuss and double-checked the geographical history of the area on his phone. He had stressed how important it was that, when back in time, they touched nothing, spoke to no one and left nothing behind.

They were about to dive off Pulpit Rock – a stack of rocks that took its name due to the way it looked – in the hope of emerging safely in the eleventh-century ocean. If anything went wrong, the only chance of being pulled to shore lay in the jaws of a shark called Aquaria. If everything went according to plan, though, they would get to the Eternus book before Leofwine had a chance to sign it. Finding the book wouldn't be easy; the sorcerer's journal was the only lead they had to go on. It was risky – insanely so – but no other plan would allow Leonard to die and for it all to be over.

The wind grew stronger, as they navigated their way along the dust-whipped pathway. They walked over a flattened limestone platform that led up to the monumental landmark. All three of them marvelled at the scale of what overshadowed them; a square slab of rock, three times their height, leant diagonally against an enormous cube-like stack, looking every bit as its name suggested, a giant's pulpit facing out to the congregation of waves that swayed some fifty feet below.

As he stood gawping, Ed sputtered, 'Does anyone else's

pants need changing, or is it just mine?'

'It'll be all right.' Aquaria placed her hand on his shoulder, as she stepped past. 'Just think of it as a diving board.' Arriving at the rock face, she reached onto the cold surface, found her footing and began to climb. Looking back at Ed, she added, 'Don't forget, you've signed the book. You can't die.'

Ed turned to Zoe. 'Why does that make me feel worse?'

'Come on.' Zoe was next to clamber up the rock. 'Let's just get it over with.'

Ed closed his eyes, just for a few seconds, and listened to the sound of the waves crashing into the rocks below. He chucked the polythene bag up to Aquaria, then began his ascent.

After stepping across the top and joining the other two at the furthest edge, Ed stopped and looked over at the swaying deep water far below. Arcs of white water rebounded from the rock, roaring like baying onlookers taunting them to jump.

Zoe shivered as she peered down. Every nerve ending in her legs tingled for her to step back. Looking over at Ed, she could see his hands shaking as he removed the blunderbuss from off his shoulder. Aquaria gave them both a reassuring look.

Ed powered up the time-gun and made some final adjustments. Taking a long steady breath, he held the gun still. Squinting through the sights, he took aim at the water. On the small LED display on the side of the gun, numbers span then stopped. 'Trajectory, all set,' he announced. 'Eleventh century, here we come. Hopefully.'

Aquaria pulled the zip on her jacket up tight. 'And you're sure that gun is waterproof?'

Gripping the blunderbuss, Ed pointed it towards the deepest part of the ocean. 'Airtight and waterproof. It has to be, or else the whole gun could backfire.' He looked at Zoe and Aquaria through anxious eyes.

Zoe caught his expression. 'Which would be bad, I take it?'

He drew the sight up to his eye level once more. 'Well, you could kiss goodbye to this reality, if that happened.'

'Ah.'

He squeezed the trigger.

Aquaria felt the long loose curls of her blonde hair, blown about by the wind, suddenly pull in the opposite direction as if magnetised by the activated gun. A flicker of static charge rippled over the fluted muzzle as Ed adjusted his stance, bracing himself. Back in the workshop, the trial had only required the gun to open a vortex big enough for a wellington boot. This was entirely different.

The air in front of the gun warped out of shape, like a tubular heat-haze, before a ray of neon blue energy burst out and blew a hole out of the surface of the furious waves below. Ed spread his legs wider as the force of the beam pushed him back. As his jaw vibrated, he cried out, 'Shi-i-i-i-i-it.'

'It's working,' gawped Aquaria, pointing below them. 'Look at the size of the thing.'

Zoe stared in awe. A huge whirlpool, with streaks of pure white light crackling around inside, lay open in the water below.

Ed released his finger. With all his body pushing forward against the force of the beam, when it cut out, he nearly toppled off the cliff edge.

'We good?' Aquaria stepped forward. She passed the polythene bag back to Ed.

'I reckon so,' replied Ed.

Aquaria took a deep breath, gave both of the rings on her fingers a good-luck kiss, then opened her arms out straight like an Olympic high-diver. 'I'll see you in the past.' Bending her knees, she sprang from the rock. As she arched down towards the ocean, she slapped her hands together with a bright flash.

Zoe and Ed leant over for a better look, just in time to see the tail of a blue requiem shark vanish into the vortex.

'Incredible,' gasped Ed.

From behind them, back on the pathway, came the sound of voices.

'We should check that,' said Zoe, walking over to the other side of the summit. In the distance, Zoe spotted three teenagers dressed in wetsuits, making their way along the path. 'Looks like we have company, Ed.'

Checking for himself, Ed groaned. 'Tomb-stoners.'

'Who?'

'It's what they call themselves. I saw images of them, cliff-jumping, when I googled this place on the way here.'

Zoe gave him a worried look. 'Won't they discover the vortex?'

'We should get a move on.' Ed shoved the bag down his pants, then strapped the blunderbuss across his torso. 'As soon as I pass through the vortex, the dimensional stabilisers on the blunderbuss should close the entrance behind me by default. It's one of the bugs I fixed back at the workshop.'

'Um… okay,' said Zoe. 'I hope so. The last thing we want is three adrenaline junkies gate-crashing the eleventh century.' She peered down, once again, into the whirlpool. 'Pretty big hole, isn't it,' she gulped. 'What do you think, wide enough for a tandem jump?'

'Yeah, looks like it.' Ed smiled, taking hold of her hand. 'Together on three?'

'One,' they both called out, bending their knees.

'Two.' Ed shut his eyes.

'Three.'

As they plummeted down, past the face of the mighty limestone rock and into the vortex, Zoe's ears popped, making Ed's scream sound deafeningly louder.

Journal of a sorcerer
V

15 October 1066.

'Yesterday, I betrayed my king and country.

'The men who signed the king's register no longer exist. Removed during the great battle by a simple stroke of my finger. My brother, who did not believe himself so weak as to sign the book, was struck down by a single arrow. Our brother, Gyrth, who joined us to defend the onslaught, lies dead beside him. I was only able to escape the battlefield by feigning death.

'Without the Knights of the Eternal Order, our armies never stood a chance. It took just one day for the rule of this country to be surrendered to the Normans, a heavy cost to stop the immortal savages that my brother created. But, I could not let them survive. The power of immortality is not safe in their hands. They have abused it with unspeakable acts.

'For my part, the elders have sentenced me to walk upon the earth for five hundred years before I can be allowed to die. And even then, it is under condition. As a final act of punishment, they have removed the enchantment that protected our castle. Its fate to be decided under Norman rule.

'Fearing I may be recognised, I have chosen to flee and begin life anew. I shall protect the secret of the book of Eternus. It must remain hidden, never to be abused again.'

Chapter 29
What Happens in Wandwich Stays in Wandwich

The girl dropped her half-chewed parsnip and ran as fast as she could. Her mother finished loading the remainder of the harvest onto the cart, wiped the sweat from her brow with the sleeve of her grey cloth gown and turned to the child.

'Milda,' she said.

Muttering excitably to her mother in Old English, Milda insisted, 'There's a creature, in the sea.' She reached to her mother's hand, grabbed it, and started to pull. 'Come, see.'

'Let go.' The woman spoke in the same archaic language, pushing her daughter to the wet ground. She returned to the cart, and to the scowling man sat upon it.

The man cast a disapproving glare over the weeping child, then flicked a fly off the polished brooch of his tunic without saying a word. He ran a gloved hand over his jet-black hair, reached for his whip and brought it down with a crack onto the back of the tall dark horse, tethered to the front of the cart.

Once she was sure the man had left, the woman helped Milda up. She patted the mud from her daughter's gown, ran her weathered fingers through the child's wild auburn hair and then hugged her. 'You must not talk when the lord's men are here,' she said. Brushing her own matted auburn locks from her face, she frowned at her daughter through tired eyes.

Milda pointed to the ocean. Her outstretched hand trembled as she dared to explain what she'd seen out in the water. But the sudden sting to her hand, as her mother slapped it away, stopped her. Grabbing Milda's gown by the shoulder, her mother dragged her away towards their hamlet.

***

In the ocean where Milda had witnessed her sea creature, a shark was circling the area. The vortex had recently closed, leaving a counterclockwise current which helped the sleek blueish shark glide around.

It dived down. Returning to the surface a moment later, Ed was now clinging on to its dorsal fin.

'F-f-find her, Aquaria,' he blurted, gasping for air. Letting go of the shark, he began to tread water as the shark circled him before submerging a second time into the deep green water.

All went quiet as Ed scanned the surrounding water. He looked down into the sea beneath him, trying to find any sign of movement that could be Zoe. A faint flash briefly lit up the water, a couple of metres under his kicking feet. 'Come on, come on,' he muttered. Within twenty seconds, Aquaria bobbed to the surface, back in human form. In her arms, she was clinging onto Zoe.

'She's unconscious,' Aquaria cried out to Ed. 'Get to the shore, fast.'

Swimming as hard as he could, Ed struggled to keep up with Aquaria, even though she was towing Zoe. As they got closer to land, the waves helped carry them along. As soon as they arrived, they dragged Zoe up the shingled beach and laid her down.

'Is she breathing?' cried Ed, removing the blunderbuss from his torso and carefully placing it down. He watched as Aquaria listened to Zoe's mouth.

'Yes,' said Aquaria. 'It sounds restricted though.' She moved Zoe into the recovery position, allowing sea water to pour from her mouth.

'C'mon, Zoe.' Ed gave Zoe's shoulder a shake. He noticed something small and black dribble from out of Zoe's open mouth. Getting down for a closer inspection, Ed caught sight of something lodged at the back of Zoe's throat. Shoving his fingers into her mouth, he pulled out a small seaweed frond.

Zoe let in a loud gasp, then eventually spluttered, 'Gross.'

Aquaria and Ed both gave a sigh in relief.

Only once Zoe had sat herself up, did they all take in their surroundings. They were a hundred metres from the tall rock face that would, one day, become Pulpit Rock. The sea was pleasantly calm now, the clear blue sky too. This surprised Zoe who, as she rested a moment, expected the eleventh century to be a dark, cold and wet place and not resemble a day trip to the beach. With the temperature fairly warm, at least their clothes would soon be dry.

'Okay,' said Aquaria to Ed. 'Which way to Wandwich Castle?'

Ed removed the wrapped-up journal from his pants. Opening out the map, he orientated it round and located their current position. 'We head that way.' He gestured up towards the land, and to the right. 'But first,' he tugged at his soaking wet hoodie, 'we'll need to steal some appropriate clothing to help us blend in.'

Aquaria scanned around. Up beyond the rocks of the cliff she could see two figures, a woman and child, walking away along what she assumed would be some kind of path. She suggested following them.

Keeping their distance, the three time travellers made their way up to the top of the rocks and, sure enough, they found a track. Luckily, other than the mother and her daughter, there was no one else around. On the opposite side to the cliff, about ten metres or so away, they saw what looked like a muddy field with vegetables growing.

'Well, if we get hungry,' joked Ed, 'at least we know where to find a bite to eat.'

Zoe humoured his remark with a worried smile.

When they'd walked further along the track, a few thick bushes provided them with a place to duck into, to avoid being spotted if needed.

Apart from the clothing the strangers wore, there was nothing to suggest this wasn't modern day. That was until they soon neared civilisation.

After fifteen minutes of walking, hiding out of sight, walking some more, they approached dwellings. It was as if they had arrived on a movie set. Ed and Zoe marvelled at the site. Five simple homes, four of which were nothing more than triangular straw and wood shelters. These sat beside a larger home, the walls of which had been constructed from mud and straw, the roof a basic thatch. Smoke rose out of a hole in the roof of this home – if it could be referred to as such – indicating a fireplace within, while the others had to make do with a communal fire outside.

'We should stay back,' whispered Zoe, stopping the others. 'See how the people here move about.' She ushered the other two towards some brambles.

'There's a couple of dogs over the nearside,' whispered Aquaria, pointing them out. 'We don't want them barking their heads off.'

Ed and Aquaria crouched and followed Zoe to the safety of the brambles. From there, they got a true sense of what life was like for eleventh-century folk. There were animals everywhere. Pigs, goats, chickens, not to mention rats. Dogs were tethered to stakes outside the larger house. They observed the people – dressed in the same primitive clothes as the woman and child they had followed here wore – going about their daily duties. Some were collecting eggs from a fenced off pen containing hens, others throwing rotten scraps to the pigs. A couple were tending to a boiling pot suspended above the communal fire. No one seemed to be taking much notice of what everyone else was doing. It wasn't long before the reason for this became apparent.

A young lad, barely into his teens, tripped over while carrying what appeared to be a basket of apples. He fell flat on the floor, sending the basket and its contents rolling up to the door of the larger dwelling.

Aquaria, Ed and Zoe heard a bellow come from inside. Everyone stopped what they were doing as the door swung open. A rotund man, dressed in noticeably more refined attire than the others, stepped out. He brushed his blue woollen tunic to one side, revealing a sturdy-looking wooden club. The lad got up onto his knees, shaking as he appeared to plead for mercy.

Zoe averted her eyes as the man's club pummelled the lad to the ground. The cries of agony reverberated around the area, but no one came to help. In fact, some turned back to their work and continued as though absolutely nothing was happening.

As Aquaria and Ed continued to watch in horror at the beating, they saw a woman rush across to the oppressive man. She got down on her knees and began to beg him to stop. This was met by another great swing of the man's club, but this time it hit the woman's chin. Blood spurted from her mouth, spraying the poor broken lad.

'To hell with this bullshit,' growled Aquaria.

Getting up from their hiding spot, Aquaria stormed off towards the scene before Ed and Zoe had a chance to stop her.

'Bollocks.' Still hidden, Ed flapped his hands about. 'We're screwed.'

'Hey, asshole,' called Aquaria, striding closer to the callous man.

Halting, the man glared at her.

'Yes, I mean you,' said Aquaria, pointing her outstretched finger his way.

The man appeared stunned, unable to grasp the broken language being fired his way. Speaking in Old English, he began ordering Aquaria to back away from the scene. Of course, not familiar with this language and hell-bent on taking him down, Aquaria accelerated her charge. The man raised his club, but he was too late. Aquaria hit him with a jumping kick to his head, sending him crashing backwards into some piled up clay pots.

Assessing the unconscious thug, Aquaria huffed at him, then turned to help the injured woman. The gesture wasn't met with the gratitude she had hoped for. Instead, the woman shuffled back towards her son, shielding him.

'Hey,' said Aquaria, her hands held up. 'It's okay. I'm not going to hurt you.'

The other folk muttered to each other. They began picking

up anything they could use as a weapon. From the safety of the brambles, Ed and Zoe grew agitated by the scene. 'This is why we don't interfere with the past,' said Ed, getting to his feet. He removed his phone from the polythene bag and opened up the Old English translator app.

'What are we going to do?' Zoe looked at him, then to the mob now forming a semi-circle around Aquaria.

Ed's mind went into overdrive. He scanned the lay of the area, taking note of where the peasants were stood, where Aquaria was. He spotted the clothes drying on a rudimentary line made of thin branches, over by the furthest shelter. He looked up at the position of the sun, frowned, then handing his phone to Zoe, he grabbed the blunderbuss and began punching co-ordinates into it.

Zoe began to panic. 'What are you doing? If we time travel from here, won't it be dangerous?'

'It's not for us.' Ed retrieved his phone and placed it into the pocket of his hoodie. Gripping the blunderbuss tightly, he ordered, 'When I give the signal, you go steal that washing.' With that, he headed off towards the mob.

As Ed approached, Aquaria caught sight of him clutching the blunderbuss. Bewildered as to why the villagers had turned on her for trying to help, she stood still, her hands held up. 'There's no need for this,' she pleaded. 'Go back to your work, I will leave you in peace.'

One of the peasants threw a stone towards her, which Aquaria dodged.

'Jeez,' she muttered to herself, 'tough crowd.'

'Siri, start translation,' said Ed, removing the phone from his pocket as he neared Aquaria.

'Starting translation into *Old English*,' the female voice on his phone replied.

'I command you all to step away,' Ed called out, in his best authoritative voice. Immediately, the phone's speaker repeated the phrase in a synthetic version of the archaic language.

Everyone turned to face him.

'This is your final warning.'

'He means it,' Aquaria chipped in, as Ed side-stepped towards her. Again, the phone translated this.

One of the mob called out an angry indecipherable reply, before throwing a second stone towards Aquaria. 'I'm sorry,' Ed's phone replied. 'I didn't catch that. Could you try again?'

'I hope you know what you're doing,' whispered Aquaria to Ed.

Returning his phone to his pocket, he aimed the blunderbuss at the ground between themselves and the mob, then squeezed the trigger. The gun rumbled like thunder.

The mob looked to one another, unsure what to do.

The blunderbuss fired a thick neon blue beam into the earth. Ed looked over to where Zoe was hiding. 'Now,' he screamed.

Zoe sprang into action. She arced the perimeter of the dwellings, as fast as she could. Leaping over a lamb, like some kind of woolly hurdle, she skidded to a halt beside the drying clothes. Without taking a breath, she wrenched three woven gowns. Spotting a large freshly baked loaf of bread sat on a wooden bench, nearby, she swiped it and wrapped it up inside the bundle of gowns.

Checking she hadn't been spotted, she turned back towards the disturbance. Ed was doing some kind of loud chanting. Zoe figured this was to fool the gob-smacked mob into thinking he was some sort of sorcerer, perhaps. She signalled to Aquaria that she had procured the clothing.

Aquaria informed Ed, beckoning Zoe to make her way over to them.

The mob held their positions, frozen in fear as to what this apparent mighty warlock may do to them should they attack.

Taking the same route back, Zoe hurried around the perimeter then rushed over to join the other two.

'We good?' asked Ed, holding steadfast.

'Er… think so?' replied Zoe.

'Jump.' Ed released the trigger on the blunderbuss, then

leapt into the vortex.

Aquaria and Zoe looked at each other, then to an elderly female peasant shrieking in terror at the sight of this apparent warlock vanishing into some kind of hell-pit.

'Let's get out of here,' said Aquaria.

Both Zoe and Aquaria jumped inside the vortex. They swirled around the whirlpool of crackling mirror-like liquid, before being thrown out.

Hurled three metres upwards, they both landed with a thud on top of Ed. 'Ow,' he groaned, 'that smarts.'

Getting to their feet – or in Ed's case, foot– they took in their surroundings. Their pupils adjusted to the dim light. Beside them, Zoe and Aquaria could make out the wall of the larger dwelling where, only moments ago, the rotund man had crashed into the pots. Only now, they had been cleared away.

'It's night-time,' said Aquaria. 'I don't understand?'

Zoe looked at the now familiar setting. 'We're still in the village, aren't we?'

'I threw us forward to midnight,' explained Ed, whispering. 'It was the best plan I could think of in such short notice. Aquaria didn't give me much choice.' His voice grew angry as he turned to the American. 'What the hell were you thinking? You could've completely messed up the future, pulling a stunt like that.'

'Oh, come on, Ed.' Aquaria sniffed. 'I hardly think teaching some medieval jerk a lesson could've done *that* much damage to history.'

Zoe, realising their bickering could alert more unwanted attention, signalled for them to shut up. 'Seeing as it's dark, shouldn't we take this opportunity to get away from here, and go find the castle?' Aquaria hung her head, while Ed nodded like a scorned child.

Moving through the shadows, they quickly found the track that led away from the settlement. Once further enough away, they donned the stolen gowns, ate some of the bread and then checked the map. Confident the way ahead would lead them to Wandwich Castle, they set off.

Trekking along the quiet route, they weighed up the best options for gaining entry into the castle.

'Okay,' said Ed, taking charge. 'Assuming what I recall from history lessons and documentaries is accurate, the castle will most likely be heavily guarded.'

'So how are we going to get in?' Zoe began to feel like this was something they should've given more thought to, in the safety of modern day.

'I'm thinking I should do what I did to get into your place?' Ed saw the look of doubt on Zoe's face. 'Being small, a rabbit has —'

'Its advantages,' said Zoe. 'I know that. It also makes a tasty stew for your average medieval castle resident too, I imagine.'

'It'll be dark, and I'll only need to get through a gate or window in rabbit form. I can change back immediately then work on letting you two inside.'

'It's got my vote,' said Aquaria. 'Just do it quickly. Once we're all in, we'll have to try and pass ourselves off as servants should anyone approach us, though.'

'But we don't speak Old English,' said Zoe. 'Surely we'll get found out?'

Ed took a deep breath. 'Let's just hope it doesn't come to that.'

After walking for a couple of hours, they froze in the middle of the track. In the distance, the sombre silhouette of a castle's towers and battlements jutted up from the stillness of the countryside. Zoe felt a shiver run down her spine. Aquaria rolled her hands into fists. As for Ed, he really needed a wee so ducked off behind a bush for a minute.

Ensuring the coast was clear, they edged along the final stretch of track. Again, they kept themselves close to nearby bushes and trees. To their right, they could hear the sound of the ocean. To their left, the tranquil calm of the countryside.

Deciding to stick as close to the shoreline as possible,

they were soon negotiating rocks. This proved to be good cover for them as they advanced nearer to the castle walls; their grey gowns helping camouflage them as they moved under the moonlight.

'Looks like we may have found your way in,' whispered Zoe, spotting a *postern gate*. This was primarily used as an emergency exit, should the castle's defences become compromised. The narrow, four-foot-high opening had an iron trellis gate blocking entry, impossible for an eleventh-century human to get in, easy for a twenty-first-century rabbit.

'Okay.' Aquaria placed both her hands on Ed's arms, looking him straight in the eyes. 'You got this, Bugs.'

Ed turned, then handed the Chronos Blunderbuss and the journal to Zoe. 'I've reset the co-ordinates, so if anything should go wrong, it'll send you back to the present day.'

Zoe gave him a worried nod. Slinging the time-gun over her shoulder, she then pocketed the journal. 'Be careful.'

'Well, obv's.' Ed smiled, masking his fear. He clambered down behind a tall, wide rock.

Aquaria turned to Zoe. 'I'm sure he'll be fine.' Sensing the anxiety in Zoe's eyes, she added, 'Rabbits are fast runners. Even disabled ones.'

There was a brief flash of light from behind the rock. This time, due to Ed's attire, the rabbit that emerged had grey fur, except for one of its hind feet which was wellie-boot green. It bounded over to where the two were stood. Not really knowing what to do, Zoe bent down and gave the creature a little good-luck pat on its head. 'What?' she said, seeing Aquaria's reaction.

Keeping as stealthy as it could, the rabbit hid from rock to rock until it reached the gate. Checking there was no one standing guard inside, it hopped through the trellis and vanished into the darkness.

Aquaria and Zoe took shelter behind the rock where Ed had transformed, and waited.

After twenty minutes or so they heard someone 'psst' them from inside the postern gate. Peering out from the safety of the rock, Aquaria saw Ed – back in human form – beckoning them over.

'I have a key,' he said, as they arrived. 'There's a couple of soldiers about a hundred yards along a corridor. They're fast asleep, so I managed to nab it from one of them.'

'Let's hope it fits,' whispered Aquaria.

Ed held up the humble iron key and went to pass it through the gate. A violet glow suddenly rippled across the gate, as the key struck something invisible.

'Ouch,' hissed Ed, feeling a sting on his fingers.

'What the hell was that?' said Aquaria.

Ed reached out his other hand to the gate. It passed through without any reaction. 'Weird?' he muttered.

Stepping back and looking up at the stone walls, Zoe recalled the myth about the castle. 'Isn't this place meant to be protected by magic?'

'Shit.' Ed tried again to hand the key through. As soon as it reached the threshold, the same invisible *something* blocked the key from passing through. 'Oh, that's clever,' Ed marvelled. 'Looks like there's some kind of forcefield? Funny how I could gain access through?'

Aquaria looked at Ed's hands, then to her own. 'I'm jus' gonna try something.' She held out her hand and reached into the gate without any problem. Removing it again, she gave a satisfied 'huh.'

'Okay,' said Aquaria, turning to Zoe. 'Now you try.'

Zoe obliged. Her hand caused the same violet ripple as it hit the forcefield.

'I could be wrong,' said Aquaria, 'but I reckon the magic that created this forcefield created mine and Ed's rings.'

'Of course,' replied Ed. 'The rings that give us the ability to shape-shift were created by Leonard. As, I guess, was this forcefield.'

Zoe looked at the key in Ed's hand. 'So, I'm guessing that can only be used by the guard?'

'Most likely,' replied Ed. He looked behind him, checking

no one was around. 'Which means I can't open this gate.'

Aquaria thought for a moment. She could shape-shift and fit between the trellis of the gate. But, being a water-based therianthropist limited her options. 'Okay,' she said. 'I'm going to transform into something small. Zoe, I'll need your help.'

Zoe nodded and followed Aquaria to the cover of the rock where Ed had morphed.

Ed looked behind him, double-checking they'd remain undiscovered. He didn't need to wait long to see what Aquaria would transform into. The flash of light behind the rock was followed by Zoe yelling out, 'That's gross.'

'Oh, that's really quite clever,' muttered Ed, seeing Zoe emerging from the rock holding a grey American eel in her outstretched hands.

The long grey creature slithered around Zoe's arms as she hurried over to the gate. 'Here you go,' she said, trying not to drop it.

'You know, these creatures can survive a good while out of water,' said Ed.

'Spare me the marine biology lesson, Ed.' Zoe winced as she began feeding it through the gate to him.

'Right, sorry,' said Ed, now clutching the entire eel. He placed it down onto the stone floor inside the corridor.

The eel squirmed about, curling itself up. With one flick of its tail, it slapped the tip against its side. The sudden flash of it transforming back into human form temporarily blinded Ed and Zoe. When their eyes had adjusted to the darkness again, Aquaria got up off the floor.

'Urgh,' said Aquaria, spitting slime from her mouth. 'Now I remember why I hated changing into that thing last time.'

'Last time?' smirked Zoe. 'Why would you have to?'

'For one of Lance's tricks,' said Aquaria. 'Had to slide through a small water pipe.'

There was a sudden sound of chatter from within the corridor.

'Shit,' whispered Ed, holding up his hand to shush the

others. 'We need to go hide.'

Zoe panicked. 'What am I supposed to do, just hang around?'

'Good plan,' replied Ed.

'Alone?' said Zoe. 'Outside a medieval castle?'

'You'll be fine. The dangerous stuff is inside.'

Zoe shook her head. 'Oh, joy.'

***

It had felt like hours since they'd separated. In that time, Zoe had taken cover further down the rocks. She managed to find a small, sheltered area and had sat down, occasionally nibbling at the remainder of the bread. Every now and then, she emerged and headed back up to the gate.

Although a fairly mild night, the wind was beginning to pick up. She could smell the fresh sea air wafting across to where she sat. The sound of the waves further below were growing louder. Thoughts of whether Ed and Aquaria were safe, whether they had succeeded in doing what they set out to, if it would ultimately mean Leonard could die, all fuelled Zoe's anxiety as she waited.

Eventually, she couldn't sit there any longer. She decided to distract her mind by having a wander along the side of the castle. Keeping close to the rocks, she could see the moonlight glistening on the sea below. She peered up at the great stone walls of the castle, making sure no one was looking down.

After skirting the edge for a few minutes, she found herself at a corner of the wall. With the blunderbuss slung across her torso, Zoe was careful not to let it make a sound against the wall as she sidled up to the corner. She poked her head around. What she saw made her heartbeat quicken and her anxiety heighten. Stood on a lonely rock about twenty metres out to sea, a tall dark tower cut through the sky. From her vantage point, Zoe could make out a wooden bridge that linked this tower to a walkway protected by sheer walls either side. In turn, this walkway led to stone steps that ascended into the castle. It appeared the only way to gain entry to the tower was via the castle itself.

A shiver ran up her spine. Zoe leant back from the corner, checking behind her. Although no one was around, she knew what she was feeling. Her knack of sensing when something wasn't right, the same feeling that had told her to go check on Tom at Leonard's place, was warning her again.

Peering back around the corner, she spotted a figure. A man, maybe in his late twenties, was making his way onto the bridge towards the tower. Zoe eyed something he was clutching in his hand. 'The book,' she murmured to herself. Realising who the person was, Zoe ducked back behind the corner. 'Leonard.'

Tentatively, she risked another look. Leonard – or in this time period, Leofwine – was now unlocking a wooden gate at the foot of the tower. Zoe watched as he disappeared from view. Giving a sigh of relief, she took a step backwards and immediately felt something hard and pointy press into her back.

Although Zoe didn't recognise the language being used, she knew what the man's voice was saying as he prodded her again. She raised up her hands and slowly turned to face a stocky man adorned in a long chain-mail gown, clutching a wooden spear. Speaking in Old English, the man gestured with his weapon for her to head back towards the postern gate.

Her heart raced, as she did as he wanted. Each step hoping he wouldn't harm her. As they reached the gate, she saw it was now open. The man swung the spear against her leg, ordering her inside. *At least I've gained entry to the castle*, she thought, as the man shepherded her inside.

The low, narrow corridor was dimly lit by candles set into small alcoves on the damp walls. As Zoe walked past them, they hissed like serpents as droplets of water dripped onto the burning fat. When she reached the end of the corridor, another man – slimmer than the other, but dressed the same way – stood guarding what looked like a prison cell. The primitive room had just one small iron-barred window and a single wooden door built into its stone wall – both facing onto the corridor where the guard was stood.

'Oh, great,' said Aquaria, from inside the cell window as she caught sight of Zoe. 'That's three for three.'

The slim guard opened the wooden cell door as the stocky man demanded Zoe enter. As she did so, Zoe noticed the green-footed rabbit being held by its ears in the guard's right hand.

The guard threw the rabbit into a round clay pot on the floor. He plonked a wooden lid down on top of the pot, then reached for the wooden spear that lent against the wall. Shouting something in his ancient language, he seemed to be instructing the stocky man to remove the Chronos Blunderbuss from Zoe.

Inside the cell, Aquaria stood rocking from foot to foot, watching, readying herself. The stocky man went to grab the blunderbuss from Zoe. Being the only ticket out of this century, she was not prepared to simply hand over the time-gun. The two of them tussled as the man tried to grapple the time-gun from her. The slim guard grew impatient. He entered the room and jabbed at Zoe with his spear. As she dodged the jab, she swivelled, lost her balance and toppled backwards, pulling the stocky man with her.

Spotting her chance, Aquaria smacked her hands together with a huge white flash. Zoe gasped at the twelve-metre-long grey whale shark, now swaying its tail across the cell floor and brandishing its jaws towards the terrified men. Backing against the far corner of the room, Zoe realised she'd let the blunderbuss remain on the floor. The stocky man caught sight of her and risked picking it up. As he scrabbled across and placed his hand on the gun, two things happened…

First, not knowing what the gun was and that it had powered up when it hit the hard stone slabs, the man's thumb accidentally squeezed the trigger and fired a beam directly across the cell floor at the terrified guard. A vortex immediately opened, swallowing the screaming guard and sending him hurtling into the twenty-first century.

Second, the stocky man's hand only let go of the blunderbuss when the teeth of the whale shark detached his arm from it. Writhing about in agony, the man screamed out loud as Zoe avoided a jet of blood spraying from the man's shoulder. Darting out of the cell, Zoe headed straight to the clay pot. The shark flicked its head to the side, opened its jaws and flung the removed section of arm back into the man's face, causing him to be knocked unconscious by his own elbow.

The shark snapped its jaws together as hard as it could, causing another flash of light. Zoe pulled the rabbit from the pot, then turned to see Aquaria stood in the cell, wiping blood from her mouth.

'I'll grab the blunderbuss,' cried Aquaria, looking visibly shaken by what she'd done. 'Keep hold of Ed. Let's get the hell out of here.'

The commotion hadn't gone unnoticed. As Zoe and Aquaria ran from the opened postern gate and across the rocks, they could hear the sound of soldiers pouring out of the corridor behind them like angry wasps.

'Fire the gun at the sea,' shouted Zoe. 'It's our only hope.'

Aquaria paused for a second. She looked back towards the castle at the men heading their way. There must have been at least fifteen, all fully suited up and armed with either spears or bows. Turning to the water below the rocks, she took aim and pulled the trigger.

Arrows whistled past Aquaria and Zoe – still clutching Ed in rabbit form – as they scrambled down the rocks to where the vortex had opened up. Stowing the rabbit inside her top, Zoe was the first to leap. As she spun around the lip of the whirlpool, she briefly caught sight of Aquaria back on the rocks yank an arrow from her chest before readying herself to jump.

Chapter 30
Get Back in Time

'Mummy, quick.' The young girl dropped her ice cream and ran to the woman stood next to an ice cream van.

'Just a second, Millie,' tutted the ginger-haired woman. 'Mummy's got to finish paying the man.'

'But there's a shark in the sea. Quick, you'll miss it.' Millie reached to her mother's hand, grabbed it, and started to pull.

'Sorry.' The woman blushed, as the man in the ice cream van handed over her change. 'Six-year-olds, full of imagination.'

'Not a problem, love.' The man held up a choc-ice. 'Don't forget this. Have a good day.'

'Thank you.' Turning from the van, the woman bit into the frozen chocolate and was ready for another of her daughter's vivid tales. 'Go on then, where did you see this shark?'

'It jumped out of a hole in the sea, over there.' Millie pointed beyond the bench where she'd been sitting, to the blue water.

'Oh, right, over where that rock sticks out like a fin?' The woman sighed. 'Honey, I think it was just your mind playing tricks again.'

Millie stamped her foot. 'No, Mummy, I did see it. Ask that girl down there with the trumpet on her back. She must've seen it.'

Her mother looked down the grassy slope, to the rocks beside the sea. There, a woman stood alone shouting and swearing at the waves.

'Millie, we've had a brilliant day looking around the castle, but let's just get back to the car and go home, shall we?' The mother hurried her daughter away, ignoring the screaming from the young woman down at the rocks.

***

'Ed!' screamed Zoe. She knelt upon a rock, scouring the water for any sign of him. A fin rose out of the water, about ten feet away. It moved further out, then submerged once more.

'Find him,' bellowed Zoe.

After nearly ten minutes of searching, Aquaria's hands gripped the rocks by Zoe's feet. 'He's still in rabbit form,' said Zoe, panting as she heaved Aquaria up. 'I don't think rabbits can swim, can they?'

Something had gone wrong during their journey back; the vortex had stretched, then bucked about like a wild hosepipe, shaking them around inside. Aquaria managed to change back into the grey whale shark, enabling her to ride it out. Ed, however, had tumbled out of Zoe's top and was rolled around like a rabbit beanie toy in a washing machine. When they eventually got thrown out, they were catapulted in separate directions.

Together, the two stared out at the waves in silence, expecting to see a grey rabbit rolling in the froth.

'Listen,' said Aquaria.

'What?' As the sound of the waves quietened for a moment, Zoe heard a voice calling out.

'It's coming from behind us,' said Aquaria, standing up and scanning the cliff face to their left.

Zoe focused in to where the cry of help was coming from. 'Over there,' she said, pointing up high. 'It's him.'

'Stay right there, Ed,' shouted Aquaria, as she and Zoe negotiated the moss-like seaweed lining the rocks like a slippery green carpet.

'I don't have much bloody choice,' yelled Ed from his precarious position. He peered down once more at the jagged rocks below him.

'Y'know you could just drop, right?' shouted Aquaria. 'Your healing ability would soon take care of any injury.'

'Yeeeah.' Ed winced. 'Not going to happen.' He felt his

knees tingle at the thought of leaping down onto the razor-like landing.

'There's a way further along there,' said Zoe, pointing to where the cliff lowered. 'We can get to the top, then walk above him.'

After a few minutes, Zoe and Aquaria had made their way along and approached the clifftop above where Ed was clinging on.

'If I hold onto your legs,' said Aquaria to Zoe, 'you should be able to lower yourself over the edge and pull him up.'

'If you're up to it?' said Zoe. 'I saw how you got hit by that arrow before we left.'

Aquaria immediately placed her hand over the small hole on her leather jacket made by the arrow. 'It's fine. Just a flesh wound.'

With Aquaria gripping on tight, Zoe leant over the edge and reached down to Ed. Before long, they had hoisted him up to safety.

'How the hell did you end up there?' asked Aquaria, after catching her breath.

'The vortex.' Ed exhaled. 'It threw me against the cliff. Luckily, being a rabbit, I skidded into a crevice, stopping me from bouncing off the cliff face.'

'What was going on inside the vortex?' asked Zoe, handing the blunderbuss over. She removed the polythene bag and returned that to him also. 'I'm guessing it wasn't supposed to do that?'

Ed powered up the time-gun. He tapped the tiny buttons beside the display with his finger. 'Trans-reality turbulence,' he said with a worried sigh.

'What the hell does that mean?' asked Aquaria.

'If I'm right,' said Ed, looking at the two of them, 'then we monkeyed about with history a little too much.'

'Meaning?' said Aquaria, wafting her hand at him to elaborate.

'Meaning, this is now an altered reality version of the present day.' Ed assessed his surroundings. 'In short, expect a few things to be different.'

'So what're we looking at, exactly?' asked Zoe as they began to walk up the hillside towards the ruin of Rufus Castle.

'Okay. So, we succeeded in making the small alteration to the eleventh-century version of Leonard's book,' said Ed as they climbed up the grassy slope.

'But no one saw us do it,' added Aquaria. 'So that's cool, right?'

Ed nodded. 'But we got caught by that guard on the way out of the castle. I'd factored in the book changing, but not what happened in the cell.' He stopped a moment to catch his breath. 'And, the incident back in that village must've altered history a little too. None of those events were supposed to have happened.'

'So history's been rewritten.' Aquaria rolled her eyes. 'But as long as everyone we know is the same, that shouldn't be too much of a problem, yeah?'

'The way the vortex acted, though,' said Ed, scratching his head. 'I can't help thinking we did something majorly bad... Oh.' He pointed up ahead to the top of the hill. A pair of legs were sticking out of the ground, feet upwards. Instantly, the three of them recognised who they belonged to.

Zoe gasped at the sight. 'That's... the guard from the cell, right?'

'Well, that explains that,' said Ed, matter-of-factly.

'We should probably get away from here quick,' suggested Aquaria.

'Good idea,' replied the other two, pacing off.

It wasn't long before they reached the top of the hillside, and the ruin of what was now Rufus Castle. Originally built for William Rufus, son of William the Conqueror, most of the existing structure had been built later on in the fifteenth century. Deciding they'd had enough of castles for now, they soon found a road and began the long walk south to Pulpit Rock.

***

'I have unanswered questions,' said Zoe, as they neared the car park. 'If the vortex reacted like that because of us changing history, then what will happen if we do it again to save Tom?'

'I'm hoping I've got that part sorted,' said Ed, secretly crossing his fingers. 'We just need to make sure the event of Tom's death remains a fixed moment.'

Aquaria and Zoe looked baffled.

'By that,' he elaborated, 'I mean everyone who experienced Tom's death needs to believe he actually died. Otherwise, things get really ballsed up.'

Zoe considered this. 'Because... if Tom never died, then we wouldn't be here now?'

'Precisely,' replied Ed. 'We would never have needed to mend the Chronos Blunderbuss, never found the map of Wandwich Castle, gone back in time and diddled with the book.'

'Okay, okay,' Aquaria interrupted. 'Basically, what you're saying is we gotta fake Tom's death. Right?'

'Just like Leonard faked his own in the Battle of Hastings,' said Zoe.

Ed nodded. 'I don't want to put a downer on it, but if we bugger this up, we risk creating a time paradox.'

'Which would be bad?' said Zoe.

'We're talking a self-destroying anomaly that would cancel itself, and us, out.'

'So, no biggy then,' said Aquaria.

'One more thing.' Zoe looked at the hole in Aquaria's jacket. 'How's that "flesh wound" of yours healing up?'

Ed looked at the small hole in Aquaria's blue leather jacket. 'What happened?'

'Oh, it was nothing.' Aquaria shrugged. 'A lucky shot.'

Zoe pressed her for an explanation. 'There doesn't seem to be any blood though?'

'Yeah.' Aquaria elaborated on this. 'Ed and I found Leofwine's book in a tower attached to the castle. I did *you-know-what* to it, then we got out before he returned.'

215

'I saw the tower when I was waiting for you guys,' said Zoe. 'Just before that soldier found me. There was something really chilling about that place.'

Ed nodded in agreement. 'Aquaria had to do what she did back then, in order to stop Leonard now.'

Aquaria unzipped her jacket. She pulled her white vest down and looked at the fully healed skin.

Zoe eyes widened. 'You're an immortal.'

'And it means,' Ed smiled, 'phase one of my plan has worked.'

They reached Zoe's car. Taking the keys from where she'd hidden them, she unlocked it.

'Aquaria,' said Ed as they got in to the Mini. 'You're the professional illusionist. You think you can come up with a way to fool our past selves into thinking Tom dies?'

Aquaria smiled. 'Already working on it, sugar.'

Zoe turned the key in the ignition. 'Phase two, here we come.'

Chapter 31
Let's Kill Tom

As Zoe got out of the Mini, behind Cassam's Magic Emporium, Ali and Gail opened the kitchen door. By now, it was mid-afternoon but, having been up all night, Ali and Gail were still wearing their same clothes. They rushed across the tarmac to greet their daughter.

'You're safe,' said Gail, hugging Zoe.

'My brilliant girl.' Ali beamed, enveloping Zoe and Gail with his huge arms.

Ed joined them, followed by Aquaria. 'No hiccups, I take it?' she asked, pointing over to the van in the car park.

'No.' Ali broke up the family hug to report to Aquaria. 'I can't begin to tell you how eerie it's been for Gail and me. Knowing the professor's body is strapped up inside the Zig-Zag cabinet, with his head over there.' He nodded towards his white Ford Transit van.

'The lack of blood. It's just so weird,' said Gail, grimacing. 'Don't get me wrong, I'm glad of it. But, so, so weird.'

'No one's been near the van, since we've been away?' checked Aquaria.

'No,' confirmed Ali. 'Gail's been keeping a watchful eye from the kitchen window.'

'Good,' said Aquaria. 'It's the best way to keep you all safe.'

'Well, for now,' added Ed, 'at least.' He hurried back to Zoe's car and retrieved the Chronos Blunderbuss.

The sight of the bizarre weapon made Gail twitchy. 'What in God's name is that thing?'

'It's okay, Mum.' Zoe gently rubbed her mother's back. 'It's what let us travel back in time.'

'You're not serious.' Gail laughed. 'Zoe, time travel is make-believe. Science fiction nonsense.'

'That shit's the real deal all right, Gail,' added Aquaria. 'We just had a crash course on how bleak the eleventh century is.' She glanced at Ed, who'd began tweaking the time-gun ready for the next trip.

'If you say so.' Gail dismissed the absurdity of it. 'Can I get anyone a drink?'

'No time for that, sorry.' Ed now had the blunderbuss primed and ready. In doing so, he noticed the fusion batteries were getting low on power. 'If we're to save Tom, we need to act now.'

'But, Tom's dea—' Gail was cut short as Aquaria shushed her.

Turning to Ali, Ed asked, 'I don't suppose you have a stop-watch anywhere, do you?'

Ali nodded. 'There's one in my office drawer.'

'Cool,' said Ed. 'I need it for a few hours. Well, seconds, I guess.'

Ali acknowledged him, wasting no time heading back inside to fetch it.

Zoe looked at the area where Tom had fallen; the sunlight bathed the tarmac a warm yellow. There were still traces of ash on the ground. A shiver ran down her spine. 'This *will* work, won't it, Ed?'

'Hope so.' Not making eye contact with her, he pretended to make a final adjustment to the blunderbuss.

Sensing he was holding back on something, Zoe pressed him further. 'Ed?'

'In theory.'

'Worse-case scenario?'

'Zoe, trust me, you honestly don't want to know.' He scanned the car park for a suitable spot to use the blunderbuss. With a quick check of the surrounding buildings, he also made sure no unwanted spectators were watching.

Gail whispered to Aquaria, as they stood watching Ed do his thing, 'You didn't *really* travel back in time, did you?'

'Uh-huh.' Aquaria nodded.

'What was it like?'

'Kinda shitty,' said Aquaria, 'if I'm being honest.'

'What were the people like back then?'

'I was talking about the people.'

Gail saw her husband return. 'Did you find the stopwatch, honey?' she called, deciding to leave Aquaria to it.

''Ere you go.' Holding up a chrome stopwatch on a chain, Ali called Ed over. 'It's got sentimental value. Don't damage it.'

Gail smiled at the sight of the keepsake. 'That's the one we used to time our magic tricks with.'

Ali winked at her. 'Never let us down.' He smiled, recalling some fond memories.

Thanking him, Ed took the stopwatch and pocketed it. 'I promise, you'll have it back within minutes.' With that, he gestured for Aquaria to join him.

'Here we go again,' said Aquaria. 'Let's hope the vortex is more kind to us this time.'

'Good luck,' said Zoe, giving them both a final hug then taking a few steps back. 'We'll wait for you here.'

'If all goes to plan,' said Ed, 'we'll be back here in no time.'

Holding on to Ali's hand, Zoe watched Aquaria and Ed walk over to the far end of the car park and enter the quiet alleyway.

In a matter of seconds, a loud rumbling noise filled the area. The Cassams looked on as a sudden swirl of litter spun from out of the alleyway. It seemed to hang, frozen in the air, before being sucked backwards accompanied by a loud *Snap!*

Zoe rushed over. Seeing the alleyway was vacant, she crossed her fingers.

'What's going on, dear?' called Gail.

'Time travel, Mum. They've gone back to earlier this morning, just before Tom died. Hopefully.'

'Oh, right.' Gail did her best to make sense of what was happening, gave up and replied, 'That's good then.'

***

Three minutes had passed. Zoe, Gail and Ali were still stood there when air boomed out of the alleyway. From their viewpoint, it appeared the entrance began to spin out of shape, distorting into a spiral. Pulling backwards, this bizarre anomaly became a tunnel.

Without warning, Aquaria hurtled out. She was immediately followed by a white rabbit with a furry green foot that somersaulted across the car park, skidding to a halt in front of Gail.

'Aww,' cooed Gail. 'Aren't you a pwetty little thi—' But before she had time to lift the creature up, it batted its front feet together with a flash and transformed back into Ed.

Gail jumped back. 'Sorry,' she uttered, feeling a little awkward. 'I forgot you could do that.'

'Did it work?' Zoe asked Aquaria.

Catching her breath, Aquaria removed the Chronos Blunderbuss from her shoulder, nodded, then pointed towards some metal bins in the car park. 'The stopwatch,' she gasped, 'is it there? Is it underneath?'

From the middle of the car park, Ali had watched in awe. He strode over to the bins, got down on his knees and looked underneath them. 'Incredible,' he said, retrieving his stopwatch. 'How did it end up here?' Turning back to the others, he stood and dangled his beloved timepiece on its chain for the others to see. 'I gotta hand it to you, Aquaria,' he called out, grinning like a Cheshire cat, 'that's a great trick.'

'It's no trick.' Aquaria spotted the gap in his smile where his silver tooth once sat. 'I've heard of better.'

Taking the stopwatch from Ali, Aquaria checked the time. 'It worked. Look.'

'It says nine hours, twenty-seven minutes,' said Ali. 'I don't understand? It was reset to zero?'

'It's how long ago Ed placed it there,' said Zoe, joining them. 'Right?'

'Yup,' replied Ed.

Ali scratched his head. 'So you really did just go back in

time?'

'Uh-huh,' confirmed Aquaria. She seemed to be counting her steps from the bins to the middle of the car park. 'The spot that Tom died is fourteen paces away, Ed.'

'Well, I have absolutely no idea what's going on,' remarked Gail. 'Can someone please enlighten me?'

Zoe explained. 'Ed's plan was to start the stopwatch at the exact moment Tom had been killed, then stow it somewhere they could find it. Returning back to now, they can retrieve the stopwatch, giving them an accurate time in which to set the blunderbuss. The time-gun thingy, Mum.'

'Okay,' said Gail, really trying to grasp the concept of time travel. 'So, how is that going to save his life?'

'Keep watching, you'll be amazed,' said Zoe, as though hosting her own magic show. She turned to Ali. 'Hey, Dad. You'll love the next part.'

'We need to make a small fire,' said Aquaria. She looked to Ali and Gail. 'Can you find us some newspaper, please? Oh, and a metal trash can or pail.' Gail went off to get the items.

'Don't forget something to light them with, thanks,' added Ed, as he inspected the blunderbuss.

Gail paused before entering the kitchen, 'Anything else, while I'm at it?'

'Nah, we're good.' Aquaria smiled. 'Thanks, Gail.'

Now used to Ed and Aquaria's bizarre double act, Gail decided to just get what they needed.

Once she had returned with the items, Gail handed them to Aquaria, then moved back to Ali and Zoe to see how everything was going to unfold. Aquaria placed the metal bucket down on the tarmac close to where Tom had previously turned to ash. She scrunched up pages from the newspaper and set about packing them inside. Next, she took a match, struck it against the matchbox and lit the paper. When the contents had completely burnt out, Aquaria checked the ash inside. 'Smoke and mirrors,' she whispered to herself, feeling the fine grey powder in her hand. 'I think we're all set, Ed.'

'Cool,' said Ed, powering up the blunderbuss one last time.

Aquaria handed him the stopwatch so he could enter the correct info into the time-gun. When he was ready, he told everyone to stand back. 'This should happen fairly quickly.' He aimed the blunderbuss towards the tarmac. 'There's a good chance Tom's in for a bumpy ride.'

The blunderbuss fired into life as Ed squeezed the trigger. The thick neon beam tore into the car park, churning a hole like sand in an hourglass.

Both Gail and Ali stood hypnotised by the spectacle in front of them. Zoe looked on, keeping her fingers crossed, as Ed steadied himself against the force of the blast. Stepping close to the edge of the vortex, Aquaria stood gripping the bucket tightly in both hands.

When he was sure the vortex was at full size, Ed released the trigger on the Chronos Blunderbuss. 'Come on, Tom,' he called out.

The vortex crackled with pure incandescent light. The whirlpool of silver liquid that had only moments ago been a section of car park, pulsed and vibrated like a bass speaker being overdriven to the point of exploding.

With a flash, Tom's body was launched out high above everyone's heads.

Tracking his trajectory, Ali cried out, 'He's gonna land on the rooftop.'

Everyone's heads moved in sync, as they watched the arcing body. Tom hit the old roof of the Cassam's building with a thud, cracking tiles on impact. Together, the four onlookers winced as his body rolled down and impacted onto the hard tarmac in front of the kitchen door.

Rushing to him, Zoe knelt down. 'Tom!' She rolled him over, gasping at the sight of his blood-splattered face. 'Tom, say something. Anything.'

'Urrgh,' groaned Tom. The bridge of his nose began to glow as the healing power started to snap the nasal bone back into position, along with a couple of ribs. Forcing a single eyelid open, he saw Zoe's smile. 'You're okay,' he croaked. 'I... I thought Leonard...' His eyelid fell shut again. 'I thought he was going to kill you.'

'I'm fine.' Zoe wiped a tear from her cheek. 'You had us worried for a while.'

Back over at the vortex, Aquaria was tipping the remaining ash from the bucket into the whirling hole. 'It's closing up,' she said, looking at Ed. Both of them waited until the vortex had fully shut before stepping away.

Turning to Ali and Gail, Ed couldn't help himself. He placed the blunderbuss down, took a bow, then flung his arms out. 'Tah-dah.'

Chapter 32
The Hidden Page

Tom sat on a kitchen chair, hugging his cup of coffee. After they'd brought him inside, he'd listened to the others recount the events that led to this moment. Despite being a little in shock, he was trying his best to take in all that had happened. All these people, who he'd recently met, had risked so much to help him.

Zoe was stood leaning against the sink. She stared at him, half in disbelief. The plan had actually worked. And, as far as she could tell, no one's memory of Tom's 'death' earlier had altered. Aquaria and Ed had pulled off one hell of an illusion, thought Zoe.

'So, let me get this straight,' said Tom. He pointed to the Chronos Blunderbuss on the kitchen worktop next to where Ed was standing. 'That's the actual thing that threw me ten years into the future, where I ended up in the Penmoor?'

'Yep,' replied Ed. 'You mentioned some of this before. When we were in Zoe's car, fleeing Leonard's workshop. Remember?'

'To be honest, mate, it was still a bit hazy. But, it's all come back to me now.' Tom rubbed his temple. 'Everything. I remember it all.' He took a moment to go over what had happened that night, ten years ago. 'I remember how Leonard had come visiting my dorm room at university and had revealed how the book gave both him and me the power to self-heal, before he tried to erase my name from it by gunpoint. I panicked, escaped and fled. I drove as far away as I could, not knowing what to do.

'Deciding the best action was to hide the book, I placed it inside an old biscuit tin I found in the boot of my car, and buried it in the middle of nowhere. But, when I returned to where I'd hidden my car, somehow Leonard had been able to track me down. I took the blunderbuss from Leonard's Land Rover. I thought it was a weapon. I accidentally activated it, after Leonard tried zapping me with that wand of his. That's when I fell into that time-tunnel—'

'Vortex,' corrected Ed, getting a stern look from Zoe.

'Sorry. That *vortex*. Next thing I remember is waking up at the foot of the cliff in the present day.'

'Which is when you first met me,' added Ed. 'Well, in rabbit form.'

Tom glanced at the Chronos Blunderbuss again. 'And you've just used it to go back in time 900 years, to when Leonard created the book of Eternus? That's insane.'

'Well, 955 years, to be precise,' said Ed. He brought the book over and joined Tom at the table. 'And, also what we just used to grab you from this morning's near-death experience.' Ed gave Tom a brief salute. 'You're welcome, by the way.'

Aquaria entered the kitchen from the car park, having excused herself so she could check something on her motorbike. 'You feeling okay, kid?' she asked, with a relieved expression.

'Think so,' replied Tom. 'So, if we have a way to travel through time, could we not just use it to go back and stop Leonard from—'

They all cut Tom off in unison. 'No.'

Shifting a little in his chair, Tom decided to turn his attention to the book. 'You said Leonard smeared blood over my signature earlier, when we were trying to save Zoe?' He looked around at them. 'So how can I still be alive?'

'That part was my idea,' said Aquaria. She came over to the table and opened the book to where Tom's signature should be. 'Take a look.'

'I don't understand,' said Tom. 'It's blank?'

Aquaria carefully peeled a sheet of greaseproof paper from the page. 'What about now?'

Tom's eyed widened. 'You covered it up. When?'

'When Ed and I travelled back earlier, before we hid the stopwatch I sneaked into the kitchen.' Aquaria gestured to the kitchen table. 'Since I knew the book had been left on here when the earlier versions of us were all in the shopfront, sorting out the guillotine, I just had enough time to tack the paper inside. No one was any the wiser.'

'Amazing,' said Tom, smiling at her.

She flipped the book to the first page. 'That's not the only part of the book we messed with.'

Tom looked at the first page. Leofwine's signature was top of the list. As it had always been. 'I don't understand?'

'What you're seeing there,' said Aquaria, 'isn't the real first page. Well, not since we altered history at least.' She unzipped the top pocket of her leather jacket. Removing a folded piece of thin paper, she handed it to Tom. 'Here's the actual first page of Leofwine's book. Go ahead, open it out.'

Tom did so. To his amazement he saw what looked to him like an autograph. 'Is that… yours?'

Aquaria gave him a wink. 'I'm the bona fide Prime Eternee.'

'And I reckon,' said Ed, interrupting, 'that explains why, originally, she had a knack for healing quicker than normal.'

Tom recalled the discussion he and Ed had had regarding Aquaria's youthful looks. 'What, you're saying Aquaria has *always* had the same ability as me?'

'Kind of,' said Ed.

'It's tricky to explain,' said Aquaria, hijacking the conversation. 'Ed reckons it's because I signed the book as an adult, but back in history way before I was born. Somehow, I was born with a sort of skewed version of the Eternus power.'

'But now she's back in the present,' said Ed, jumping in to finish the explanation, 'she's got the full whack of it. It's how she can see all the signatures in the book now, and knew which page to stick the greaseproof paper onto.'

'Yeah,' Tom winced, rubbing his temples with his fingertips, 'you've lost me there.'

'Thank God I'm not the only one,' said Gail, as she and Ali entered the kitchen from the shop.

Ed rolled his eyes at Aquaria, before stowing the loose page back into the book.

'Basically,' exclaimed Zoe, 'all you need to know, Tom, is that you, Aquaria and Ed all have the same ability as Leonard now.' She looked at Aquaria, adding 'Oh, and Lance Goldstorm too.'

'Of course.' Aquaria glanced out the window at the hatbox strapped to the back of her Harley-Davidson.

'I can't believe you all risked so much, just to save me?' He turned to Zoe. 'I don't know what to say?'

'You don't need to say anything, Tom.' Zoe's face beamed. 'I'm glad you're back. We all are.'

'Right,' said Ali, sucking his teeth. 'What are we going to do about you-know-who?'

'Well,' said Zoe, 'we're certainly not going through with Aquaria's original plan.' She looked to the American. 'No offence, but we're just not.'

Aquaria shrugged. 'If you think you can reason with Leonard, by all means go ahead. Personally, I'm still unconvinced.'

'I have to agree with Zoe,' said Tom. 'All Leonard wants is to be allowed to die. If we can give him that, then hopefully all this will be over. Right?'

'I'm with Aquaria.' Ali moved over to his daughter. He placed his hand on her back. 'Sorry, Zoe. But having seen what he's capable of, I think it's too risky to awaken him.'

'All of us have been affected by the prof's wrath,' added Ed, looking down at the wellington boot where his foot should be. 'However, Aquaria's now got the power to drop Leonard in an instant.' He looked around the room to everyone. 'Let's bring him back and give him the choice: die or live forever as a head in the bottom of the ocean. What do we think?'

After deciding on the more humane of the two options, it was agreed Leonard's head was to be brought back inside the building. But first, they would need to place Leonard's decapitated body back onto the chair in the shop.

'I'll help Aquaria,' Ali offered, feeling unsettled by the task.

'But, I want Zoe and Gail safe.' He turned to them both. 'You can stay upstairs.'

Zoe cast her father a stubborn look. 'I don't think so—'

Straightening his back, Ali mirrored his daughter's stance. 'I have spoken.'

'Please, Zoe,' insisted Tom, 'you've already risked so much.'

Zoe sighed, then reluctantly agreed. 'I suppose I'll be keeping Mum safe.'

'I'll stay here, keep an eye on the van,' said Ed, as Ali and Aquaria left the kitchen.

Walking over to the front door of the shop, Ali pulled down the roller blind, hiding what was about to take place from any passers-by. The Zig-Zag cabinet had been placed vertically across the shop floor. With its garish paint job, it resembled an Egyptian sarcophagus.

Both Ali and Aquaria approached, knelt and carefully unclipped the brass clasps around the edges of the small doors on the front of the magician's prop. Removing a handkerchief from his jacket, Ali mopped the sweat off his bald head before cautiously undoing the last clasp. Standing, they took a quick step backwards and waited a few seconds. Just in case.

The box remained silent. Ali reassured himself, *It's just a headless body, it's perfectly safe.* He looked over at Aquaria, who was staring at the cabinet with a steeled expression, and waited.

She took a deep breath. 'Ready?'

Ali nodded. 'Ready.' Feeling his heart pound against his chest, he took another cautious step back.

Aquaria returned to the cabinet and opened the topmost door, decorated with the image of a woman's head. She wasn't surprised to see this section empty; it was a headless body inside, after all. She opened the middle door depicting a woman's torso.

'Shit,' she said, backing off towards Ali. 'It's empty.'

Ali spun around in a panic, his eyes flicking to every inch of the shop. Hearing the remaining door fling open on the Zig-Zag cabinet, he turned back as a headless black rooster launched itself directly at his face. 'Wah di *hell*,' he blurted in his native Patois. Ducking down, just in time, Ali felt the bird's toes scrap over his head. It flew up into the nearest shelves behind him, sending boxes of magic sets tumbling to the floor.

Before Aquaria could stop it, the rooster's body had flown up onto the highest shelf. 'Get down here,' she cried, before remembering it couldn't actually hear her. 'Damn.'

Hearing the commotion, Tom and Ed entered the shop.

'Look out,' gasped Ed, as Ali thwarted another attack by the headless winged assailant. Tripping backwards, Ali fell into the glass display cabinet in the centre of the shop, sending it crashing to the floor.

Rushing over to help Ali up, Ed shouted to Aquaria, 'Get Leonard's head from the van. Now.'

Aquaria sprinted out the back.

Tom grabbed a velvet cloth from by the window, tried to throw it over the flapping body and missed. The bird changed direction and came right at him. Dodging to his left, Tom brought his right elbow down hard onto the back of the creature, slamming it to the floor. Seizing the opportunity, Ali booted it across the room like a rugby ball, causing it to land back inside the Zig-Zag cabinet. 'Close it,' he boomed.

Both Ed and Tom jumped at the cabinet and slammed the doors shut.

'Jesus wept,' heaved Ed.

***

Aquaria had opened the back of Ali's van. She stared at a square wooden chest containing the head of Leonard. Taking a slow intake of breath, she opened the lid. Inside, the head of a rooster lay.

'Whatever made you think this was a good transformation?' Aquaria burst into laughter. 'You know, you're actually quite pathetic.'

With its head resting on one side, the rooster eyed her

with piercing hatefulness at the remark. Unable to move, it blinked as Aquaria reached into the chest and picked it up between her thumb and forefinger. The beak of the rooster snapped open and shut, trying to bite her.

'I know what you're thinking,' continued Aquaria, bringing the head up to her face. 'You think you can't be killed. You're just stalling for time until the opportunity comes to steal the Eternus, yes?'

The rooster blinked.

'I imagine you've already planned when you'll change back into human form, right?' Aquaria squeezed the rooster's head, the pressure on the bird's skull making its tiny tongue shake. 'I wanted to bury you alive for all eternity,' she hissed. 'I was going to make you suffer. Make you feel how I have, ever since the night you mutilated Lance.' She eased the grip on the rooster's head. 'But then I met those guys and they showed me an alternative solution.'

Aquaria carried the head over to her motorbike. She eased the lid off the hatbox. Blinking at the contents, the rooster began crowing loudly. Aquaria quickly slid the lid back onto the hatbox, checking behind her in case anyone had heard the noise.

'Now that I have your attention, I got some news for you.' Realising the others would be waiting inside, she whispered, 'I'll make this brief. We fixed your time-gun, went back to the eleventh century and found a way to kill you. So now you can piss off to the afterlife.'

The rooster blinked.

'Oh, you don't believe me?' Aquaria grinned, almost savouring each word. 'You will, when I show you what I've done with your god-damned book.'

Chapter 33
Ashes to Ashes

Aquaria entered the kitchen, clutching the rooster's head in her hand. Spotting a small kitchen knife on the sink, she picked it up with her other hand, then slid it into her jacket pocket. Next, she grabbed the book from off the kitchen table and headed into the shop.

'Keep back,' she ordered, entering the room. Ushering everyone towards the kitchen door, she placed the book on the shop counter then walked across the wooden floor. Broken glass from the fallen display cabinet crunched under her leather boots as she approached the chair, previously used to tie up Leonard. As the others looked on, she dragged it over to the Zig-Zag cabinet.

'Aquaria? What are you doing?' Ed watched, as she opened one of the doors of the cabinet, threw the rooster's head inside, then returned to the counter to retrieve the book.

'Don't worry, Ed. I know what I'm doing.' Aquaria stood in front of the chair. She held the book open in one hand, the loose page reinserted. With her other hand, she removed the knife from her jacket and held her thumb poised on the tip of the blade. 'His blood's harmless now, but mine...'

There came a flash from inside the cabinet.

'Come out, Professor,' commanded Aquaria, 'and take a seat.'

Tom, Ed and Ali all stared as Leonard's hand curled over the side of the Zig-Zag cabinet, like Dracula emerging from a coffin. Aquaria didn't blink once as she held her stance, ready to act if needed.

Leonard lifted himself up. His first focus was on what Aquaria was holding. He gave her the sort of smile a chess player might give, after realising their opponent just moved a piece across the board to checkmate. Silently, he stepped out of the Zig-Zag cabinet, straightened the knot of his black tie, and lowered himself down in the chair.

The old sorcerer's eyes widened as he saw the new signature on the inserted page in the book, in Aquaria's hand. Looking over to the others, stood by the door to the kitchen, he grinned. 'I got to hand it to you, Ed. I didn't think you'd ever get the blunderbuss working again.' He gave his lodger a slow clap. 'Bravo.'

'Oh,' replied Ed. 'I'd known for a while how to fix it. I just made sure to keep my thoughts to myself, especially when around you.'

'Touché.'

'Enough,' said Aquaria. 'You now see my signature is the first. I'm *Prime Eternee*.' Her voice seemed to dominate the room more with every sentence. 'I hold the power to kill you.'

Leonard's brash facade began to wane as he stared into her eyes. 'As you wish, my dear.'

Tom looked at the old professor. His mind replayed what had happened over the last few days. How Leonard had befriended him, betrayed and then tortured him. And yet, sat there looking defeated under Aquaria's ascendency, Tom couldn't help feeling sorry for the man. 'This is your chance for redemption, Leonard,' he said, stepping forward. 'To put things right. You don't have to kill any more. You don't even have to die. Your abilities could help so many.' Tom pointed to Ed, then Aquaria. 'We all could, right?'

'Get back, Tom,' snapped Aquaria. 'I got this.'

Leonard tipped his head to one side and sniggered. 'You do realise what's happening to you. Don't you, Aquaria?'

'Just shut up.' Aquaria became more agitated, her thumb quivered on the blade. 'You do what I tell you now.'

Leonard held up a hand, then pointed to the book in her hand. 'It feeds off your darkest emotions, you know?'

'I said SHUT UP.' A drop of blood ran down the blade, splashing onto the corner of the book. 'I am the first. I AM FOREVER.'

'Aquaria, please.' Tom rested his hand on her shoulder, trying to diffuse her growing anger. 'Let him speak.' She shrugged him off.

Zoe and Gail, hearing the commotion, now arrived at the doorway.

'Ed?' whispered Zoe 'What's happening?'

'I think,' replied Ed, 'we may have given unlimited bullets to a machine gun.'

Ali kept his family from getting closer as the tension in the room swelled.

'Tell me where Lance's body is,' barked Aquaria, 'then I can end you. After all, that's what you've always wanted, isn't it?'

'Yes,' replied Leonard. 'But please, you must hear me out.'

Another droplet of blood appeared on Aquaria's thumb. She held it above Leonard's signature. 'You're running out of time, old man. WHERE is Lance's body?'

'Move your thumb away first.'

'Aquaria, please,' said Tom. 'If you don't, you'll kill him and never find out.'

Hesitating for a few seconds, Aquaria submitted to the request. She flicked the blood from her thumb onto the floor. 'Talk fast, Sorcerer.'

There was a sigh from the doorway, as Zoe and Ed could breathe again.

'Things just happen, don't they?' Leonard's shoulders dropped, his eyes falling on the book, then back to Aquaria. 'Revenge, bitterness, anger? These things can consume us all, given enough time.'

Aquaria rocked on her heels, trying not to let the words break her focus.

Leonard looked at his open hands. He let out a slow breath as he studied the long, deep creases on his palms. 'I regret what I have become. What the Eternus has turned me into.'

'A murderer?' hissed Aquaria.

'Sure, I can take that.' Leonard looked at Tom, then Ed. 'I am sorry for everything, you know? Only now, as my story comes to an end, can I see what's truly been written. The Eternus craves its own pages to be filled, it thrives off the darkness within us. Don't you see? And, in giving those who sign it eternal life, it can reap so much in return.' Leonard turned to Aquaria, his expression pleading for her to listen. 'With you being the first to sign it, my dear, I fear the Eternus will consume its greatest source.'

'It won't,' said Aquaria. 'Once Lance is returned, I'll be happy.'

Leonard gave her a half-smile. 'Perhaps.'

'Can the Eternus not be undone, somehow?' said Zoe, stepping next to Aquaria. 'The magic be removed, I mean?'

'I'm afraid there is nothing in this world,' replied Leonard, 'powerful enough to do that.'

Aquaria stared deep into the old man's eyes, then down onto his signature. It was time. 'Lance's body,' she said. 'Tell me what you've done with it.'

Leonard shut his eyes tight. 'Let me show you.'

Aquaria pressed her thumb on the knife. She hovered it once more over the page. 'Quit stalling, Leonard.'

Zoe felt a sudden wave consume her body as though she was no longer in control, her thoughts like someone else's. Her left hand swung down hard onto Aquaria's thumb causing the blade to slice the tip open. 'No,' cried Aquaria, dropping the book to the floor.

Tom grabbed Zoe back as Aquaria turned to punch her. Blinking, Zoe appeared stunned as to what had just happened.

'What have you done?' screamed Aquaria.

'I-I don't understand?' stuttered Zoe. 'I didn't do anything?'

Ali took hold of her. 'It's all right, child.' He stood between his daughter and Aquaria. 'I got you.'

Aquaria looked down at the blood-splattered book on the floor. Slowly, she turned to face Leonard, 'You controlled her mi —'

But instead of the professor, there sat a motionless grey

statue-like figure. The room fell silent.

Ed approached the book and picked it up. The blood from Aquaria's wound sizzled over Leonard's signature as it erased it from the vellum page. At the same time, Gail rushed towards Zoe and held on to her hand. Everyone stood stock-still at the sight of the ashen corpse of Leonard.

'He's crumbling away,' gasped Gail. 'Please tell me this isn't a trick?'

Leonard's nose crumbled into dust, followed by his ears then his entire face. Gail, Zoe and Tom all looked away from the vulgar sight. Ali, Ed and Aquaria, however, continued staring as Leonard's arms disintegrated to dust on the floor. In one sudden avalanche, the rest of his remains fell into a pile of ash onto the floor, sending a fine cloud into the air.

'Urrgh,' spat Ed. 'I think I just swallowed a bit.'

Aquaria snatched the book from Ed, then fell to her knees. 'Bastard.' She thumped her fist on the open pages. Her eyes welled with anger. 'I should've known not to trust the old fool.' Turning to Ali, she cried out. 'What am I going to tell him now?'

Ali, confused by this outburst, simply replied, 'Sorry?'

'Lance, you big oaf.' Rocking, Aquaria hit her head with the palm of her hand. 'I swore I would find his body.'

'Aquaria,' said Gail, as she came over and knelt to hug her, 'I think you're in shock. Lance is gone, my dear.'

Aquaria pushed her back. 'No. He's waiting outside.'

'Huh?' Gail looked at Ali for help. In return, Ali just shrugged.

'The hatbox,' said Zoe. She recalled how Aquaria had looked at it through the kitchen window, when his name was mentioned earlier. 'He's in there, isn't he?'

Aquaria nodded and stood back up.

'What... alive?' blurted Gail.

'Of course alive,' snapped Aquaria. 'He's immortal.'

'All right,' snorted Gail, standing up and moving away. 'No need to have a go at me.'

Tom shushed them. He pointed to the pile of ash. 'Erm... I

think something's happening.'

As everyone watched, smoke started rising from the centre of the pile on the floor. The ash began to glow, like embers.

'Should I get the fire extinguisher ready?' said Gail, trying to be helpful.

'Wait,' said Ali. 'Something's growing in the middle. Aquaria, protect the book, just in case.' She gripped it tight, stepping back from the ash.

In the centre of the burning embers, a single purple flame ignited. Below the flame, something white and oval emerged.

'What *is* that?' said Zoe. 'Looks like some kind of egg?'

'Whatever it is,' exclaimed Ed, as the purple flame blew out, 'it's breaking open.' He rushed off and returned with the gold wand. Pointing it at the egg, he made the tip of the wand glow pink.

'Stay back everyone,' said Ali. The embers died away with a final wisp of smoke. Bracing themselves, everyone waited.

A beak suddenly pecked out of the side of the egg.

'Is that a bird?' asked Gail.

'Well, of course it's a bird, Mum,' replied Zoe.

'Well, it could've been a snake,' mumbled Gail, 'or, I dunno, a lizard?'

'With a beak?'

'Oh… bollocks,' said Ed as the side of the egg fell open, revealing a fiery orange and red wing. 'That's no ordinary bird.'

'But, it's not possible,' said Aquaria, astounded by the bright crimson head poking out from the broken shell. The bird blinked its glimmering emerald eyes at her, tilted its head, then breathed a small plume of fire from its beak. 'It's a—'

'Phoenix,' gasped Ed.

'How?' Aquaria looked at him. 'Not only is that a creature of two elements, but one is *fire*.'

'It's trying to fly,' said Tom, as the phoenix clawed its way across the remains of the eggshell and stretched out its fiery wings. 'What do we do?'

'I'm guessing the book's useless now, right?' said Ali. He

pointed to the wand in Ed's hand. 'I hope you know how to use that thing?'

'To be honest,' whispered Ed, 'it's more for show.'

'Oh, great,' tutted Ali.

In just over a minute, the phoenix had tripled in size to that of an eagle. It shook flames from its wings, flapped and rose up onto the back of the chair. There it perched, flicking its head at everyone.

Tom looked at Aquaria who seemed transfixed by the fiery creature's eyes. 'You okay?' he asked her. Aquaria remained still, her eyelids slowly opening and closing.

'Aquaria?' Tom waved his hand in front of her face to no reaction. 'Guys, I think she's hypnotised?'

'Impossible,' said Ed. Striding over, he repeated what Tom had done. 'Shit,' he exclaimed, 'she's hypnotised.'

The bird gave off a caw unlike any they'd ever heard. The sound had a strange metallic resonance to it, almost like someone twanging an electric guitar.

Again, it cawed.

'Could we not just open the door,' suggested Gail. 'You know, shoo it out maybe?'

'Actually, Mum, that's not a bad idea.' Zoe backed slowly away out of the room and into the kitchen. She headed to the rear door and opened it. Returning, she pointed to the exit. 'You can go. We can't stop you.'

The phoenix cawed.

'I understand,' muttered Aquaria. Her voice sounded slow and hoarse, like it was being dragged over a gravestone. 'The A-hole will open.'

Everyone stopped and looked at her.

Ed, of course, couldn't resist a smirk.

'The way is clear,' said Aquaria. 'The A-hole will open.' With that, she shook her head then dropped to the floor like a rag doll.

'Aquaria.' Zoe rushed over, rolling her onto her side. 'She's breathing.'

Tom joined her. 'White as a sheet, though,' he said to Zoe.

Zoe lifted up Aquaria's legs and instructed Tom to place them on his lap. 'I think she's just fainted.'

The phoenix cawed one last time. Beating its wings down hard and sending a cloud of ash curling across the room, it flew past everyone, straight out of the shop, through the kitchen and up out into the sky – leaving behind a trail of smoke where it soared.

***

'She's coming round,' said Zoe. 'Aquaria, you okay?'

Aquaria blinked and looked up at the cream-coloured ceiling of the shop. 'The phoenix,' she said, abruptly, 'is it here?'

'No,' said Tom, smiling. 'Hey, I'm the one that's supposed to pass out. Not you.'

Aquaria ignored him and got up. 'I need to go after it.'

'Erm... no.' Zoe looked at her, then to the others for backup.

'She's right,' said Ali, stood by the shop counter with Gail. 'Leonard's gone. But, so has his signature. Surely that means we're safe?'

'You don't understand,' said Aquaria, looking visibly shaken. 'That phoenix, it showed me the way.'

'It seemed to be hypnotising you,' said Ed. 'What happened?'

'Somehow it projected a series of images in my brain.' She smiled. 'It showed me the ancient stone up on the moor. Only it was a doorway, open to another world. The phoenix was waiting for me to enter.'

'Aquaria,' said Zoe, 'what if it's some kind of trap?'

Aquaria rushed outside before anyone could stop her.

As everyone made their way across the car park, they could see Aquaria had already removed the lid off the hatbox, on the motorbike. She appeared to be talking to it as they all approached her.

'Aquaria?' said Ed. 'You going to introduce us?'

Aquaria tilted the hatbox so they could see inside.

Ali's mouth dropped. 'Well, paint my arse blue and call me —'

'Alister Cambell,' said the head of Lance Goldstorm, in his Mid-South American accent. 'How fantastic to see you again, buddy.'

Everyone stared in awe. The blond-haired, deep tanned, bodiless head beamed a highly whitened smile at them from the comfort of the red-velvet lined box.

'Cambell?' muttered Ed, turning to Zoe.

'It's Dad's real surname,' replied Zoe. 'Before he jazzed it up for show business.'

'I have sooo many questions right now,' said Ed, staring back at the head in the box.

'Abigail, how the hell are you?' Lance gave Gail a well perfected wink. 'And, as for everyone else, it's an absolute pleasure to make your acquaintance. I'm sure I don't require an introduction.' Even his chuckle sounded perfectly rehearsed.

'Leonard's no longer Prime Eternee,' said Aquaria. She briefed Lance on what had happened, how he died but his spirit had returned as a phoenix.

'Damn, Sugar-pop,' said Lance, surprised by the news. 'That guy just doesn't like leaving a stage, huh? How're you holding up?'

'I've had better days.'

'Erm… guys?' Ed interrupted the tête-à-tête. 'I hate to break up this lovely moment between a woman and her lover's decapitated head, however…' he flung his arms up, 'what the hell is going on?'

'Sorry,' said Aquaria, stroking Lance's hair, much to Ed's unease. 'Now you see why I have to get Lance's body back to him.'

'I thought you said Leonard was the only one whose head remained conscious after being cut off?' said Tom.

Ed nodded in agreement. 'That's what I was always told too.'

'To be honest,' said Aquaria, 'that's not strictly true. But, as far as I'm aware, only Lance and Leonard are able to.'

'I gotta be honest, girl.' Lance looked up at Aquaria. 'I reckon ol' Lenny threw my body into whatever lies inside that stone. Bet that's what you're thinkin' too, right?'

'I reckon so,' said Aquaria.

'You think that's where he went?' asked Zoe. 'I mean, where the phoenix went?'

'Only one way to find out,' said Lance. 'Guys, it's been brief. If I had arms, I'd give y'all hugs, high fives, etcetera.' He gave them all a wink instead. 'Sugar-pop, shall we?'

Aquaria replaced the lid on the hatbox, then strapped it down.

Watching, as Aquaria mounted the bike, Tom asked Ed, 'Do you honestly believe the A-hole is a gateway to some other, erm...'

'Dimension?' replied Ed.

'Right. Some other dimension.'

'Hey,' said Aquaria. She picked up her helmet, pulled it down onto her head, then tipped back the visor. 'If what I saw was right, and there's a way through, I gotta try.'

She placed a key into the Harley's ignition and started it up. The others took it in turns to say their farewells. Ed gave her a high five. 'You coming back?'

'Hope so,' she said. 'In the meantime, keep training. If I do return, I want you up to at least a level three therianthropist.'

'We'll see.' Ed stepped back from the motorbike. 'Have a safe journey. And keep a cool head, yeah?'

Aquaria paused for a second, as though composing herself, then replied, 'I won't become like Leonard, y'know. I give you my word.'

Everyone watched as the Harley-Davidson growled away off the car park.

'Right,' said Gail, clapping her hands together and rubbing them. 'Who would like—'

'Not more tea, Mum.' Zoe tutted.

'Actually,' said Gail, 'I was going to say, who would like to go to the pub?'

Zoe smiled, then looked at Ed. 'We might get there in time for poker. Ready to get thrashed again?'

'Ho ho,' chuckled Ed. 'Aren't we the funny one.'

As the Cassams walked back towards their kitchen door, Ed stopped and turned to see Tom stood alone. 'You coming, mate?'

'I guess.'

'What's up?' Ed saw the look in Tom's eyes. 'I'm pretty sure Leonard's not going to return. No matter what that phoenix was, his spirit or something else, I reckon he's found peace.'

'I guess.' Tom scuffed the sole of his shoe on the tarmac. 'You know, everyone's been so kind to me. But, maybe I should be moving on. Find somewhere to live?'

Ed stood next to him. He grabbed Tom's shoulder, then pointed to the Cassams. 'Dude, we helped you out because it was the right thing to do. But, when we were off on our little mission, it became obvious just how much you mean to Zoe.'

Tom looked over to the kitchen window. Inside, Ali and Gail were busy while Zoe was stood looking out at him. She smiled and beckoned Tom and Ed to hurry up.

'There's people here who care about you. I totally understand you wanting to go find yourself, to see if there's family out there waiting for you. But for now, stop being a knobhead and let's go have some fun.'

Ed shoved Tom forward. 'And as for a place to stay,' he added, as they crossed the car park, 'we've literally got Leonard's place to ourselves. I'm thinking biiiig party.'

Epilogue

'I'm sorry, Marty,' the exhausted-looking man told his four-year-old son as they arrived at Cassam's Magic Emporium.. 'The sign on the door says it's reopening next week.'

'But Daddy, I want a magic set,' demanded the neatly dressed child. 'You promised.' He stomped his feet in protest.

'I know, but there's not much I can do about it. If the shop's closed, it's closed.' The man ruffled the boy's short brown hair, much to the child's annoyance, then said, 'Maybe if you're good, Santa will get you one for Christmas this year.'

'But—'

'Who would like some ice cream?'

Marty, in that instant, couldn't care less about a magic set. 'Me, me, me,' he revelled. 'I want raspberry ripple.'

'Of course.' His father smiled, looking relieved.

They both walked down the street until they reached the Copper Kettle Café. Opening the door, they stepped inside. Luckily for the father, there was just one person being served at the counter.

As they waited, Marty pointed at the carbon-fibre prosthetic foot of the young man stood in front of them. 'Daddy,' he asked, 'is he a cyborg?'

'Shush, Marty. That's rude.' The father blushed at the young man, stood in front of him, as he turned round. 'I'm so sorry,' he mouthed.

'Hey, not a problem.' Ed smiled at the boy. 'I got this after battling an ancient sorcerer.'

Marty laughed. 'My daddy says there's no such thing as magic, not in real life anyway.'

'Aww, you got me there, kid.' Ed shrugged at the man, who smiled.

Beryl placed a tall glass of banana milkshake on the counter. 'Here you go, Ed. Is that everything?'

'Yep. Thanks, Beryl.' Ed said goodbye to Marty and his father, then went over to the table near the window to join Tom and Zoe.

'So, anyone heard from Aquaria?' he asked, sitting down. 'I mean, the news article last week said those tourists were positive they heard the sound of a motorbike from *inside* the A-hole.'

'I dunno.' Zoe took a sip of her cappuccino. 'I have a feeling we'll never see her or Lance again.'

'Maybe it's for the best,' said Tom. 'We still have the book.' He leant over and kissed Zoe on her soft cheek.

Ed slurped his milkshake through a paper straw. 'Anyway, what happens next?'

'The shop reopens next Monday, life continues as normal in Penworthy.' Zoe frowned at Ed, 'What's that look for?'

Ed tipped his head to one side. 'I mean, what happens next for the book. I guess it's our responsibility to guard it, right?'

'It's safe, don't worry.' Tom smiled at Zoe.

'Why are you two grinning?' Ed leant in. 'What've you done with it?'

Both Zoe and Tom pretended to ignore him.

'Oh, come on, guys. I thought we were a team now.'

'We decided something *that* special, should be...' Zoe prolonged the sentence, watching Ed squirm.

'Well?' said Ed, shifting in his seat. 'Should be *where*?'

'On display.'

'What?'

Both Tom and Zoe burst out laughing at Ed's reaction.

'Oh, very funny.' Ed tutted. 'Seriously though, I hope you've hidden it well.'

'You could say we're keeping its whereabouts,' said Tom, 'safely under our hat.'

Ed shook his head. 'Oh... whatever.'

***

Back at Cassam's Magic Emporium, Ali opened the door from the kitchen and took another look into his newly refurbished shop. He took in a deep breath through his nostrils, savouring the smell of fresh paint and floor polish.

'The place has never looked better,' he said, admiring the neatly arranged products sat on the gleaming glass shelving.

Gail stepped behind him and wrapped her arms around his waist. 'Did you see the new display that Tom and Zoe did in the window?'

'They've finished it?' he asked.

Walking out onto the street, they stood and admired their new installation.

'You don't think it's too obvious, do you?' said Ali.

'I shouldn't think so, honey.' Gail turned to look at the contents in the window. 'What's the saying again? Hidden in plain sight?'

In the shop window, the huge new automated rabbit waved a shiny golden wand side to side above the large black top hat.

'It really adds that magical touch.' Gail smiled. 'Don't you think?'

'Absolutely,' replied Ali, before kissing his wife's cheek. '*Real* magic.'

The End...

Ten years ago

'Hello? I'm looking for a… Thomas Last?' came the muffled voice from outside the door, as whoever was there knocked again.

'Yes, just hold on a minute,' shouted Tom. Seeing the damp old book of his on the desk, he could worry about why it had spontaneously burst into flames later. He turned back to his bed and flipped the damp duvet over. Shutting his wardrobe door, he walked over to the door to see who was bothering him so late in the evening.

'Hi, yep, I'm Thomas Last. What can I do for you?'

A smartly dressed, elderly gentleman with long white hair and a matching beard stood in the hallway. 'Hello, Thomas. My name is Professor Leonard Goodwin. I wonder if you could spare me a moment of your time?'

'It's a bit late, Prof,' replied Tom, thinking the man's three-piece tweed suit far too posh for such a late hour. 'But, I guess so, come on. Do you work at the uni? I don't recognise you.'

Leonard entered the room. 'Er… no, although, I have met the principal on a number of occasions.'

Tom gestured for the professor to take a seat on the chair next to his desk.

'Thank you. Ahh, swatting up on history, I see.' Leonard pointed at Tom's computer screen.

'Yeah, Last-Minute Last, that's what my mates call me. They're all off in town getting pissed, but I've got an exam tomorrow morning. Should've revised more but, anyway, what can I do for you?'

'Well, it's rather an unusual ask. I'm trying to track down something that belongs to me. It went missing a few years back, you see.' Leonard leaned forward on the chair, pressing his fingers together. 'It's a book, actually.'

'Okay,' said Tom, sitting himself down on the edge of his

bed. 'Not entirely sure where I fit into this? Go on.'

'Well, the thing is, Thomas, it's a rather old book. About a thousand years old, to be precise. It's very important that I get it back.' Leonard leant back in the chair, 'I did manage to track down its whereabouts a while back. Unfortunately, the man who was in possession of it, left it on the back seat of his rather flamboyant Ferrari, which was unfortunately stolen. But, that's idiotic celebrities for you, eh?'

'If you say so,' said Tom.

'Now, it seems the person who stole that car had a son. And that son, appears to have been the only survivor of a recent plane crash.' He paused, prompting Tom to make the connection. 'The book to which I am referring is currently in your possession.'

Tom flicked his eyes to the desk, then quickly back to Leonard.

'That's right,' said Leonard, turning round and sliding the old book towards him. 'It's this one. Now, if you wouldn't mind, I shall take what belongs to me and be on my way.'

Leonard stood, but Tom got up and held out an arm, blocking him from leaving. 'Whoa there, Professor. That's a keepsake, it's important to me. I can't just let you walk off with it.'

Leonard reached into his suit jacket and removed a pistol, taking aim at Tom's head.

'Let me be clear, Thomas. The book does not belong to you. I'm taking it with me.'

Leonard lifted up the book in his free hand. Cautiously, so as not to take the gun off its target, he opened the book and glanced at the pages. 'So many new entries, I should never have let it out of my sight.' He turned to the final page of names. 'Oh, Thomas,' he tutted, 'you foolish boy.' Lifting up the book to show Tom, he tapped the end of the pistol's silencer on the bottom of the page. 'You've signed it. Oh, you stupid, stupid boy.'

'What? I don't understand. It's no big deal. Right?' Tom raised his hands; he didn't dare take his eyes off the gun. 'Loads of people's names are in there. Sorry if mine has devalued it in some way. Worth much, was it?'

Leonard's eyes widened. He lowered the gun, aiming for Tom's left knee, and pulled the trigger. The silencer muffled the shot, enough so as not to be heard above the noise from the other dorm rooms.

Tom cried out in agony, falling back onto the bed.

'Do be quiet, Mister Last. You'll be fine in a few minutes.' Leonard watched, as Tom gripped his blood-soaked knee.

'Fine?' cried Tom, writhing. 'Shit. Look what you've done. You psychopath. How in the hell does that look anything close to fine?'

'Ten, nine, eight,' whispered Leonard.

Tom held his knee, the burning agony searing throughout his leg.

'Three, two, one.'

The burning intensified in Tom's knee. 'It's on fire,' he blurted. Releasing his hands from it, he saw what looked like steam rising from the wound. 'What's happening? Make it stop.'

'It's the *Eternus*, the magic that binds you and the book together, Tom.' Leonard was almost enjoying the spectacle in front of him. It wasn't often he got to witness the spell at work on another.

'What the hell is that supposed to mean?' spat Tom, through gritted teeth.

'It means you're self-healing.' Leonard pointed to Tom's knee. 'Take a look, go on.'

The shock coursing through Tom's veins caused his hand to tremble as he rolled up his sodden-red trouser leg. As he did so, the small bullet fell out onto the floor. Tom stared at the blood-stained skin. 'What the...? But that's not possible.' He rubbed his hand along the wound, now almost completely healed.

For a brief second it almost looked like the skin had been glowing. But now, it was as if nothing had happened. He watched as the blood completely evaporated. 'How? How did you do that?'

Leonard placed the pistol on the desk behind him. He held up the book. 'I just told you, it's this, the *Eternus*. Which means you'll heal from every injury within minutes. Your life will be extended too. I lost this book three hundred and forty-two years ago. Since then I have longed to find it again.'

'That makes no sense,' said Tom, struggling to believe what he'd just seen. 'No one lives to be that old. How can that possibly be true?'

'I just damned-well told you, lad. Are your ears painted on? This book makes you heal, it makes you live far beyond your years, and I created it. I was the first to sign it. The *Prime Eternee*.'

Tom took a couple of deep breaths. 'If you've already signed it,' he said, 'why come back for it?'

'In the past 945 years since I signed it, I've seen those I have loved grow old and die, again and again until love lost all meaning. I have fought in battles, civil wars, world wars. Again, being witness to death while *I survived*.

'I've witnessed the horrors of mankind. Tell me, where is the kindness in violence, murder, slavery, corruption, greed? I'm sick of it all. I have lived through the destruction of this planet. Mass deforestation, the industrial revolution polluting air, water, earth. Atom bombs, nuclear missiles. Dictators, terrorism, death, destruction.' His face grew redder and redder as he spat the words out.

'I am tired, Thomas. Mankind is hell-bent on destroying everything and taking the whole rotten planet with it.' Disgusted, he slapped the book back onto the desk. 'That book is my only ticket out of this.'

'Okay, so you're pissed off with everything,' reasoned Tom. 'I get that. But, you just came in here, threatened me, then shot me in the knee. How does that make you any different?'

Leonard took the pistol and aimed it him again, his temper heightened. 'Do not dare try and make *me* out to be the villain. You know NOTHING.'

Tom held out his hands. 'Okay, I'm sorry. That's not what I was implying. Just take the book and go do what you want with it. I'll carry on doing whatever it is us invincible people are supposed to get up to. How does that sound?'

Leonard grinned, an unsettling sight given the old man's current mood. 'Oh, my poor boy, I am sorry, but tonight your unique ability must come to an end. You see, my curse for being the first to sign the book, means there's only one way I can be released. I must erase every name from those pages. Which means, in short, you must die.'

Tom felt woozy. Adrenaline did its best to shake him into fight or flight; he had to get himself and the book away from Leonard. Right now.

'You won't escape me,' said Leonard, as though somehow reading Tom's mind. He saw a craft knife sticking up from a plastic desk tidy. 'We've wasted enough time, already,' he said, pressing his thumb down onto the upright blade.

Tom glanced at the pistol in Leonard's hand. The old man had lowered it while he was distracted by the knife.

Leonard turned to face Tom. He held out his thumb so Tom could see. 'My cut is already starting to heal itself.' Turning his attention back to the book, Leonard glared at Tom's signature. 'A simple smear of my blood onto your name should suffice. Then, you will cease to exist.' He hovered his thumb over the page.

Tom eyed the small maroon droplet, just centimetres above the page. *This can't be real*, he thought, but wasn't prepared to find out.

Leonard focused on his thumb, now just millimetres from the page. 'My name is Leofwine Godwinson,' he announced, as though starting some kind of ritual. 'First Earl of Kent, brother to King Harold, keeper of the sacred gate. I was born in the year ten thirty-five and my—'

'Bollocks to this,' shouted Tom, leaping forwards. With a hand clenched into a fist, he punched the pistol from Leonard's hand, sending it flying across the room. Leonard swivelled round in the chair.

Instinct kicked in, and with all his strength Tom booted

Leonard as hard as he could in the groin. Leonard dropped to the floor, curled up into a ball – his howl an octave higher than normal.

Tom didn't think twice about booting Leonard again, this time in the head. 'Bloody shoot me, will you?' he barked. *Shit, what do I do now?* Tom looked around the room. *Okay, get the book, the gun, get away.*

He rushed over and picked up the pistol, his hand shaking. *But what if someone catches me with it? The window, yes.* Sprinting over, Tom swung the window open, and threw the pistol down into the bushes below. *Okay, now for that book.*

Leonard remained in a foetal position, groaning on the floor.

Tom jumped back to Leonard. *Is it wrong*, he thought, *to kick an old man when he's down? He did just try to kill me though. Balls to it.* He gave him another boot to the groin. 'Stay down.'

Chucking the book onto the bed, he rushed to the wardrobe, opened it up and grabbed the satchel from inside. Opening it up, he threw the book inside.

Grabbing his brown peacoat jacket from the hook on the door, Tom put it on and checked the pockets to make sure his car keys were inside. Picking up the satchel, he looked down at Leonard, still very much curled up in agony. 'You're never getting this book from me,' uttered Tom. 'Sorry.' He pulled the door open, sprinted off down the corridor, down the staircase and outside, not stopping until he reached his car.

***

The Triumph sped through the countryside. The further Tom drove, the quieter the roads had become, until barely a car passed by. Along the way, Tom tried to make sense of what had happened, and what he was going to do now.

The car's headlights lit up a signpost ahead. He was five miles away from Cornwall. *Think, Tom. You need a plan, you can't just keep on driving.*

After a mile, he saw another sign indicating to take the exit for Penmoor. That was when Tom had an idea. If what Leonard said was true, those who signed the book could only die if the old professor wiped the signatures with his blood. But if Leonard could never find the book, then surely Tom would be safe. He took the exit and headed to Penmoor.

Following a narrow country lane until it became a dirt track, Tom eventually arrived at a quiet area next to an old disused shed. He switched off the engine. *Okay, I'll just bury it somewhere no one will find it. That will be the end of it.*

He got out of the car and opened up the boot. He removed the book from the satchel. Spotting an old biscuit tin which he used as a makeshift toolkit – comprising of a small oil can wrapped up in a cloth, some Allen keys, and a small ratchet set – a thought crossed his mind. *If I bury the book as it is, will the pages rot? What happens to me, if it does?*

He emptied out the contents of the tin. Wrapping the book in the oily cloth, he placed it inside the biscuit tin and pressed the lid down firmly.

As he locked the car, he could hear a vehicle in the distance. *Shit, what if Leonard's followed me? No, you're just being paranoid.* Still, Tom was not going to take the risk. He looked over at the shed. Rushing over to the wooden doors, he found it was unlocked. He swung them open. Empty. Perfect.

With the lights off, he reversed the car inside. Exiting the shed, he shut the doors and pulled the old bolt across. 'Right,' he said, looking at the biscuit tin, 'let's do this.'

In the dark, with no idea where he was going, Tom spotted an opening in the trees ahead. He jogged through, eventually finding himself stood on the edge of a steep drop. Not wanting to risk falling, he chose to take the long way down. Skirting the edge, he walked down the left-hand side. Once at the bottom, Tom could hear the sound of a babbling stream. *Need to get further away*, he decided, and paced off down the valley until he arrived at a gate.

After hopping over it, he stood on a dirt track. 'Damn it,'

he cursed, 'must find somewhere more isolated.' Following the track, he came to an open area of long grass. Running across it until he reached the far side, he soon realised he'd come to a dead end. He took a moment to compose himself. 'What the hell are you doing, Tom?' He shook his head. 'You're going insane.' He knelt down and started scooping away at the soft earth.

Questions were vying for his attention, as he dug. *Is any of this real?* His knee getting shot, then miraculously healing seemed pretty real. *Is the professor telling the truth about the book... living for so long?* And, *How had he found me?* Tom decided to get this job done then go and find somewhere to lay low for a while. Somewhere safe. There was no way he could return to the university campus now, that much was certain.

After burrowing into the ground for what felt like ages, Tom's fingers were now cold, sore and covered in mud. He picked up the biscuit tin from beside him, placed it into the deep hole, then began to refill the earth.

Eventually, after stamping his feet over the ground, he slumped down into the long grass and let out a long exhale of relief. It was done. He allowed himself a few minutes to look up at the clear starry sky as he considered where would be safe. He had the satchel full of cash back in his car. It was unlikely he'd be using it to get him through university now. Well, not that one anyway. *Maybe, I could move to Scotland*, he thought, *or France? Would the Professor find me? The old bastard can't kill me now I've hidden his book, at least.*

Deep down, Tom knew that Leonard – a man who'd been searching years for that book – was not going to simply cease looking for it. *God, maybe I'll have to change my name?* He thought about getting a whole new identity, what it would entail, would anyone want to know his reasons for doing so. A thought stopped his paranoia from escalating further. He remembered the men who had shown up at his parents' funeral. *They had said to contact them, should I need a favour.*

He looked at the state his hands were in, then down at the mud covering his grey jeans. 'Okay, Tom,' he said, pulling himself together. 'Find a hotel and get cleaned up first. You can deal with all the other crap afterwards.'

***

After retracing his steps, he was now creeping back through the trees, near to where he'd hidden his car. As he crept closer, he felt his heart pound. Parked in front of the shed was a green Land Rover. Tom ducked down behind a fallen tree trunk. Maybe it was nothing, just a horny couple looking for a quiet spot, or someone else having a sneaky spliff? *Any number of different people could have reason to park a Land Rover here*, he thought. It didn't have to be...

Tom felt the blood rush from his head. 'Leonard.'

Panicking he watched the old man get out of the vehicle, look around, then walk up to the shed doors. *Bollocks, he'll find my car.* Tom looked down at where he was crouched. Finding what he was looking for, he picked up a stone and threw it at some far-off trees. The stone bounced off a tree trunk with an echoing knock.

Leonard turned round and crept back towards his Land Rover. He stood there, a minute or so, looking over to where the noise had come from. Reaching into his jacket, he removed what looked like a gold stick and held it out in front of him.

The old man then strode off to investigate.

Waiting until it was safe to do so, Tom made his way over to the shed, being careful not to make a sound. When he got there his worst fear was true. Leonard had parked too close to the shed doors for him to get his car out. He cursed the professor under his breath. Stepping over to the driver's side of Leonard's vehicle, Tom tried the door handle. To his surprise, it was unlocked. He checked to see if the keys were in the ignition. No such luck. Maybe, if he released the handbrake, he could somehow move it? Checking the ground in front of the Land Rover, it seemed possible, given it was parked on a slight incline. He'd need to act fast.

Taking a big inhale of air, Tom readied himself. He reached into the Land Rover and placed his hand on the handbrake. As he did so, something caught his attention. Sat on the passenger seat was a large gun. An odd-looking thing, Tom thought, sort of like an antique shotgun but with what appeared to be the pipework of a trumpet bolted onto the side of it. Tom lifted it up. He studied the various cables, dials and tiny LED displays attached to the strange contraption.

Tom's attention snapped back into the moment, as he heard the sound of something crackle through the air towards him. He looked up just as the window of the passenger door exploded, showering his head in glass. Jumping into the driver's seat, Tom yanked the door shut.

Another blast hit the vehicle, this time bouncing across the bonnet. 'The guy's a bloody maniac,' gasped Tom, reaching for the bizarre shotgun. 'How the hell does this thing work?' He tried to see if the weapon was loaded. Twisting dials, tapping buttons, he would just have to take aim and hope for the best.

Pointing the gun through the smashed window, to where he thought Leonard was, he pulled the trigger. Electronics inside the contraption began to whir and vibrate. 'What *is* this bloody thing?' uttered Tom, hitting more buttons.

'Step away from the vehicle, Thomas.' Leonard called, from a distance.

Tom peered over towards the trees. A streak of green lightning arced from the metal wand-like stick and skimmed across the roof of the vehicle.

'Give up, lad. You can't get away.'

Whatever it was the professor was shooting at him with, Tom knew there would be no way he could move the Land Rover now. His only chance was to run for it. He readied himself to make a dash. *Okay, here goes nothing.*

Like a greyhound out of the starting gate, Tom fled the vehicle, still clutching the gun. He dashed across the clearing.

Leonard, brandishing the gold wand from his outstretched hand, yelled, 'Get back here! That belongs to me.'

Green lightning bolted from the tip of the wand once more. Tom hopped as shots hit the ground in front of him. He tried the gun again, but still the trigger just clicked. A green bolt hit the trunk of a nearby tree as Tom swerved past it. 'Bollocks.'

Another bolt hit his foot, causing his entire leg to give way in agony. The gun clunked to the ground in front to him as he fell over. He grabbed his ankle, feeling for the wound. Adrenaline forced him back up. He grabbed the gun and hobbled away, finding cover down an embankment. Something within the strange weapon began to rumble.

A minute had passed before Tom realised Leonard was no longer shooting at him. He paused to catch his breath, clutching the gun in both hands like a soldier in a bunker. Looking behind him, he recognised the sheer drop just yards from his feet. *I've gone round in circles.*

A couple more minutes passed by, and still there was no sign of Leonard. *Maybe he's given up?* Nevertheless, he couldn't stay there all night. He stepped up to the edge of the cliff, just for a moment, to look down.

High above him, in a nearby tree, a large black eagle opened up its wings and dived. With speed, it flew directly into Tom, knocking him to the ground.

The eagle backed up, then launched in for a second attack. This time its talons clawed at Tom's face. Tom swung the gun, like a baseball bat, hitting the bird's head. The shotgun whirred into life in his hands. Unabated, the bird came at him again. Stumbling backwards, Tom lost his footing and tumbled over the edge.

As he tumbled, the gun flew from his grip and hit a rock. A spiralling beam of neon blue light ejected from out of the weapon's fluted barrel, ripping a hole through the valley floor below. The earth span into a whirlpool; a time vortex had opened.

Tom continued to bounce, break and tumble down the cliff until he reached the swirling vortex and was sucked inside.

In the centre, he could just make out what appeared to be

a large hole. The wall of the vortex melted into liquid, as though now a whirlpool. Cyan sparks rippled across the mirror-like surface. Tom sank into it as he spun. All he could do was try to keep himself afloat.

The liquid, thicker than water, as reflective as mercury, gave off an incandescent light which seemed to crackle whenever he moved his limbs. All around him, he heard a pulsating noise.

At the centre of the whirlpool, the hole suddenly ejected a flash of light that shone past him. Becoming more anxious now, Tom was closer to falling through it. He struggled to fight against the current, *Shit, shit, sh...*

Another flash.

As Tom approached the centre, he could now see through it. He saw what appeared to be fields and woodland, hundreds of feet below. His breathing became rapid, his heart beating faster.

He tried kicking his legs out, thrusting his arms against the liquid. It felt thicker at the centre, although that could've been fatigue.

'It's dragging me down,' he cried out, hoping someone, anyone, could hear him. 'Please, help!'

Too late, he'd reached the centre. The pulsating sound was at its loudest. He could feel it coursing throughout his whole body as he slid into the hole. Down he fell, into a world ten years ahead of the one he'd left behind. The land rushed towards him and within seconds he collided onto the rocks of the cliff causing bones in his limbs to shatter. Over and over, he tumbled down into the valley.

When his body finally came to a stop, it lay there lifeless. For now, at least.

ACKNOWLEDGEMENT

I want to thank everyone who has helped me along this journey, from those who supported me to my awesome (and honest) proofreaders.

Special thanks to Chris Jones for inventing ideas and characters that made this story so much more enjoyable to write.

Thanks to Gary Smailes (Bubblecow) and Anna Paterson (ADL Editorial) who shaped the final version.

To my parents, thank you for helping to fund this project.

And lastly, BIG thanks to you, the reader! If you enjoyed this story please recommend it to others and leave a review on Amazon, as every sale will help to fund the next book.